T0267516

FATE BE CHANGED

A TWISTED TALE

Fate Be Changed

A TWISTED TALE

FARRAH ROCHON

DISNEY • HYPERION
Los Angeles • New York

Published by Disney • Hyperion, an imprint of Buena Vista Books, Inc.
No part of this book may be reproduced or transmitted in any form or by any means,
electronic or mechanical, including photocopying, recording, or by any information storage
and retrieval system, without written permission from the publisher.

For information address Disney • Hyperion,
77 West 66th Street, New York, New York 10023.
Printed in the United States of America
First Hardcover Edition, April 2024
1 3 5 7 9 10 8 6 4 2
FAC-004510-24018
Library of Congress Control Number 2023031245
ISBN 978-1-368-07795-8
Visit disneybooks.com

SUSTAINABLE FORESTRY INITIATIVE

Certified Sourcing

www.forests.org
SFI-01681

Logo Applies to Text Stock Only

Dedicated to the memory of my own Mama Bear.
I will love and miss you forever, Mama.

—F.R.

PROLOGUE
Merida

Princess Merida of Clan DunBroch squinted, bringing the funny-shaped knot on the tree trunk into focus. When she had been here a fortnight ago, she'd managed to hit it from thirty paces. This time, she backed up *fifty* paces. If she made this shot, it would prove that she was the best archer in all the Highlands. It didn't matter that no one other than her was there to see it.

Merida straightened her shoulders and concentrated on pulling in slow, steadying breaths. She shut out the sounds of the forest critters going about their day. It was just her and the tree. For the next few minutes, nothing else existed.

She homed in on the knot, focusing on the center of it.

She reached behind herself and pulled an arrow from her quiver. Merida slightly relaxed her grip on the bow, remembering the instructions her father had given her when she was but a wee lass. Too much tension could send the arrow flying past her target.

She fit the bowstring into the notch on the tail end of the arrow, pulled it back, and—

"Princess Merida!"

"Bloody—" Merida stopped herself before the rest of the curse could move past her lips.

"Princess, where are you?"

She released a frustrated sigh and turned in the direction of the voice.

"Over here, Thomasina," Merida called to the woman, who worked as one of the queen's maids. "What is it?" Merida asked, though she did not need to hear Thomasina's answer. She already knew why the maid was here and who had sent her.

A moment later, Thomasina's covered head crested the short ridge.

"Oh, Princess, there you are," she said, puffing slightly as she climbed the rest of the way. "You must come now. You need to get ready for the evening meal."

Merida frowned. She thought the maid had been sent to call her in for her lessons, not to prepare for dinner.

"Now?" She looked up at the sky. The sun was still high. "We won't sit for a meal for some time."

"The queen wants you washed and dressed in your formal *léine* and DunBroch tartan," the maid said.

Merida drew her head back. "Why?"

She wore her formal léine only on special occasions. Why would the queen want her dressed in it for dinner? So that her three rambunctious brothers could cover it in whatever food the cooks had prepared?

"Do you not remember, lass? The King and Queen of Sinclair Kingdom are in residence tonight. Your mother wants you in your best attire. And for you to be on your best behavior," Thomasina added with no small amount of judgment in her tone.

"Oh, bugger!" Merida exclaimed.

"Princess!" Thomasina shouted.

"Sorry," Merida said. She had completely forgotten about the Sinclairs' arrival, and what would be required of her because of it.

Merida resented nearly every single aspect of being a princess, particularly those as trivial as keeping up appearances. But during her many lessons on her duties as a member of the royal family, her mother had imparted the importance of presenting a united front when visited by the heads of other sovereign kingdoms. Clan Sinclair was as formidable in eastern Scotland as Clan DunBroch was in the north.

At least she would not have to speak all that much at the evening's meal. Her mother would expect her to sit like a docile lamb and eat dinner while the adults at the table discussed boring kingdom business. She would take her cues from her mother, laughing when she laughed and remaining stoic when she did.

That should please Queen Elinor.

One thing that would *not* please her mother was if her daughter smelled like the forest when she sat down for dinner. Merida brushed her fingers through her hair and came away with several twigs.

"Perhaps I could do with a bath," Merida muttered. She gathered her bow and quiver and, with Thomasina trailing behind, headed back to Castle DunBroch.

The castle was brimming with activity by the time Merida returned. She dodged servants carrying armloads of linens, platters, and other items that would be used to adorn the Great Hall. Her mother would insist it had nothing to do with impressing their guests, but Merida had attended enough of these gatherings to know better. Success would be measured by the amount of favorable chatter regarding the dinner that spread throughout neighboring clans.

Merida quickly made it to her room and, after scrubbing

her skin to within an inch of her life, sat at her vanity while a maid fussed over her hair and gown. As usual, her riotous curls would not be contained, and after a half hour Merida told the maid to leave them be. She would rather have shown up for dinner with unruly hair than shown up late.

In the end, it did not matter.

Merida entered the Great Hall, head held high in perfect posture, only to learn that the King and Queen of Clan Sinclair had been delayed by weather. They would not be joining them that evening after all.

"Ah, look who got all dressed up for dinner." Her father, King Fergus, laughed as he gestured to Merida with a pheasant leg.

Merida stared at the rest of her family, all wearing normal everyday attire.

"Why did no one tell me that we would no longer have guests?" she exclaimed. Her father only laughed harder.

Merida growled. "I am going to change," she said, turning on her heel.

"Oh, don't be foolish," her mother called. "Come and sit before your dinner grows cold."

"I do not care about eating cold pheasant," Merida said as she marched toward the Great Hall's entrance. "I am—"

"Merida," Queen Elinor announced in her most queenly voice.

Merida stopped. She turned, making sure her expression conveyed her disapproval, but she would not get into an argument over such a trivial matter. When it came to her mother, she knew which battles were worth fighting. Having to eat pheasant in a starched léine was not one of them.

Taking a reluctant seat at the table, Merida dodged a barrage of peas that one of her brothers catapulted at her.

"Boys!" she barked.

"Harris, Hubert, Hamish, not tonight," her mother said.

The redheaded triplets all sat up straight in their chairs, wearing innocent expressions. It was the reason they got away with everything. No one could resist those sweet faces.

Merida picked a stray pea from her hair and started on her dinner. She had to admit that her mother was right; the pheasant, peas, stewed kale, and oatcakes were best enjoyed hot. She shoveled the food into her mouth, suddenly realizing how ravenous she was after an afternoon of archery.

Merida mumbled answers to her mother's inquiries regarding her whereabouts that afternoon, and quickly changed the subject, pivoting to the King of Clan Sinclair. But when the discussion turned to the Sinclair princess's impending nuptials, Merida wished she had just admitted that she had been out with her bow and arrow. She detested all this marriage talk. She would never understand why so many lasses wished to tie themselves down before they had a chance to *live*.

"Are there not better things to discuss at the dinner table?" Merida lamented.

"What could be better than love?" her father asked. He leaned forward, a smile lifting the corners of his mouth. "Did I ever tell you the story of how I met your mother?"

"Please, Dad, not again." Merida rolled her eyes.

"Ah, it's your family history, Merida." He turned to the triplets. "Boys, listen up, this is a great one."

Merida sighed. "You were on the way to Clan MacCameron to deliver a message from the chieftain," she recited under her breath.

"I was on the way to Clan MacCameron to deliver a message from the chieftain of Clan DunBroch," her father said at the same time, lifting the other roasted pheasant leg from the platter before him.

Merida looked to her mother, who returned an indulgent smile as her gaze pivoted to her husband.

"You see," her father continued, a far-off gaze on his face, "Clan DunBroch was under the rule of King Douglass MacCameron at the time. And while we were . . . friendly," he said, gesturing with the pheasant leg as he spoke, "our clans were . . ."

"Not friends," Queen Elinor said.

"We were friendly competitors," King Fergus amended.

Elinor rolled her eyes. "If you say so."

"Where was I?" Fergus asked.

Merida jumped in. "You were on a journey to deliver a message from the chieftain when your horse was spooked by a hare. The horse threw you, you hit your head on a big rock, Mother rescued you and nursed you back to health, and the two of you fell in love. The end."

"No, no. You missed all the good parts," her father said.

Merida sighed. She had been hearing this story since she was a wee lass. It was her father's favorite. Well, his second favorite, right after the one where he single-handedly defeated the sinister monster of a bear, Mor'du.

"It was a sensitive matter of great importance," he continued. "I had been sent because I was the chieftain's most trusted soldier—and his favorite son," he added. "My da knew that I would get word to King Douglass without delay."

"But he did not know that you would be felled by a wee bunny rabbit," Merida teased.

"That's right!" Her father hooted, slapping the table with his massive palm and causing his goblet to teeter. "That little bunny shot from behind a tree like a bolt of lightning. Spooked my horse good. You would have thought the monster from Loch Ness himself was chasing us. I held on for as long as possible, but he still managed to throw me."

"And that's where I first saw your father—sprawled in the grass like a wounded animal," Queen Elinor said.

"But you were brave," Fergus added, pride beaming in his eyes. "She recognized my DunBroch tartan and was ready to put up a fight."

"Until I remembered that we were to be *friendly* to Clan DunBroch," Elinor said.

"She helped me climb onto her horse and brought me to MacCameron Castle. Of course, there were others in her clan who would have left me injured in the forest." Merida's father reached for her mother's hand and captured it in his own. "She nursed me back to health, even though there were others with more skill to do so."

"I felt responsible for you," the queen said.

"I think you felt something else for me," the king said, his eyes twinkling with mischief.

"Oh, Fergus." She slapped his hand, her cheeks turning as red as Merida's hair.

As much as Merida lamented hearing this story over and over again, she always found herself smiling when they reached this part. To look at them, many would say her mother and father were an ill-matched pair. But if there was one thing she was certain of, it was that they loved each other fiercely. And her father loved to tell people about it.

"You will one day have your own husband to contend with," her mother said to Merida.

Merida tutted. "Not if I have anything to say about it."

"It is your duty as a member of this family to marry so that you may begin assuming more royal responsibilities and maintain the peace between the clans. This kingdom depends on it, Merida. It is your fate."

Her mother's voice was resolute, but Merida would not be bullied into something so life-altering.

"Well, I refuse to believe that," she said. "There must be another way to maintain peace without marriage being involved. Besides, I do not see why I must be concerned with any of that. There are others to help with running the kingdom."

Her mother and father shared a look that put Merida on edge, but just as she was about to press harder, Hamish snatched a sweet from a platter and sent the entire thing crashing to the floor.

Chaos ensued. The dogs scarfed down all the cakes before anyone had the chance to rescue them. Harris and Hubert jumped out of their seats and started running around the dining hall, bumping into their caretaker,

Maudie, and sending the basket of bread she was carrying flying into the air.

The dogs attacked the bread as fiercely as they had attacked the pastries.

"Boys!" Merida's mother yelled.

Meanwhile, her father chortled, gaily helping himself to another piece of pheasant and a swig of mead.

A typical night at the dinner table in Castle DunBroch. Little did Merida know this rowdy meal with her family would soon be the least of her problems.

CHAPTER ONE
Merida

Three months later

Merida's heart beat wildly as she marched behind her mother. She ignored the stares of the people who had just witnessed the most brazen act of defiance Merida had ever dared perform against her parents. When she hid the bow and arrows on the dais with the intention of shooting for her own hand at this year's Highland Games, she had known that it would enrage her mother.

She did not care.

Nor did she care what the people of their kingdom who were gawking at her with such astonishment thought about her. They knew nothing of the pressure she felt—the weight of the responsibilities she carried as the daughter of the king. They could attend these games without worrying that their freedom hung in the balance.

Merida kept her head held high, never wavering throughout the journey across the grounds and into the castle and finally into the sitting room. Once they reached their final destination, her mother slammed the door and lashed out.

"I've just about had enough of you!" her mother hissed.

"You're the one that forced me—"

The queen pointed at the door. "You embarrassed them. You embarrassed *me*! I told you before that this marriage is your fate! It is your responsibility to this kingdom!"

"But that is unfair! It is not my fault I was born into this family. Why must I suffer the consequences for something I never asked for?"

Back and forth they went, talking over each other, each trying to get her point across.

"I will not be forced to marry!" Merida yelled.

She drew a claymore from the display stand, not because she thought she needed the long sword for protection, but because she felt more at peace with its heavy weight in her hand. Her mother had never understood her. She wanted Merida to be like her, a prim and proper royal lady. But Merida had never felt drawn to that life. She wanted to be free.

She relished the feel of the wind in her hair as she raced her horse across the glen. Delighted in the exhilaration of hitting a target from fifty paces away with her bow and arrow, or tumbling in the dirt with her three brothers.

She was her father's fierce lass, not her mother's proper princess.

Years of pent-up frustration and resentment poured forth from Merida's mouth. She knew she should stop. She knew her mother deserved her respect, not the venom she was now unleashing on her.

But she could not help it. She'd held in her feelings for too long, and look what it had led to: her mother believing that she could marry Merida off to some bumbling stranger just because he shot an arrow at a target. Was that all she was worth to her parents?

She would not stand for it.

"You're acting like a child," her mother said.

"And you are a beast!" Merida returned. She marched over to the tapestry her mother had been working on for years and poked at it with her claymore.

"Merida!" Her mother gasped when Merida twisted the sword's tip into the fabric. "No! Stop that!"

But Merida was too far gone to see reason.

"I'll never be like you!" Merida cried. "I'd rather *die* than be like you!"

She slashed the tapestry, ripping a huge gash right down the center.

What followed tore a hole through Merida's soul. Her mother grabbed her beloved bow and threw it in the fire.

Merida fled the room. In moments she had reached the stables and climbed onto the back of her trusted horse, Angus.

"Yah!" Merida yelled, pressing her feet against his flank while snapping his reins. The horse shot out of the stable.

She could hear the people still enjoying the Highland Games, but she wanted no part of it. She no longer cared about the event; let them have it. She needed to be alone.

Unable to stop the tears from falling, Merida clutched Angus's neck and wept like a baby as the horse galloped at full speed across the glen. Sobs tore from her chest. Fierce, tormented sobs. The mass of fury, hurt, and disappointment fueling her cries seemed to grow the farther they traveled.

She could not shake the image of her mother's furious expression from her head. Worse than her mother's fury had been her father's look of disappointment.

What had they expected? That she would just go along with their plan? That she would marry that dolt from Clan Dingwall without objection? Or that cocky Macintosh lad? Did they not know her at all?

She reached the edge of the open glen, but instead of

turning around as she had first planned, Merida encouraged the horse to keep going. Angus continued into the forest. Low-hanging tree limbs slapped her face, their knobby branches scraping her skin and pulling her hair.

Suddenly, Angus drew up, his thick hooves skittering along the ground. Merida couldn't fight against the momentum that propelled her forward. She lurched, then went sailing off her horse's back.

She hit the ground with a painful thud.

"Angus!" Merida called in an accusatory voice.

The horse ignored her cry as he stomped around in a tight circle, neighing and huffing and carrying on as if he'd been spooked by a ghost.

A brisk wind began to blow. Merida moved her hair from her face and pushed up from the ground.

"What . . . ?" she started. She slowly twirled, staring in stunned silence at the towering menhirs that now surrounded her. Angus danced around the outskirts of the stone circle, pawing at the ground and huffing his disagreement with this entire situation.

Merida started for him, but a strange noise caught her attention. She whipped around, searching for its origin. And that was when she saw it—a tiny ball of blue hovering above the ground.

"A wisp," she breathed.

Few people believed in the magical beings, brushing them off as folklore. But Merida knew they were real. She had seen them before, back when she was but a wee lass. Legend claimed that the wisps would lead you to your fate.

What were the odds she would see one that day, the day of the contest, of all days? It could not be a coincidence.

The floating lights multiplied. "Come on, Angus," Merida whispered to her horse. He neighed again, shaking his head. "Angus," she said more forcefully. She started forward, not wanting to lose sight of the wisps.

Merida tiptoed behind the tiny floating fairies, being careful not to slip as she traversed the dense forest floor, which was dotted with downed tree limbs and boulders. She was relieved to hear Angus behind her, but kept her eyes forward. Deeper and deeper they traveled, going much farther than Merida had ever ventured. The trees were massive, their trunks covered with thick vegetation. Their gnarled, spindly branches twisted and twirled, stretching above her.

At last, they came upon a clearing with an abandoned structure that had been swallowed up by the forest.

"Why would the wisps lead me here?" Merida wondered aloud. She slowly made her way to the door, surprised to find it unlocked. She pushed the wooden door aside and entered the dim cabin. Her brow furrowed in confusion at the sight of countless wooden bears.

"Oh, look around!"

Merida swiftly turned at the voice.

A short woman with wrinkled skin and a head of thick gray hair stood next to a large carving. "You holler if you see anything you like. Everything is half off."

"Who are you?" Merida asked.

"Just a humble wood-carver."

In an instant, the woman was at her side. Merida gasped, wondering how the old woman had made it across the room so quickly.

The wood-carver took her on a tour of the display room, pointing out the various offerings for sale. The woman held out a rather ingenious carving of a bear fishing for salmon. Merida's brothers would have had a grand time playing with this toy. Before they broke it into a million pieces.

A swishing sound grabbed Merida's attention.

She turned to find a straw broom sweeping the floor, without any help from anyone.

"Your broom!" Merida cried.

The woman responded with a quick explanation that Merida barely registered. There was something strange about this place. A feeling in the air that she couldn't quite explain.

She came upon a crow that appeared to be the only thing that wasn't carved out of wood in this entire cabin. In fact, it seemed . . . real.

"Oh, ah, ah," the wood-carver said in a warning tone. "That's stuffed."

Merida poked a finger at the crow's beak, and it snapped at her.

"Staring is rude," the crow squawked.

Merida gasped. "The crow's talking!"

The crow flapped its wings and started singing. Confusion and fear rippled through her. What was she seeing? This could not be real.

Then it dawned on her.

"You're a witch!" Merida shouted at the woman.

"Wood-carver!" the woman rebutted far too quickly.

Merida knew it. She knew there was something strange—something mystical—about this cottage hidden so deep in these woods. She thought she would be more terrified if she ever came face to face with a real witch. Instead, Merida felt a sense of hope.

"That's why the wisps led me here," she murmured.

"Wood-carver!" the woman said again, demonstrating how expertly she carved wood.

"You'll change my fate," Merida said, excited now. This must have been the way the will-o'-the-wisps could do it, by leading her to a witch with the power to alter things. "You see, it's my mother—"

"I am not a witch!" the witch cut her off. "Too many unsatisfied customers. If you're not going to buy anything, get out." The woman snapped her fingers and a dozen weapons appeared. Merida jumped back, her heart pounding against her chest as she stared at the gleaming blades. Axes, hatchets, daggers. All shiny and sharp and pointing directly at her.

Merida backed away, bumping into tables and stools. The door opened, illuminating the dark room with blinding sunlight.

"Get out! Shoo!" the witch proclaimed.

"I'll buy it all," Merida shouted, thinking quickly. "Every carving." She reached behind her neck and unhooked the pewter chain she'd been given as a child. In the center hung a pendant emblazoned with the DunBroch crest, three bears disposed in a circle.

The weapons fell to the ground. The witch tried to take the pendant, but Merida held it out of her reach. "Every carving . . . and one spell." She quickly explained what she wanted, making it clear she was serious.

"Done," the witch said before snatching the chain from Merida's hands.

The short woman walked out into the clearing. Then

she turned and led Merida back to the cottage, but Merida didn't enter. She stood in the doorway, once again stunned into silence.

The carvings were gone. There was not a bear in sight, wooden or otherwise.

The witch began telling a story about some long-ago prince, but Merida barely heard the words. She was trying to get over the shock of what she was seeing. A black iron cauldron stood in the middle of the dark room. The witch clapped her hands, and a fire ignited underneath it.

She continued with her story of the prince who had sought a spell to change his fate.

There was that word again. *Fate.* It rang in her ears.

"My mum thinks she knows what my fate is, but she's wrong," Merida said.

"Is that so?" the witch asked, tilting her head to the side as she studied Merida. "Your mum is trying to control your destiny, you say?"

"Yes, but I will not let her. My mum does not understand that I have much to do with my life before I am married—if I am *ever* married." She began to pace. "This is all happening too soon. I need my freedom! I need more time! I cannot be tied down in a marriage. I will not stand for it!"

"So it is more *time* you seek?" The witch tapped her

finger against her chin. "Time," she repeated. "And a different fate."

Merida nodded.

"I had a spell in mind, but I believe there is another that suits this situation even better," the witch said. She reached into her garment and retrieved a glass vial. She tossed its contents into the cauldron, along with various other objects.

The liquid sizzled and popped, changing color with every item it consumed. Without warning, the witch slapped her hand over Merida's eyes. Even with her eyes covered, Merida could feel the energy from the bright light that shot out from the cauldron. She heard Angus neighing outside, clomping around after being spooked yet again.

"Now, let's see. What have we here?" the witch said.

She lifted a pair of metal blacksmith tongs and lowered them into the thick sludge that bubbled in the cauldron. She retrieved a small disk of some sort and carried it over to a table.

The disk was . . .

"A cake?" Merida asked with an incredulous frown.

"You don't want it?" the witch asked.

"Yes, I want it."

Unsure that a simple cake could be the thing that altered her future, Merida asked the witch if this spell would change her mother. If she could change the queen and her rigid adherence to tradition, perhaps her mother would not be so determined to see Merida married.

"Trust me. It'll do the trick, dearie," the witch answered. She wrapped the cake in cloth and handed it to Merida. "Give this to your mother, and a great transformation will be made. And *you* will have all the time you need to do the things you want to do before you are required to marry. Now, off you go," she said, shoving Merida toward the door.

The witch spouted off something about Merida's purchase—she'd already forgotten that she'd bought hundreds of wood carvings. The only thing Merida could think about was this cake, and the power it supposedly held. This small, unassuming sweet was her ticket to the life she'd hoped for.

Merida held the package against her chest as she left the cabin and headed toward Angus.

She thought she heard the witch's voice. "Did you say something?" she asked over her shoulder. She turned to find the grass-covered cabin had disappeared. Just like that, she was standing in the center of the tall menhirs.

"How . . . ?" Merida breathed. How had she ended up back in the ring of stones? She'd walked at least a dozen yards before she'd reached the cabin, hadn't she?

What did it matter? She had her answer now. Wrapped

in this piece of cloth was the thing that would put her mother—and her—on a new path.

But as she considered returning to the castle, all Merida could think about were the things that *wouldn't* change, despite the witch's spell.

Even if her parents became more accepting of Merida's wishes, it wouldn't alter the archaic tradition her people had adhered to for centuries. This spell wouldn't change the expectations of those three lords, who all believed their sons had the right to her hand in marriage without any thought to what Merida wanted.

This was not only about her mother. This was about *her* and where she fit in this world.

Even if the witch's spell changed her mother, Merida would still be the Princess of DunBroch. And, as princess, she would be expected to marry, because that was their custom. It was as her mother said: it had become her fate the moment she was born into the royal family.

If Merida wanted any authority over her own life, *she* was the one who needed to change. Not her mother.

She stared at the package ensconced in her palms.

With shaking fingers, Merida peeled the fabric away, revealing the tiny cake. She felt the wings of a thousand butterflies fluttering about her stomach as she brought the cake up to her mouth.

"With this, I will win my own hand," she whispered.

And then she took a bite.

Merida grimaced at the tart, gamy flavor. The witch's cake might have looked appealing, but that was where its pleasant qualities ended. The chalky texture stuck to the roof of her mouth. If she were to lick the sandy shoreline that ran along the edge of the river at the bottom of the gorge, it would probably feel this way. She had thought the gooey center was made of her favorite dark cherries, but it tasted more like dirt.

She stood in the middle of the ring of stones, impatiently waiting for something to happen. She was not quite sure *what* she had expected to happen, but she had been assured by the witch that *some*thing would.

"Well," Merida called out. "Why am I not changing? Why is your spell not working?"

Frustration bubbled up in her veins. She should have known better than to trust that charlatan, with her mystical phrases and stories of past princes whom she'd helped. The witch was nothing but a trickster. Merida wouldn't have been surprised if the woman had no magical powers at all.

How could she have been so gullible? The triplets were but wee lads, but surely they wouldn't have fallen for the ruse. She had been so desperate that she had been willing to believe anything.

"Magical cakes," Merida muttered.

Of course, there still was no explanation for the broom that swept the floor on its own. Or the crow that talked. And there was the matter of the hundreds of bear carvings that had disappeared in the blink of an eye.

It had to have been a trick. If the witch's spell were real, Merida would have felt *something*.

She took a step toward Angus but stopped mid-stride.

Something was . . . off.

She felt woozy, as if the ground had started to undulate beneath her feet. Merida stretched her hands out, reaching for an invisible wall on which to steady herself. The imposing menhirs surrounding her swayed back and forth, as if the thick stones were doing an old Scottish folk dance.

Merida turned in a slow circle. The menhirs had doubled. So had the trees. There were scores of them all around. Their leaves and branches waved as if caught up in a strong wind.

She looked for Angus and saw two horses. Both neighed, stomping their hooves against the trampled grass. She blinked hard, bringing her horse into focus. He was still fuzzy around the edges, but at least there was only one of him now.

"Ang . . . Angus," Merida muttered.

She tried to walk to him, but instead of moving forward, each step took her sideways. She moved the other way, tumbling to the right. Then to the left. Then right again. Her head spun like the wooden top her brothers played with back home.

"Angus," she said again, the word barely making it past her lips. Dark clouds drifted overhead, casting sinister shadows around the ring of stones.

The last thing Merida saw was the glow of a wisp before she passed out.

CHAPTER TWO
Elinor

Cognizant of the short window between when lute practice ended and when her lessons on the kingdoms of ancient Scotland would begin, Princess Elinor MacCameron moved about her bedchamber with haste, shoving her thinnest kirtle and hose into a linen sack, along with an extra pair of slippers.

She reached for her hairbrush, but then decided against it. Her head would be covered for much of her journey. She would secure a new hairbrush once she reached her destination. She had to keep the sack as light as possible. Anything too heavy would only slow her down.

Elinor stopped, her hands arrested on the bag.

She tilted her head to the side, listening intently to the

sound of footfalls in the corridor. She halted her breath as the seconds ticked by.

The footsteps grew louder, and louder still. Just as she was about to stuff the sack underneath the bed, they stopped.

Elinor closed her eyes and sucked in a relieved breath, but then she quickly returned to the task at hand. Time was of the essence, and she could not waste any more of it.

She picked up three tallow candles she had pilfered from the wall sconces in the east wing and tucked them into the sack. They were all partly burned, but her presence would be questioned if she were to go to the chandlery for new candles. Besides, she could not spare the time. Her maid would be here to call her soon.

Elinor gathered the last of her supplies, including the dagger she had taken from the castle's armory. She had a knife of her own, of course. Every lass in the kingdom received one once she reached a certain age, but she could not escape to the Lowlands with the modest blade she had been given to celebrate turning five and ten. The dagger she had stolen from the armory was for protection, not ornamentation.

Elinor hoped she would not have to use it, but she was prepared to do so if need be.

Her hands shook as she tried to close the open end

of the sack with a sash from one of her night rails. Rope or twine would have worked better, but she would have encountered the same questions she would have received from the chandlery maids were she to go to the stables or kitchens inquiring about rope or twine. Princesses had no use for common household items.

Elinor took a moment to calm her frayed nerves.

She could not panic. Panic was her enemy. Panic would cause her to make a misstep. And a misstep could very well cost her the one thing she coveted most.

Her freedom.

The weight of her impending betrothal squeezed against her chest like a corset pulled too tight. So little of her life was her own; once betrothed and married, she would control nothing. Any decision she made would have to be approved by her husband, just as any she made now had to be approved by the king and queen. She was in danger of having her entire life dictated by others.

It was why she had to leave.

She deserved to taste freedom, to know what it felt like to rise in the morning and not have the weight of an entire kingdom on her shoulders. To go about her day doing the things *she* wanted to do, and not what others demanded of her. Just the thought of having such liberty sent a jolt of anticipation down her spine.

She retrieved her favorite pewter-colored cloak from the wardrobe, but just as quickly shoved it back. She needed something old and dingy, something that would not stand out in the forest. Elinor searched through the kirtles and gowns, determined to find a more appropriate garment.

That was when she spotted it: the worn brown cloak she had borrowed from Ewan, the stable hand, back when she had been caught out in the rain. She had meant to return it ages ago but had held on to it for some reason.

"This is the reason," Elinor whispered, holding the cloak up to her chest.

It was a sign. The universe must have approved of what she was doing. Why would it provide this cloak if her true destiny was to remain here at MacCameron Castle and take her place as the future queen?

She bundled the cloak up in her arms and raced to the bed. Elinor glanced out the window on her way back to the wardrobe and did a double take. She could have sworn she had glimpsed a streak of red among the trees.

Could it have been a bird? No, it was too big for a bird. A deer, maybe?

An uneasy feeling settled in the pit of Elinor's stomach.

She would ignore it. She had to. Fear was as detrimental to her plans as panic. She would not allow either to deter her.

"Princess! Princess, it is time for your lessons."

No!

This was what she got for dawdling.

Elinor grabbed the sack and stuffed it in the bottom of her wardrobe just as the maid entered the room.

"Princess, your lessons," Orla, her mother's most trusted maid, said.

"I shall be there soon."

Orla gave her a look that closely mimicked the one her mother, Queen Catriona, would have given had she come to fetch Elinor. Her spirits sank. The queen's maids were loyal to a fault, Orla more than any of the others. She would not leave Elinor's side until she had delivered the princess to her lessons, just as Queen Catriona had ordered, no doubt.

"I shall follow you there now," Elinor amended.

Orla gave her a firm nod.

She had missed out on her chance this time. She would not make the same mistake again.

CHAPTER THREE
Merida

Merida tried to lift her head, but it felt as heavy as the chain mail that hung from the suits of armor lining the halls of Castle DunBroch. Twin throbs beat at either side of her head, the rhythmic thumping worse than any headache she'd experienced before.

The air was redolent of the forest, musty earth and decomposing leaves. Thin blades of grass pressed against her cheek. She could feel them imprinting on her skin but could not summon the strength or will to do anything about it.

She needed rest, even though it felt as if she had been sleeping for a fortnight.

And as much as she wanted to spend the rest of the

day snoring atop her grassy bed, Merida knew she could not. She had to get home. Her parents would be wondering where she was. She mustered just enough resolve to push herself up from her prone position and into a kneeling one.

She had to steady herself on a nearby boulder, the throbbing in her head intensifying as she attempted to stand. Merida clasped her head in her hands and discovered a chicken-egg-size bump near her right temple. She gingerly pressed around the tender flesh, pulling back fingers that were sticky with blood.

"Well, that's just great," Merida groused.

She looked down, noting the impression her body had left in the grass.

Just how long had she been lying here? She was lucky some wandering clansman hadn't trampled her with his horse.

Horse?

Angus!

"Angus!" Merida called. She moved on wobbly legs, trying to shake off the dregs of sleep. She had to find her horse. "Angus! Angus, where are you?"

Her already weak limbs shook in relief when she heard him neigh. Merida rushed toward the sound and found her horse hiding behind one of the menhirs. He was skittish at first, backing away from her.

"You're well, boy," she said, trying to coax him from behind the stone, but he refused to leave its safety. She moved slowly toward him so as not to spook him.

"You're well," Merida said. She ran her hand along Angus's thick mane, grateful that he'd started to calm down. As she comforted her horse, Merida noticed that something didn't seem quite right with the menhir. Frowning, she swiped her hand along the smooth, grassless surface. She could have sworn the bottom half of the stone towers had been covered in moss, the kind of moss that grew over time.

The lack of moss on the menhirs was not the only thing that gave her pause. The trees also seemed different. Many of them were shorter and their trunks were not nearly as wide as she remembered. And there were more of them standing. She was certain at least a dozen of the trees that now stood tall around the ring of stones had been on the ground. Their stumps had been covered with the same moss that had covered the menhirs.

Clearly she had hit her head quite hard after eating that blasted cake.

"Come, Angus," Merida said. She untied the bow she'd taken before leaving Castle DunBroch and draped it across her chest. Then she tightened her grip on Angus's reins. "Let us go home."

She had no doubts that her mother would be in a snit

when she returned, but Merida did not care anymore. After all those hours on the cold ground, she could think of nothing better than standing before the warm fire that burned in her bedchamber.

She ran her hand through her knotted hair and came up with several blades of grass.

There *was* something better than standing before the fire. Soaking in a nice warm bath and washing the events of the day away along with the grime sounded heavenly.

Merida tugged on Angus's reins, urging him to come along. She was still feeling somewhat dizzy and did not trust herself to climb atop the horse, especially after the way he had thrown her. She decided it would be better to make the first part of this journey on foot. She would mount Angus once they reached the glen, where the terrain was flatter and littered with fewer hazards. She started walking west toward home.

At least, she *thought* this was the way. She had never journeyed this far into the forest before, and after all the time that had passed since she'd stormed away from the castle in tears, she could not be sure she had not been turned around.

Merida heard what sounded like thunder coming from somewhere in the distance. She looked to the sky, but it was clear: no sign of the thick, dark clouds that had previously cast threatening shadows. She stopped to listen and realized it was not thunder she had heard; it was horses.

"Thank goodness." Merida breathed a sigh of relief. It was probably members of Clan Macintosh. Their lands were to the east of DunBroch, so they likely traveled this route to return home. She would stop one of them and make sure she was indeed heading back to Castle DunBroch.

But as the party of horsemen drew near, Merida could see that their tartans were not the red and green of the Macintosh. In fact, the purple-and-orange tartan did not belong to any of the clans of their land.

Hide, her instincts told her. *And fast.*

Quickly tugging Angus behind the trunks of two trees growing closely together, she flattened her back against one of them, grimacing as a sharp piece of bark dug into her flesh where her gown had ripped. Her heart pounded as she listened to the mounted men drawing closer.

These lands had not seen invaders since her father was a young man—well before the neighboring clans had reached an alliance. If the trespassers were here to seize their kingdom, the Princess of DunBroch would be a grand prize. She would not put herself in a position to become a bargaining chip.

But it would seem she didn't have to worry about being

captured. The group of men rode right past her. Still, Merida waited several minutes longer before stepping out from around the tree trunks.

She needed to get home. She had to warn her father and the other chieftains about what she had seen. Their four clans were no longer enemies; they would band together to fight these marauders.

And she would help!

Adrenaline surged through Merida at the thought of using her skill with the bow and arrow to help save her kingdom from an attack. She could show her mother that she was good for something other than playing a lute or hosting a dinner.

Or being someone's wife.

Merida gathered Angus's reins, invigorated by newfound purpose. She kept her eyes open for the landmarks she normally used to guide her when she came out for rides. She was bound to encounter the small hill that lay just beyond a group of boulders, or that massive tree with a trunk the size of three horses. She would often stop to sit underneath it. When feeling a bit whimsical, she would entertain herself by imagining it as a home for magical woodland creatures.

But the more she walked, the less familiar her surroundings appeared. Had she been traveling in the wrong

direction? She had never been on the other side of the forest, toward the lands where Clan Macintosh resided. Maybe
she had been turned around and not realized it.

Merida decided to stick to the course she had set upon.
If she *did* reach Clan Macintosh's dwellings, at least she
would know that she needed to head in the opposite direction to make it back home.

She looked up at the sky and realized the sun would be
setting soon. She would have to rely on Lord Macintosh's
hospitality for the night. Merida doubted he was feeling
very hospitable after the way she had behaved toward his
son, but there was nothing to be done about that now. No
matter how upset he was, the chieftain would not turn away
their kingdom's princess. He would direct his household to
treat her with generosity and respect.

Her mother, however, was another story. Merida feared
the queen's earlier ire was nothing compared to what she
would face when she returned to Castle DunBroch.

After more than an hour of travel, the dense clusters
of trees began to thin, an indication that she was drawing
nearer to home dwellings. Her father had taught her that
trees closest to the edge of the forest were the first to be
chopped for firewood.

Merida wasn't sure if her wobbly knees were due to
exhaustion or relief at the first sight of a thatched roof. She

quickened her steps, buoyed by the thought of getting some help and maybe a bite to eat.

"Wait here, Angus," she said, tying the horse's reins around a tree trunk. "I promise to bring you an apple." She would have to rely on the charity of others on behalf of her horse as well, having bartered the only thing of value she'd carried with the wood-carver.

The witch, Merida reminded herself. A witch who had sold her a faulty spell. If changing her fate meant getting lost in the forest, Merida wanted her pendant back.

She gave Angus's neck a reassuring rub before she took off down the trampled path that led from the forest to the edge of the small burgh she had happened upon. The strong odors of drying animal hide, dung, and fish hit her before she made it to the first structure.

Merida tried not to judge the rudimentary architecture, but if this was how the Macintosh clan lived, she'd had every right to try to get out of marrying the eldest son. The villagers around Castle DunBroch had stopped using heather and reed for their roofs a long time ago, but those seemed to be the materials of choice here. The buildings were squat and narrow.

Several skinny horses drank from a trough that sat between a blacksmith shop and a butcher. Merida's mouth watered at the sight of the plucked pheasant on display. It made her long for the succulent dishes their cook prepared for their evening meals.

She clutched her stomach. What she wouldn't give for a big bowl of mutton stew.

She entered the butcher shop, but before she could speak, the man took one look at her and said, "Nae, lass. Yer kind is not allowed. Get out."

Her head snapped back at his rudeness. "I am Prin—"

"Out!" The man shoved her. "I do not care about all the new talk about peace. Yer kind is not welcome here." He closed the heavy wooden door in her face.

Merida was too shocked to form a response. Her people were rather informal, but never had anyone treated her so. And what did he mean by *her kind*? Was it because she was a girl? Were the Macintosh so backward in their thinking that they did not believe women could buy meats?

And what *new* talk of peace? The Macintosh and DunBroch clans had forged their alliance when the Vikings invaded north Scotland. The only story her father told even more than the one about the day he met his dear Elinor or when he faced Mor'du was the story of how he saved the clans from the towering Nordic warriors who arrived in their huge boats, ready to conquer the land and all the people who resided on it.

Maybe Merida should remind these Macintosh that they

would not have businesses to kick her out of if not for her father.

She raised her fist, preparing to knock on the door, but then decided it wasn't worth it. She did not want advice or pheasant from such a close-minded man.

Instead, she ventured to the next shop—the cobbler— hoping for a better reception. The store was empty, but Merida could hear someone in the back.

"Hello," she called.

A woman came out carrying a broom. At least this one wasn't sweeping on its own.

"Hello," Merida said again. "I am hoping you can help me find my way back to DunBroch la—"

"No DunBroch," the woman interrupted. She swept dirt toward Merida's feet. "Get out. You're not welcome here."

"But—" Merida started. A new thought suddenly darted across Merida's mind. *The games.* Of course. Perhaps the villagers had already heard about what had transpired at the Highland Games. Was that why they were treating her with such harshness, because she didn't want to marry their chieftain's eldest son?

"Out! Out!" the woman continued to shout. When Merida didn't move fast enough, the woman attacked with the broom, raising it high above her head.

Merida quickly turned and raced for the exit. She ran out of the door and into the street.

"I just need a little help getting home!" she called. Several villagers stepped out of the various shops; some poked their heads out of the windows. "Is that too much to ask?" Merida pleaded as she spun in a slow circle, begging these villagers to listen.

Suddenly, she locked eyes with a woman who stood just outside a small shop at the end of the short street. Even from a distance Merida could see she had a bulbous nose that dominated her face. A dramatic lock of silver ran through her long black hair. The sun's rays glinted off it, amplifying the conspicuous feature. Her intense gaze held Merida captive for a moment. She seemed familiar somehow, like they'd met in a dream once, and Merida tried to place her . . . until the cobbler came out of her store, wielding her broom.

"I told ye to go!" the cobbler shouted. "We don't want no DunBroch here!"

Merida darted up the street, back the way she had come.

She scrambled through the brush and around the rocks protruding from the ground, putting as much distance as she could between herself and the broom-wielding shopkeeper. She was not sure what was going on, but the hostility coming from the Macintosh people seemed unwarranted. They could not be this upset because she had decided to participate in the archery competition herself.

Then again, Merida was no stranger to the pride Scotsmen took in their clan's standing within the kingdom. The villagers no doubt saw her rejection of the three eldest sons as a rejection of their people. She had very likely made an enemy of every member of Clans MacGuffin, Macintosh, and Dingwall.

Had she also made them enemies of the king and queen? Would the various clans blame Merida's parents for her defiance? She had not fully considered the implications of her actions at the games. Her guilt grew as she took more time to ponder what she had done and the possible ramifications.

"The damage is done," she muttered. There wasn't much she could do to change it, and certainly not now, while she was wandering the forest with no idea how to get back home.

Satisfied that she had at least outmaneuvered the cobbler, Merida slowed her pace as she returned to the spot where she had left Angus.

"Sorry, boy," she said when she came upon the horse. "No apples."

He neighed his discontent. As she suffered from the hunger pangs resonating throughout her own empty belly, Merida could not blame him.

"I'll find something for us both," she said.

She climbed onto her horse's back and guided him deeper into the woods, away from the village. As much as she loathed the prospect of sleeping out in this dense, unfamiliar area of the forest tonight, she disliked the thought of getting bashed in the head with a broomstick even more.

Should she try to find that witch's cottage again? Merida wasn't sure she would make it back to the ring of stones before nightfall. That is, if she could ride at all without passing out from hunger or the headache that continued to plague her.

Lucky for her, King Fergus of DunBroch was not as strict as his wife was when it came to his daughter adhering to the rules that governed a princess's existence. Her father had taught her how to survive a night in the woods. Much to her mother's chagrin.

Merida closed her eyes and tried to picture the layout of the forest. A creek ran along the western edge. She looked up at the sky to gauge the position of the sun and guided Angus in the direction of where she thought they would find the fresh water. She heard a gurgling sound and excitedly tugged Angus's reins.

"Come on, boy," she said. But when they came upon what should have been a wide creek, it was nothing more than a tiny brook.

"This is . . . odd," Merida said. She had fished in the creek during her many excursions over the years. Maybe this small brook was the start of it, which meant she was well north of DunBroch, where the creek probably widened. That was the only explanation that made sense.

"At least we have clean water," she said to her horse.

Merida and Angus both drank their fill from the brook. She then used the water to freshen up, grimacing as she washed the caked dirt from her face and hands. She looked down at her dusty, torn gown. Was it any wonder the butcher and cobbler had shooed her from their businesses? Typically, she didn't care much about appearances, but even she had to admit she must have looked a fright.

Gathering the hem of her gown, she dipped a tiny portion of it into the water. Then she gently dabbed at the knot on her head.

Now that she had quenched her thirst, she needed to find something to fill her belly. The creek near DunBroch was overflowing with salmon and trout, but this brook wasn't deep enough to sustain fish. Merida settled Angus near a patch of grass where he could eat, then crept around the trees and brush, seeking out something she could have for dinner.

Out of nowhere she heard a horse's strident blore, followed by a loud thump.

Merida dropped to the forest's floor. Her muscles tensed as sweat broke out across her forehead. Sucking in quick, shallow breaths, she closed her eyes and focused her attention on the area where the sound had come from. Several heartbeats later, she heard the *clump, clump, clump* of horse hooves again.

She remained in the crouched position, hovering there until her knees quivered. Merida bit her lip. She was unwilling to risk being seen by whoever was here in this forest with her. It was only after she was sure the horse was long gone that she finally rose and continued her hunt for food.

She spotted a wild hare lurking near the brook.

She pulled an arrow from her quiver and sent it careening from the bow, striking the hare on her first try.

"Let's see perfect, dutiful Queen Elinor do that," Merida said, retrieving her kill.

However, cooking her dinner proved to be much more difficult than catching it. She dug a small hole in the ground and encircled it with rocks, then went about gathering twigs and kindling for a fire. She grabbed her bow and a sturdy stick and tried to remember the steps her father had taught her when it came to making a fire. She vigorously sawed the bow back and forth across the stick until finally, after a half dozen tries, a flame sparked.

She had left home without a dagger, so she had to use the pointed tip of one of her arrows to skin and clean the hare. Sacrificing one of the arrows, she used it as a spit, slowly rotating it above the flames to roast the animal.

After what felt like an eternity, Merida was finally able to enjoy her dinner. The bland, gamy flavor made her appreciate the cooks at Castle DunBroch even more. She would never complain about a single dish they made ever again.

But at least she had some food in her belly. She could be grateful for that.

The sun had already set by the time she finished eating, and as much as she wanted to keep the fire going for both warmth and light, Merida knew better. Her father had taught her that fire was a beacon for the enemy. And she had not forgotten about those men with the unfamiliar tartan, nor could she be sure that the person on horseback who had been near as she was hunting would not return. She did not want to lead any unsavory company to her, especially when she felt so poorly.

After securing Angus's reins, Merida wrapped her arms around her knees and leaned against a tree. Her head pounded, the knot near her temple still tender to the touch. Coupled with the exhaustion of this long, harrowing day, it made for an agonizingly rough night's sleep.

The next morning, Merida awoke to the same throbbing headache, along with stiff shoulders and a pain in her side. She opened her eyes. Then sucked in a swift breath.

There was the gleaming blade of a deadly-looking dagger pointed directly at her face.

CHAPTER FOUR
Merida

"Who are you?"

Merida's eyes darted from the jagged knife mere inches from her nose to the girl a few years older than her clutching it in her hand. The stranger's grip on the handle was so tight that the skin strained stark white over her knuckles.

"What are you doing here?" the young woman asked. "What do you want?"

What was it about this village? Was everyone so hostile?

Merida contemplated her chances of survival if she tried to roll away, or knock the knife from the girl's hand. Neither seemed a smart choice, especially with the tattered, bulky gown weighing her down and the persistent headache that refused to go away.

"Are you going to answer me?" the young woman asked again. She looked over her shoulder, then back to Merida. "Well?"

There was something about her striking features that stole Merida's ability to speak. Her pert, aquiline nose flared as she waited for Merida's answer. Despite the dusty cloak she wore, the fine braided trim at the neckline of her garment told of a position of wealth. Especially compared to the woman Merida had spotted in the village the day before, with the silver streak in her hair.

"I shall ask you but once more," the girl snarled. "Who are you?"

"My name—" The words came out raspy. She cleared her throat. "My name is Merida."

"And what are you doing on our lands, Merida? Have you come to steal from the king?"

"Of course not," Merida said. She cleared her throat again. She needed water. The sound of the brook a few paces away taunted her. "The only thing I want is to get back to Castle DunBroch."

The stranger drew up short, her eyes narrowing in suspicion. "You are of Clan DunBroch?"

Merida nodded. "Yes. Do you know how to get there?"

The girl ignored her question, her eyes roaming over Merida's face. "You do have that brash hair of the

DunBroch." She regarded Merida with a touch of sympathy in her expression, as if her red hair was something to be pitied.

"You still have not told me what you are doing on our lands," she said.

"I would, but it is hard to think clearly with a dagger pointing at my face," Merida answered. "Can you please put it away? I am a defenseless visitor. There was no need for you to draw your weapon on me while I was sleeping."

"You are not defenseless," the girl stated. She jutted her chin toward the bow and quiver that Merida had left near the firepit.

Merida cursed her misstep. She had been taught to never let her weapon out of her reach. Her father would be so disappointed.

"I cannot even reach my bow," Merida argued. "Can you please draw back your blade? I promise, I am harmless, and I need to think."

Suspicion teemed in the young woman's eyes, but after a moment, she stepped back and dropped her hand. She continued holding the knife in a tight grip at her side, no doubt waiting to pounce if Merida tried anything untoward.

"Get up," the stranger ordered. "Over there." Her dark auburn hair whipped over one shoulder as she motioned for Merida to move away from the tree where her bow and arrows sat.

Merida lumbered clumsily from the ground. For a second, she considered making a run for it, gauging how long it would take to mount Angus. In the state she was in, she would likely fall off her horse's back. If she managed to mount him at all.

"Over here." The girl pointed to a spot near a short boulder. "I know we are supposed to trust the DunBrochs now that we are in an alliance, but you should understand why I do not. That is, if you really are a DunBroch."

"I am," Merida insisted. She wondered why everyone seemed to talk about this alliance as if it were a terrible thing. Were the villagers of Macintosh so unhappy with their neighbors? Was this a recent development, truly connected to Merida's performance at the games? Or had Merida not known about a simmering rocky political situation? She usually didn't concern herself with such matters, but maybe it was time she started to pay attention.

The stranger leveled a challenging glare at Merida. "Now, tell me what you are *really* doing here."

"I got lost in the forest," Merida said. "I just want to go home."

"And where is home?"

"I told you. I live in Castle DunBroch. I am Princess

Merida of Clan DunBroch. My father, Fergus, is the king. My mother is—"

"King?" the girl interrupted her. She huffed out a laugh. "Just like a DunBroch to declare himself a king simply because of the alliance. You tell *Chieftain* DunBroch that there is but one king, and he is a MacCameron."

MacCameron?

The only Clan MacCameron Merida knew of was her mother's old clan, but most of their members had been killed in a battle with Vikings shortly after her mother and father were married. According to the stories Merida had been told, what was left of her mother's original clan resided far south, near the tip of the country. Merida had never had the chance to meet any of the MacCamerons. Both her parents had declared that it was far too dangerous to chance taking Merida and her younger brothers on the journey south.

Absently, Merida tried to sweep the hair from her face. She winced as pain shot from the knot on her head. How far had she traveled?

"What happened to your head?" the girl asked.

"I don't know," Merida answered. "I fell yesterday. I think I may have hit it on a rock."

"I am not sure I believe you," the stranger said, her deep brown eyes narrowing. "The chieftain of Clan DunBroch has never sent a lass before. His emissaries have all been elite warriors." She peered at Merida with a cynical frown. "You do not look like an elite warrior to me."

Merida could not argue with her. She might have been an expert archer, but she was no warrior.

"And what is this?" The young woman gestured to the rudimentary firepit, which held the remnants of Merida's dinner.

"I caught and cooked a hare last night," she explained.

"And you expect me to believe you are from DunBroch." She shook her head. "If the chieftain had sent you to deliver a message to the *real* king, he would have provided enough food to last your entire journey. You would not have had to skin your own hare."

"I was not sent as an emissary, but I *am* of Clan DunBroch," Merida said, unsure what else she could do to make the girl see reason. "I left the castle in haste; I did not even think to bring my plaid with me," she said. "The Highland Games are taking place there right now. You can ask anyone."

"The Highland Games are almost a fortnight away," the stranger answered.

Merida frowned, rubbing her sore temple. None of this was making sense.

"Can you please just point me in the direction of home?" Merida asked.

Suddenly, the young woman held up a hand. "Shhh," she said. She looked right, then left. "Down," she whispered intensely. "Get down."

Merida dropped to the ground, but not before she noticed men wearing the same purple-and-orange plaids that she had seen the previous day, making their way through the brambles several paces away. There were at least a half dozen of them, riding atop broad-chested horses. These were no peasants, not with such fine steeds. These men were part of some chieftain's army.

"Who are they?" Merida whispered.

The suspicion that continued to lurk in the stranger's eyes deepened. "You say you are of Clan DunBroch, yet you do not know who those men are?"

"I have never seen that particular tartan before," Merida answered.

"And I thought *my* father kept *me* sheltered," the young woman said. "At least I know a hostile clan when I see one."

So she had been right to hide from those men before. At least her instincts were still intact.

But Merida's head hurt too much to think about it more deeply. She needed to get home, and as much as she hated to admit it, she needed this young woman's help to do it.

"Are you going to assist me, or aren't you?" Merida asked her.

The young woman arched her brow, and Merida sucked in a breath.

She had seen that look before. Often during a firm dressing-down by her mother, following some misguided action on Merida's part.

It cannot be.

But hadn't the young woman said her father was a MacCameron? This stranger must have been related to her mother. The resemblance was too strong for it to be mere coincidence.

"What is your name?" Merida asked her.

The girl raised a hand again, silencing her. She looked over both shoulders. "I think the men are gone. I must continue. You have held me up long enough."

"No!" Merida said. "No, please. You do not understand. I have no one else. I have been lost in these woods since yesterday. I hurt my head. My horse—"

She looked around in a panic. She had to stop losing her horse!

"Angus?" Merida called.

"Your horse is fine," the stranger said. "He is tied up to a tree next to mine." She finally sheathed her knife, tucking it in a scabbard tied to her belt. "Those men are gone now, but they may come back. It is not safe for a young lass like yourself to be in these woods alone."

"*You* are alone."

"Yes, but I know these woods. You, clearly, do not."

"Are you really going to leave me here?" Merida asked.

"I must," the young woman insisted. "My father's men will soon be here looking for me. I am sorry, but I cannot help."

"Who are your father's men?"

"Warriors in the king's army," the girl said distractedly as she straightened her belt. "My father is King Douglass MacCameron. I am his daughter, Princess Elinor."

CHAPTER FIVE
Elinor

Elinor did not know what to think as the stranger named Merida put a hand on her arm, demanding her attention. Elinor was about to protest, but stopped as she took in the girl's expression. Merida stared at her wide-eyed, as if she had seen a ghost. Frowning, Elinor felt an eerie sensation come over her, like she somehow knew this girl very well, and Merida knew her.

Then, just as quickly, the princess shook off the feeling. Many from the surrounding villages had never set their eyes on the royal family. Merida was obviously stunned at the sight of the princess. That was all.

"What did you say your name was?" the girl asked.

"My name is not as important as leaving before those men from Clan Bruce come riding back," Elinor answered.

She had her eyes trained on the girl with the fiery red hair, but kept the rest of her senses on the surrounding area, particularly the path that led to MacCameron Castle, anticipating more unexpected visitors. No doubt her absence had been discovered by now, which meant her father had likely dispatched a troop of men to search for her.

After all, this wasn't the first time she had fled.

She was, however, determined it would be the last.

But then the girl let out a little whimper. She tried—and failed—to get up.

Elinor felt a stab of sympathy despite herself. The girl was lost, both physically and mentally, if she thought the Highland Games were already taking place. If she left this girl to her own devices, who knew what would become of her. She might venture even deeper into the woods, so deep she might never be found. And then what?

What if the roles had been reversed and Merida decided to leave her for dead?

"Fine. I will help you," Elinor found herself saying.

Blast.

She had never gotten this far before. Her father's sentries usually stopped her before she was able to make it past the thirty-foot-high stone wall that surrounded the castle. But she knew she couldn't in good conscience leave the stranger. And if she was honest with herself, it was more than a sense of altruism that had her rethinking her plans.

Stumbling upon this lass was the most interesting thing that had ever happened to her. She had so many questions for Merida. How had she come to be here alone, and with such a fine horse? Her gown was torn, but Elinor could tell the garment was of good quality. How had she come to own it?

And how had she learned to kill and skin a hare?

"Where is my horse?" Merida asked again.

"I already told you he is tied to a tree next to *my* horse."

Elinor wondered if Merida should be seen by the physician. It was possible her injury was affecting her memory. She had heard of such things happening after warfare, as well. Although, when she considered some of the stories the warriors told when they gathered around the table at MacCameron Castle, forgetting their days in combat was probably a good thing.

Had this girl seen things she wanted to forget during her time alone?

Traveling through this forest was not for the faint of heart. Legend had it that a mystical bearlike creature roamed these woods, seeking retribution after a spell was cast on him by a wily witch. Several villagers claimed to have seen the beast throughout the years. Others were quick to dismiss it as a fable meant to scare would-be intruders.

Elinor had a healthy respect for the legend of Mor'du. She had given much thought to how she should respond if she were to encounter the beast during her escape but had not come up with a satisfactory solution.

"I should check on Angus," Merida said.

"He is a handsome shire," Elinor remarked as she held out a hand to help the girl into a standing position. "You are lucky I am the one who found you. There are others around here who would have had no issue slitting your throat as you slept just so they could make off with your horse."

Her father had at least a hundred like it; she knew how valuable they were.

"Did you steal him?" Elinor went on. "Because if you did, you are going to bring more trouble on your head."

"Of course I did not steal him. He is mine," the girl said haughtily. She took a step and would have crumpled to the ground if Elinor had not been there to stop her fall.

There was no doubt about it. This girl, Merida, needed immediate medical attention, followed by a warm bath. The girl's bones must have been chilled from a night of sleeping outdoors. Elinor would have the apothecary whip up a tisane to help stave off fever.

She pulled her plaid from the linen sack and wrapped the thick wool around the girl's shoulders, securing it with the pin imprinted with the MacCameron crest.

"Stay right here," Elinor told her. "I will bring the horses."

The girl nodded. "Thank you, El—Elinor."

"You're welcome, Merida."

Merida.

It was a pretty name for a girl with a pretty face.

Elinor walked over to the horses. She untied Alistair, the jet-black Friesian she had been given for her thirteenth birthday.

"Next time," Elinor whispered to him, running her hand down his neck. "Next time we are going to make it all the way to the Cheviot Hills and beyond."

Elinor wrapped Alistair's reins around her hand, then turned to Merida's horse. She could tell by his broad chest, shiny coat, and lush mane that he had been well cared for, which made her wonder yet again where this girl had come from. Was she really of Clan DunBroch? If so, why were there not scores of those redheaded louts looking for her?

There were vagabonds throughout these lands, wanderers who had been cast out of their clans. But this girl did not appear to be a castoff. She wore no clan's colors. Elinor had no doubt she belonged to someone.

Was she foolish to trust her? Was she inviting the enemy into her family's home? What if the redhead's injury was all an act? Some ruse to breach MacCameron Castle?

The alliance between the various clans that inhabited MacCameron Kingdom and its surrounding lands was fragile at best. If the treaty were to be infringed upon, she would bet her prized lute that the one to shatter it would be from DunBroch. The clan of feisty Highland warriors had at one time been Clan MacCameron's fiercest enemy.

What if this strange girl was a harbinger of bad news? And Elinor was the one who unleashed her onto her family?

But what if she wasn't?

No, Elinor's conscience would not allow her to leave the girl to fend for herself. The best she could do was pray that her instincts were not wrong, and that Merida was not faking her injuries.

Untying the shire from the tree and wrapping his reins around her free hand, she escorted the horses back to where she had left the girl.

Except Merida was no longer there.

CHAPTER SIX
Merida

Merida decided then and there that she would never forgive her mother for making her wear this ridiculous gown. She dropped her skirts, stood, and immediately grabbed on to the tree that she had dipped behind to relieve herself.

Once she felt steady enough to walk, she rounded the boulder to find the brown-haired young woman pacing in front of the two horses.

Elinor. An Elinor who was also of Clan MacCameron. The coincidence was almost too astonishing to believe.

Merida stood there for a moment, studying this girl who resembled her mother more than Merida herself did, who even shared her mother's name. Was she a distant cousin?

Angus huffed, clearly agitated by Elinor's pacing.

"Do not be alarmed, Angus," Merida said to the horse as she approached. She grabbed on to his neck, both to comfort him and to give herself something to hold on to.

Elinor whirled around and blasted Merida with a fiery glare. "Where did you go off to?"

"Over there," Merida said, pointing to the tree. She refused to say anything more. She might not be as proper as her mother, but there were some things she would not discuss with strangers, like relieving herself.

Merida took a step forward, intending to retrieve the plaid the girl had given her, but the dizziness returned with a vengeance. She would have hit the dirt if not for her reluctant rescuer wrapping her arms around her waist and steadying her.

"You are not well," Elinor said.

Merida groaned. The trees swayed, just as they had right after she had eaten the cake from that witch. Why was this still happening? How was it getting worse?

"Which is the way back to DunBroch?" Merida asked the girl, attempting to focus.

Elinor let out a sharp laugh. "You are in no condition to travel to DunBroch," she said. "It is at least three days' journey by horse."

Three days' journey?

Her head was still woozy, but Merida knew she had not traveled three days before reaching that wood-carver's cabin. She had been on Angus for barely an hour before he threw her.

"I am not sure you know where Castle DunBroch is," she told the girl.

"Of course I know," Elinor replied. "I traveled there with my father shortly after the alliance was agreed upon between the clans. You must get stronger before you can make that ride." She paused. "I will bring you to MacCameron Castle."

She looked at Merida's head, her eyes narrowing on the spot where Merida felt the knot growing.

Merida studied the other girl's face. This Elinor could not be more than a year or two older than Merida. If her mother had a relative who was so near Merida in age, wouldn't her mother have mentioned it? Could it be that her mother did not know about this girl? Was there an offshoot of the MacCameron clan closer to DunBroch than they'd thought?

Maybe she could learn more about this intriguing development, and rest, all at the same time. When she was well enough, she could take the news back to her parents.

"How far is this MacCameron Castle?" Merida asked.

"Not very far, unfortunately. Or, I guess it *is* fortunate for you that we will not have to travel very far. I doubt you would make it otherwise," Elinor said. "You'll ride with me. And I shall hold on to your horse's reins. Wait." The girl put up her hand before Merida could protest.

Merida heard the sound that she had heard the day before, the one she had mistaken for thunder.

Elinor put a finger to her lips. "Let us go before they see us," she whispered.

"Who?" Merida asked.

"I do not know," she answered. "But a group of men encountering two young lasses in the forest is never ideal, especially if they are my father's men."

"Why would . . ." Merida said, but the young woman had already started for the horses.

Elinor guided her horse over to the boulder Merida had used to support herself earlier.

"Climb up here and mount. I will be here to steady you."

She held Merida's hand as she made her way onto the black horse. Elinor hopped on expertly in front of her.

"Hold on to my waist," she told Merida. "You can rest your head on me. I do not want you getting dizzy and falling off."

Merida did as she was told. As she rested her head

against Elinor's back, she was surprised by the sudden onslaught of emotion that welled up within her. This small act of kindness was overwhelming after the tumult of the past twenty-four hours. Even if it was coupled with a reproachful tone.

The clamor of horse hooves grew louder, causing both Merida and Elinor to sit upright.

"We must depart," Elinor said. She snapped the reins, and the horse started forward. As they ascended a modest mound, Merida caught a glimpse of the men on horseback.

"Wait!" she said.

"Shhh!" Elinor warned.

"But . . ." Merida continued looking over her shoulder. The men wore the DunBroch tartan. The ocean blue, scarlet, and green colors of her clan were unmistakable. She was unable to tear her eyes away as five men dismounted from their horses and attended to something on the ground.

Merida's mouth fell open as she watched them lift an unconscious man and drape him across the back of one of the horses. A large figure with fiery red hair.

Just like her own.

She caught the briefest glimpse of the man's face and sucked in a breath.

"It cannot be," Merida whispered, her mind refusing to register what she was witnessing.

"Shhh, lass," Elinor said.

All the pieces began to fall into place, forming a picture that could not possibly be real. She had heard this story countless times, relayed in her father's jovial voice, with her mother reining him in when he started to embellish. A story she'd heard again not three months earlier . . .

Merida recalled the horse she had heard neighing last night, and how it had galloped away just before the hare she had killed for her supper had appeared.

"It cannot be," Merida said again.

"What cannot be?" Elinor asked in a harsh whisper.

Merida pulled back slightly and peered at Elinor's face, drawing her gaze over every inch. The girl had the same slim nose and high cheekbones as her mother.

"Why are you staring at me that way?" Elinor asked, her eyes widening with agitation.

And that was when Merida saw it.

Right there, in the corner of Elinor's left eye, was the same tiny gray dot that her mother had. When Merida was a child, her mother would jokingly tell her the mark gave her special powers that allowed her to see everything that Merida was doing.

Merida's head felt muddled, the mixture of confusion and disbelief making her dizzy.

"Do you know King Fergus?" Merida asked Elinor.

"There is no King Fergus," the girl replied. "I told you; the only king is my father."

"Just Fergus then. Fergus of DunBroch? His father would be the clan's chieftain."

Elinor shook her head. "I do not know of any Fergus. There are too many of those DunBrochs to know each by name."

"You said there was a peace alliance between your two clans. Do you know if someone from Clan DunBroch was due to arrive with a message from their chieftain?"

"I would not be surprised," Elinor answered. "Chieftains often send emissaries to my father, from Argyll to Strathaven and all points in between. Why?"

Merida shook her head. She was not sure what to make of any of this. It made no sense.

Was it possible she was still sleeping? That this was all a dream? Would she wake up to find herself still in the forest, with the Highland Games still taking place at Castle DunBroch, and her mother still expecting her to marry Lord Dingwall's son?

She needed to think through this, but her head pounded

too much to focus on what she *thought* was happening. And there was no way what she *thought* was happening *really* was happening. It could not be.

They started in the direction that Merida was certain she had traveled from when leaving the ring of stones, but she and Elinor didn't encounter anything that looked remotely like the menhirs she had stumbled upon the day before. Angus walked dutifully alongside them. Merida wished she could be on his back right now, if just to feel something sturdy and familiar beneath her. She hated feeling helpless. Being in such a vulnerable position—having to rely on strangers—it was not Merida's way. And at present it could be very dangerous indeed.

In a short time, they reached the edge of the forest. Merida could make out a large stone curtain wall. It had to be at least a hundred hands tall.

Elinor brought them to a stop.

"We will have to leave your horse here for a short time," she said as she dismounted her own horse and held out a hand for Merida.

"What? No," Merida protested.

"It will not be for long," Elinor said. "There are dozens of MacCameron horses, but our stable hands know them all. If we arrive with such a big, healthy horse, people will question who he belongs to." She bit her lower lip. "People will question who *you* belong to."

"I already told you, I belong to Clan Dun—"

"If you are really a DunBroch, then I should not have to explain to you why broadcasting such news would not be to your advantage," Elinor said, cutting her off. "This peace alliance is still new. If I bring you into our castle, people will question your presence. Everyone knows that your chieftain would not send a young lass out alone. They may assume that you are here to cause trouble."

Elinor bit her lip again as she looked between Merida, the curtain wall surrounding the castle grounds, and Angus.

"We should hide your hair." Her eyes roamed over Merida. "One look at it and anyone will know you are either Clan DunBroch or Clan Carruthers. Neither will win you any friends in the castle. Here." She pulled a shawl in the MacCameron tartan from the sack she carried and wrapped it around Merida's head.

Merida flinched when she got close to the knot on her forehead, but Elinor was surprisingly gentle, making sure not to touch the injury.

"That is better," Elinor said. "At least this will get you into the castle without arousing suspicion. You will have to remove the head covering when the physician arrives, but he will not hold your status as a DunBroch against you if I vouch for you." Then Elinor leaned in close. "But if this is all a ruse, I will take my own dagger to your throat."

Merida's head snapped back.

"It is not a ruse," she said. "I promise. I . . . I just need a bit more sleep, and then I will be able to think more clearly."

And she needed to find that witch.

CHAPTER SEVEN
Elinor

Elinor squinted as she tried to pass the slate-colored silk thread through the eye of her needle. She had known this part of the tapestry—one of dozens that told their clan's story throughout history—would be difficult. Why couldn't she weave a meadow of bright flowers and soft blue skies instead of MacCameron Castle? Its muted hues were so hard to distinguish from one another. Or from the gray of this blasted needle.

As she examined the design, Elinor acknowledged that this piece, which she had worked on tirelessly for the past two years, inspired very little joy. She feared she was no longer capable of experiencing such an emotion while living within these walls, not after that small but delicious taste of freedom she had sampled before finding the redheaded girl in the woods.

To dwell on what she had lost would only bring heartache, so she would embroider. She would embroider and play the lute and direct the staff and do all the other things a proper princess was expected to do.

For now.

Elinor released a sigh as she returned her attention to the needle and thread. She squinted, trying to bring the needle's slim eye into focus so she could pass the thread through it.

"Stop biting your lip."

Elinor snapped to attention. She looked up to find her mother standing in the doorway to the drawing room.

Anyone who did not know Queen Catriona would assume her severe frown was a sign of unparalleled displeasure, but Elinor recognized it as her mother's normal expression. The matriarch of Clan MacCameron was not known to smile, especially when in the presence of her only daughter.

"I apologize," Elinor said. She straightened her spine, lest she give the queen something else to harp on. "I have encountered difficulties threading the needle."

Her mother entered the room and snatched the silk thread and tapestry needle from Elinor's hands. With precision, the queen inserted the delicate silk through the narrow eye on the first try.

"Maybe if you spent more time practicing your sewing instead of gallivanting around the countryside on that horse, you would be better at it."

"I apologize," Elinor said again. It was a frequent refrain, and it was never enough where her mother was concerned.

Queen Catriona looked down her regal nose at her. Elinor could only guess at what fault she found in her daughter that day.

"Tell me. Who is this girl you have brought into the castle?" her mother asked.

So, she had gotten word about Merida. Elinor had wondered how long it would take before the queen was informed. Her father had been apprised of Elinor's return moments after she had entered the castle, along with word of the young girl with a head injury that she had found in the woods.

But she wondered how much Queen Catriona knew of the situation. Her mother was not usually privy to all the details her father received, something Elinor suspected was a bone of contention between the king and queen. After all, Elinor's mother was the one of royal lineage, yet it was her father who had been given the authority to preside over the kingdom.

The practice galled her. If she were to ever serve as queen, Elinor would insist the rules change. She would demand to be an equal partner to her husband in the running of the kingdom.

Elinor answered her mother's question: "The girl is of no importance. She was lost and injured. I could not leave her in the forest to fend for herself, not in the condition in which I found her."

"*You* should not have been in the forest," her mother snapped. "What were you doing there?"

"I took Alistair out for exercise," Elinor lied. "There was too much activity in the bailey, so I decided to take him out for a ride in the woods. It was such a lovely morning, I lost track of the time."

Her mother continued to stare at her with a look of singular disapproval. Elinor fought to keep herself from squirming.

"You are the future queen of this kingdom." Queen Catriona began her oft-repeated diatribe. "You must conduct yourself as such. I have explained this to you on more than one occasion, Elinor. Princesses do not race their horses through the woods, and they certainly do not do so unaccompanied. What if you had been kidnapped?"

"But we are at peace—"

"Silence!" her mother hissed. "You are not so

dim-witted as to believe that one of these clansmen would not make away with you if given the chance. Peace accords be damned."

Her mother paused, seemingly to collect herself.

"It is not only rogue clansmen that pose a danger, Elinor. What if you had gotten lost or injured like this girl? Would you be able to get back to the castle on your own? What if . . . what if you had encountered Mor'du?" The queen's voice shook with rarely displayed emotion. "The perils that could befall you are too numerous to name. You mustn't put yourself in such danger again."

Witnessing her mother's concern for her was both surprising and rather comforting. Elinor did not doubt her mother's love for her, but the queen meted it out as if it were rare gold coins.

"I will make better choices in the future," Elinor promised.

Her mother's expression returned to its usual frostiness.

"Must I also remind you that you are to be married soon?" her mother asked. "I will not be here to hold your hand and teach you how to be a queen forever, Elinor."

Elinor put a hand to her stomach. Just the mention of her upcoming betrothal brought on a case of the vapors. She did not need her mother to remind her of what awaited her in the very near future, because it was all she could think about.

It was the reason she had to make her escape. And quickly.

She had been promised to the son of her father's most loyal chieftain since birth, but to say Elinor abhorred her impending groom was putting it mildly.

Yet Elinor knew she could not allow anyone to see just how much she loathed the thought of marrying her betrothed. She had to let her parents think that she was still their dutiful daughter, ready and willing to go along with centuries of tradition.

"Reminders are not necessary. I am well aware of my betrothal." She held out her palm. "May I please get back to my sewing?"

Elinor tried to keep her fingers from shaking as she returned to her tapestry, knowing the queen was watching her every move. She surreptitiously sucked in a deep breath as she pierced the fabric, then released, pulling the needle through. Her body remained tense, waiting for her mother to unleash more criticism.

But after several long, anxiety-riddled moments, Queen Catriona turned and walked out of the room without saying another word.

Elinor wilted the moment her mother cleared the doorway. She had survived another encounter with the queen unscathed.

Unscathed, but not unbothered.

Her mother made an important point about the dangers of the forest. Elinor was unsure how she would fare if any of the calamities the queen listed had occurred during her escape. Maybe she was not as prepared for the grueling journey south as she first thought.

But she knew someone who was.

Merida. Elinor had been shocked that a girl so young would have ventured into the forest on her own. And yet, what she had found even *more* shocking was how well Merida had survived her night in the woods. The girl had been able to build a fire and procure her own food, two skills Elinor did not possess but absolutely needed if she was going to be successful in her future escape.

A plan began to take shape.

Merida would be taken back to her clan once she recovered. If Elinor was allowed to accompany her, she would be able to use the journey as her means of escape. DunBroch's lands were to the west of MacCameron, past a small mountain range. She could reach DunBroch, then head south.

Her shoulders slumped as reality settled in.

If her father discovered Merida was of Clan DunBroch,

he would send word to the chieftain and request that the girl be retrieved as soon as possible. The king would not take the chance of sending her with his own men; if something happened to Merida while in MacCameron hands, it would break the delicately held peace alliance between their clans. The longer Merida remained here, the more of a liability she presented.

But that was only if anyone discovered that she was from DunBroch.

Elinor had to keep Merida's identity a secret for her plan to work. It should not be all that difficult. Even the physician did not know. He had examined the knot on Merida's forehead without removing Elinor's shawl.

All they needed was a fortnight, maybe even less. That should be enough time. Merida possessed all the skills Elinor needed to learn to survive her journey to the Lowlands.

She just had to convince the girl to teach them to her.

CHAPTER EIGHT
Merida

Merida woke to the sound of heavy feet shuffling back and forth across a stone floor. Several things struck her as odd as she lay upon the woolen mattress. The fact that she was in a bed and not on the hard ground seemed peculiar, but welcomed. And she was no longer cold. After spending the night in the forest without even her plaid to keep the chill out, she was just realizing how numb she had been.

The most stunning discovery was her clear head. Though still foggy, she did not suffer from the persistent pounding she vaguely remembered from the day before.

Had that been the day before? She had lost track of time.

She had also apparently lost track of where she was.

She had hoped she would wake up to find herself back in her bedchamber at Castle DunBroch. She would have done anything for that—even put up with her three brothers being a pain in her arse. Or her mother, for that matter.

But as she turned her head on the feather-filled pillow, Merida could tell she was not in her own bedroom. This room's windows were much smaller than those at DunBroch; it made the room even more drab. The heavy tapestry hanging on the wall was one she had never seen before. The scene depicted men engaged in a fierce battle. She looked to the right and noticed the dark wooden table next to the bed was bulky, not delicate like the one in her bedchamber.

Merida lowered the soft counterpane that covered her and sat up on her elbows.

"Ah, you're awake," came a voice thick with a heavy Highlander brogue. "I thought you would sleep more."

A plump woman dressed in a gray kirtle over a white tunic stood at the hearth on the far side of the room.

"As soon as I am done with this, I'll get the physician to check on you again," she said. She fed a layer of peat into the fireplace, and the dwindling flames immediately roared to life.

"Where am I?" Merida asked.

"You're in a guest chamber at MacCameron Castle. I thought they would stash you in the servant quarters, but I guess because the princess brought you here, they put you in one of the better rooms. You're a lucky one, lass," the woman said with a gentle smile.

The details of the past few hours came flooding back to her.

The woman walked over to Merida and reached for her head, but Merida pulled away.

It was the girl, Elinor, who had wrapped her head in this shawl for her own safety. It was Elinor who had rescued her. She was the princess the servant spoke of.

And possibly Merida's mother.

She needed answers more than she needed to be seen by a physician.

"Can I have some privacy?" she asked the servant.

"Of course, lass. And how about a bite to eat, as well? It's late, but there is leftover stew." She tilted her head to the side as she looked at Merida. "But I wonder if that may be a bit heavy for you, you think?"

Merida's stomach answered with a loud growl.

The servant laughed. "Or maybe not," she said. "I'm Orla, by the way. I tend to Princess Elinor and her mother, Queen Catriona."

"Catriona," Merida repeated.

"Yes." Orla nodded.

That confirmed it. Even taking into account the girl's name and her looks and that gray mark in her eye, Merida had still tried to tell herself that the Elinor who had rescued her could not possibly be the Elinor who now served as the matriarch of Clan DunBroch. But the grandmother Merida had never met was named Catriona. Which meant this Elinor MacCameron, who could not be more than twenty years in age, was indeed her mother.

But how?

"The cake," Merida whispered.

"What was that?" Orla asked.

"Oh, nothing," Merida said. She put a hand to her head. "Just a bit woozy."

"Should I get the physician now, then?"

"No, no!" Merida said.

The bedchamber's door opened, and another woman walked in. She was younger than Orla, with a long light brown braid sticking out from underneath her kerchief. But it was the girl's striking blue eyes that grabbed Merida's attention. They shimmered like ice.

And they looked just as cold.

"Can I help you, Aileen?" Orla asked.

Aileen? From what Merida could recall from her studies, the name meant "ray of sunshine" in the old language.

If this lass was a ray of sunshine, Merida did not want to see what a gloomy day looked like.

"I was sent for the chamber pot," Aileen answered. "Apparently, the queen's maids are above such lowly tasks, so they sent for someone in the kitchens to do it."

"It is empty," Merida said quickly.

The girl flashed those cold eyes at her for only a moment before returning her attention to Orla. The tension that stretched between the two women was so thick Merida could practically feel it on her skin.

"You heard the girl," Orla said. "The chamber pot is empty. I shall have someone call for you when you are needed."

"Or maybe the maids can do their jobs."

"That will be all, Aileen," Orla said.

Merida looked on in fascination as the girl stuck her pert nose in the air and left the bedchamber. Orla's disapproving glare followed her. Merida did not pay much attention to household politics, but surely she would have sensed if such hostility had been present among their staff at DunBroch.

The maid turned back to Merida and smiled, though it seemed more strained than it had been prior to Aileen's interruption.

"Where were we?" Orla said. "The physician. Should I fetch him?"

"No," Merida repeated. "Thank you for tending the fire and for offering supper, Orla, but I do not think I can hold anything down."

"Are you sure I cannot do anything more for you, lass?"

"I am sure. What I need most right now is more sleep."

"I understand," the woman replied with a nod. "I'll be on my way. And I'll make sure no one disturbs you."

Merida waited several minutes after the woman had left the room before she jumped out of bed. She was certain she was on the right track when it came to that blasted cake. Something about the spell hidden within it had set all of this into motion.

Orla had mentioned that it was late, past suppertime. Remaining in this bed would not get her the answers she desperately needed. She had to get to the witch's cottage.

Merida looked around for her slippers and found them in front of the hearth. She closed her eyes and released a sigh of pleasure as she slipped her feet into the warm shoes. She did not look forward to going out into the cold night, but these would stave off the chill. At least for a while.

But as she wrapped the tartan shawl Elinor had given

her around her shoulders, Merida realized how foolhardy it would be for her to leave this castle in the middle of the night. She was not familiar enough with these woods to navigate them during the day. How much more difficult would it be to do so in the dark?

She sank to the floor.

Making such rash decisions had landed her in this position in the first place. Maybe she should seek out Elinor and try to get more information from her instead.

But what information could the girl—her mother—give her? If Princess Elinor had known who Merida was when she happened upon her, she certainly would have said so by now. And this younger Elinor had been adamant that she did not know of King Fergus.

Because there *was* no King Fergus. Her grandfather, Douglass MacCameron, was the reigning king of this area of Scotland. And her father—the man she had known as the King of DunBroch her entire life—was very likely still a young clansman.

A young clansman who was supposed to have been rescued by Princess Elinor in the woods, Merida realized. A sinking feeling came over her. Instead of her mother rescuing her father and nursing him back to health, Princess Elinor had discovered Merida in the forest. It was as if she had taken her father's place when, in reality, she should not have even been born yet.

Merida covered her face in her hands. Confusion riddled her senses, making her head spin with questions that continued to grow every minute.

And then, in front of the warm hearth, Merida fell into a restless sleep.

The physician greeted Merida with a smile the following morning.

"You're lookin' much better. Even for sleeping on the ground." The man had the cheeriest disposition Merida had ever seen on someone who witnessed sickness and death on a routine basis. He'd barked out a laugh when he'd seen her in front of the hearth, startling her awake, then escorted her back to bed. "How's your head?"

"It no longer feels as if my horse is grinding his hoof on it," Merida said.

"That sounds better to me," the man said with another laugh. He used two fingers to press lightly at the skin around Merida's injury. "Looks as if that bump has gone down some, but you've still got a nice egg there." His finger got closer to the knot, and Merida flinched.

"Still tender?"

She nodded. Her head felt better than she was letting on, but Merida figured if she could buy more time by convincing the physician that she needed extra rest, she could keep the staff away from this room. It would give her the opportunity to slip out and go in search of the witch's cottage.

"I will have someone from the kitchen bring up a little porridge to break your fast. Then you can get more rest," the physician said. "Here in bed, preferably."

Merida nodded. She was not going to turn down her morning meal after skipping supper last night. Besides, she needed the sustenance if she was going to spend her day searching for the cottage.

Another servant—one much younger than Orla, but whose eyes and nose showed a strong family resemblance—arrived with a bowl of hot porridge sweetened with honey, along with an oatcake. Merida practically inhaled it all.

When the young maid returned to retrieve her breakfast tray, Merida said she would be following the physician's orders and going back to sleep.

"The physician advised that I not be disturbed for the rest of the day," she told the girl. "Can you make sure the servants and Princess Elinor are informed of his orders?"

The maid nodded, then backed out of the door and closed it behind her.

Just as she had done the night before, Merida waited

several minutes before getting out of bed and slipping on her shoes. She went over to the window, but it was well fortified. Not a surprise; it was the same way at Castle DunBroch. One could never be too careful, and according to Elinor, the peace between the clans surrounding MacCameron land was still very fragile. Any good king would make certain his home was impenetrable. Which meant it would be more difficult for Merida to sneak out.

She walked to the wooden wardrobe against the wall. Her legs went weak with relief upon finding several kirtles in various shades of gray and green. Compared with her gown, one of these would blend in much better with the forest.

Merida disrobed, folding the woolen shift she had been given to sleep in and setting it on the floor of the wardrobe. Then she retrieved a dark green kirtle and pulled it over her head. It had obviously been made for someone taller than she; the hem dragged on the floor. But it would have to do.

She slipped on her shoes, gathered her skirts in her hand, and made her way to the door. Merida put an ear to the cool wood, listening for footsteps. She heard none.

Was it because the rest of the household staff was off attending to their duties, or because the door was so thick that she could not hear through it?

There was one way to find out.

Sucking in a deep breath, she opened the door a crack

and slowly stuck her head out. She looked from left to right, her heart beating like a flock of wild geese. The glow from the candles illuminated the corridor, but they did not cast any shadows on the opposite wall; it was empty.

She had been too groggy to pay attention to the layout of the castle when she was brought in the day before, so Merida thought back to what she knew of the one at DunBroch.

All castles were, first and foremost, military fortresses, designed to shield the royal family by keeping them as far from enemy invaders as one could. The guest chambers would be closest to the front of the gallery and Great Hall, with the family's sleeping quarters near the keep—the safest part of the castle.

Taking a chance that MacCameron Castle had been designed with similar intentions, Merida slipped out of the door and moved left, flattening her back against the wall as she hastily shuffled toward the front.

She heard the murmur of voices just as she reached a shallow alcove. She ducked inside and cursed herself for not choosing a gray kirtle. It would have blended in better with the walls.

The voices grew louder. They spoke in thick brogues, so thick that Merida could barely make out the words. She heard Elinor's name and what sounded like the queen's, but she could not be sure. As they drew closer, she closed her eyes and tried to come up with a plausible excuse.

"The king is with his council," came a voice that sounded vaguely familiar. "We must wait until he is alone."

"The king is never alone," a craggy male voice returned. "We must wait."

Merida frowned as she tried to place them, but she had been in this castle for less than a day. She did not know anyone here well enough to distinguish one voice from another.

After several agonizing moments, the whispering and footsteps retreated, going the opposite way.

Merida slowly leaned forward out of the alcove, looking both ways. The narrow corridor was once again empty, but if the past five minutes were anything to go on, it would not remain that way for long. She gathered her skirts and tiptoed faster, making her way through the gallery and past the banquet hall.

A human-shaped shadow appeared before she had the chance to hide. Merida gasped, but it looked as if luck was still on her side. The shadow belonged to a young maid who carried an armful of linens, stacked high and blocking her vision. Merida lowered her head and turned her face away from the maid as she passed her in the corridor.

Just as she rounded a corner, she heard someone call out, "Who goes there?"

She panicked. She did not know if she had been seen, and she would not take the time to find out. She quickly ducked into the first room she could get to, flattened her back against the door . . .

And screamed.

CHAPTER NINE
Merida

Merida covered her mouth with both hands and cursed herself for being such a ninnyhammer. She then cursed the stuffed wild boar head mounted on the opposite wall for scaring her.

After taking a moment to catch her breath, she finally took the time to look around and realized she was in the drawing room. Sometimes drawing rooms had . . . She looked around and spotted it.

Yes! There was a servants' entrance, and Merida would have bet anything that just off the servants' entrance was a passageway to the scullery, larder, and courtyards.

She crossed the room and slipped through the small doorway, and within minutes found herself outside in the bailey. She remembered where she and Elinor had entered and quickly made her way to the side gate.

Rushing forward, Merida was hit with a wave of emotion when she spotted Angus standing near the tree where they had left him the previous day. He grazed on the grass as if enjoying a typical morning meal, oblivious to the fact that both of their lives had been flipped upside down.

"Hey there, boy," Merida greeted her horse. Angus neighed happily when he spotted her, dancing in a circle before pummeling her with his head.

"I've missed you, too."

She climbed onto Angus's back, and they took off in the direction Merida and Elinor had traveled from earlier. As they rode deeper into the forest, the thick leaves shielded more of the sun, making it harder to distinguish the path from the rest of the forest floor. They were just cresting a short mound, Merida wondering which direction she should try next, when she caught sight of a soft glow out of the corner of her eye.

"Hold, Angus," she said, drawing up the horse's reins.

She focused on the area where she had seen the light. There it was again.

"A wisp," Merida breathed.

There was another one. Then another.

Finally—a lead!

"Come, Angus," she whispered. She directed the horse to follow the little blue flashes of light, even as trepidation floated around in her stomach.

She wasn't sure she should trust the wisps, considering what had happened the last time she followed them. Then again, the wisps were her best chance of finding that wood-carver's cottage.

Maintaining her distance, Merida stayed several yards behind the tiny blue sparks as they scurried through the woods. She frowned when the wisps stopped, flickering brighter for a moment as they gathered, then disappeared.

"Here?" she asked, stopping Angus at the start of the stone path. The wisps had guided her back to the village that she had been chased away from the day before.

If it was true that wisps were meant to lead her to her fate, then her fate must have been to get her head bashed in with a broom.

She tied Angus's reins to a post next to a trough and left him to drink water while she ventured farther down the path, her feet moving quickly. She walked past the butcher, remembering his less than warm welcome, choosing instead to visit the blacksmith.

A bell chimed above her head as she entered the shop.

"Hello," Merida called.

"Well, hello there, lass," a man wearing a dinted face

shield greeted. "What can I do for you?" He set down his tongs and lifted the shield, revealing a gap-toothed smile.

Merida returned his smile, immediately feeling more at ease from this vastly different reception. It was nice to know there *were* some pleasant people in this little village.

"Good day to you, sir," she said, walking farther into the shop. "Uh . . . this question may seem a bit . . . odd, but do you know of an old wood-carver who specializes in bears? She has wiry gray hair and keeps a pet bird."

His wrinkly forehead creased even more with his frown. "Only one wood-carver here, lass. Well, two, if you count her daughter. I don't know about no pet bird. And both their hair is as black as the coal in this here forge," he said, pointing to the smoldering hearth in the center of his shop. "Though the daughter has that silver streak. Folks say she was struck by lightning."

Merida remembered the woman who had caught her eye during her previous visit. She'd had a streak of silver in her hair.

"Can you tell me where to find them?" she asked the blacksmith.

"I wouldn't bother if I were you." He scratched his scruffy beard, then motioned for Merida to come closer. Leaning toward her, he whispered, "Trust me, lass. Stay away."

The bell above the door chimed and another man, wearing a saffron-colored léine, entered. The blacksmith's face lit up.

"Sir," Merida called, but the blacksmith had already turned his attention to the other customer.

Merida left the shop. After checking on Angus, she started for the next thatched-roof building—a leatherworker, according to the sign above the door. Just as she reached for the handle, an unsettling feeling raced up Merida's spine. She caught sight of a figure in black out of the corner of her eye.

Merida turned and spotted the woman—the one with the protrusive nose and silver streak in her hair. She must have been the wood-carver's daughter the blacksmith had spoken of.

She stood outside a tiny building at the end of the dirt road and stared at Merida. Her piercing gaze made Merida uncomfortable, but there was something familiar about her. Merida could not pinpoint what it was that drew her in. She started in the direction of the woman, but a man hitching his horse to a post outside the leatherworker's shop caught her by the arm.

"You don't want to go there, lass," the man said. He nodded in the direction of the woman. "She's a strange one."

"What do you mean by strange?" Merida asked.

"I won't say more." He shook his head and looked over his shoulder. "But you would be better off staying away," he said, echoing the blacksmith.

Merida considered heeding their warnings, but decided to keep going. After all, *she'd* been considered an interloper not twenty-four hours ago. Approaching the shop with caution, Merida glanced up at the building. There was nothing indicating what type of business was housed there, just a plain wooden door with a jagged groove carved down the center, as if someone had taken a chisel to it.

Merida knocked, even as she recognized how silly it was to do so, given that this was a business that was opened to the public. But unlike the previous shops she had visited, it did not feel right to just barge in.

There was a faint voice behind the door, which Merida took as an invitation. Yet when she walked in, the shop was empty.

Of everything. No items for sale, no shelves, no people. Only four bare walls.

"Hello?" Merida called, searching for any sign of life.

"Oh, hello there!"

She jumped. She turned to find a much older woman with raven-black hair and striking gray eyes walking through a side door she had not even noticed was there.

"Welcome, welcome, welcome," the woman greeted.

"We are altering the shop, so all our carvings are in the back room. Follow me."

The woman flew past Merida and headed for the opposite side of the room. She knocked three times on the bare wall, and a panel opened.

Merida's mouth fell open.

There were camouflaged doors at Castle DunBroch, intended to mislead intruders and give the household time to escape, but none as seamless as this one. How had they managed to conceal the doorway so well, and why would a shopkeeper need such a well-designed secret door? This did not seem like the kind of occupation that required quick escapes.

"Well, are you coming?" the woman called out to her.

Merida hesitated for a moment, then followed her into the back room. She stuttered to a stop the moment she crossed the threshold.

Bears. Hundreds and hundreds of bears. The carvings were everywhere and in all sizes, just as they had been at the witch's cottage.

"Who sent you here?"

Merida spun around. It was the other woman she had noticed standing outside the shop, the one with the streak of silver in her hair. She came charging toward Merida, grabbing her by the arm.

"What are you . . . ?" Merida said.

"Freya, you do not treat customers this way," the older woman said.

"I do not think she is a customer, Ma," the younger of the two answered.

The older woman shrugged and walked over to a tree stump that had been sliced in half.

The one called Freya slapped at the wall, and yet another hidden door opened. Still holding on to Merida's arm, she pulled her into a smaller room that had nothing but a lone bench sitting in the middle of it. Then she turned and plopped her hands on her hips.

"Did someone from the Council send you?" she asked.

"Council? What council? I have no idea what you are speaking of," Merida answered.

"Do not lie to me." She leaned forward and sniffed Merida's hair. "I smell the magic on you. You can tell the Council that I have not practiced another spell since their last reprimand."

"Spell?" Merida took a step back. "You *are* a witch."

"Well, aren't you the claymore calling the broadsword dull," Freya said with a huff.

"What does that even mean?"

The woman looked over her shoulder and, in a hushed voice, said, "It means that it takes a witch to know a witch."

"But I am *not* a witch."

Freya's eyes narrowed. She sniffed at Merida's shoulder, and again at her hair. "If you are not a witch, then why do I sense magic coming from you? Who are you? What is it you are seeking from me?"

Was it possible that this woman could help her?

"I am seeking answers," Merida said. "I need to know how I got here."

"You got here by horse. I saw your steed outside."

"Not *here* here," Merida said with a sigh.

Freya pointed an accusatory finger at Merida. "Look here, girlie. You had better—"

"Oh, my goodness!" Merida gasped. She finally recognized it, the thing she had not been able to pinpoint about the woman earlier. It was in the hand gesture and the way she twisted that bulbous nose.

"You're the old woman who gave me the cake," Merida whispered. Her eyes roamed over the woman's face. She shook her head, unable to process what she was seeing. "This cannot be." Her throat suddenly felt tight. She took several steps back as if putting physical distance between herself and the woman could change what was happening. This, even more than what she'd witnessed in the forest and on the way to MacCameron Castle, was alarming confirmation of what she suspected.

Somehow, she had traveled to a time before she was born. Before her parents had even met, back when their respective clans held very recent memories of being sworn enemies. "But how . . ." Merida asked in a weak voice.

"You start a question, but you do not finish it," Freya said. "Spit it out."

"I need to sort through what has happened," Merida said. "You see, I made a deal with a witch, and I believe that *you* are that witch. But you were much older. You sold me a cake that was supposed to change my mother, but I ate it instead, and now I am here." Merida cradled her head in her palms. "This does not make any sense, but there is no other explanation."

"Let me see if I understand this correctly," Freya said. "You are saying that you came to *me* for a spell? And the spell that *I* created sent you back in time?" Excitement danced in her eyes. "Do you know how powerful a witch has to be to create such a spell!" She clapped her hands together and squealed. "How long did it take? Was I confident in my ability, or did I seem afraid? Did I make any mistakes, or did I get the spell correct on the first try?"

"This is not about you," Merida practically shouted. "I do not belong here. You did this to me!"

"Me!" Freya jerked her head back. "It seems to me that *you* did this to yourself. You sought a spell to change your mother, but instead you used it. Do I have that right?"

"Yes," Merida answered.

"Well, you cannot just go around using spells intended for others. That is not how these things work."

"How do we fix it?"

"Why should I fix it? I did not break anything."

"Please," Merida pleaded. "I have nowhere else to turn."

Freya stared at her with a skeptical lift to her brow. After a moment, she took Merida by the hand and brought her to the bench.

"Before we can figure out how to fix it, we must figure out exactly what has happened," Freya said. "Now, start from the beginning."

Merida did just that, from how the wisps led her to the cottage hidden deep in the forest, to the deal they struck, to when Merida decided to eat the cake herself and woke up inside the ring of stones.

"I cannot be certain, but I am fairly sure that there are still quite a few years before I am even to be born," Merida finished.

"Is that so?" Freya asked. A self-satisfied smile curved up the corners of her mouth. "It sounds as if I am a very powerful witch in my old age." Her shoulders slumped. "Unfortunately, my current skills are . . . uh . . . not so powerful, shall we say." She put both hands up. "I am getting better every day, but I am still learning.

"Oh, I know!" Freya jumped up from the bench. "Wait right here."

Moments later, she returned with a parcel of worn animal hide secured with twine. She sat the package on her lap and the twine unraveled on its own, as if invisible fingers were untying it.

Merida gasped. "How did you do that?"

"I may not be an all-powerful witch—yet," Freya added, "but I do have some abilities." She lifted a book of bound linen sheets from the parcel. "Now, tell me what it is you were seeking when you inquired about the spell. I shall try to find the one I used."

"You did not consult a book," Merida said.

"I didn't?" Freya's eyebrows shot up. That cagey smile returned to her lips. "I must be an even better witch than I imagined. I hope I charged you a hefty price for this spell. Ma says I devalue our wood carvings all the time, but I think it is better to get some payment than no payment at all."

"Can we get back to the matter at hand?" Merida asked impatiently.

"Yes, of course," Freya said. "So, if I understand correctly, the formidable spell I created sent you back in time."

"Yes." Merida nodded. She hesitated for a moment, then said, "But that is not all."

She realized that if she wanted Freya to help her, she would have to share everything that had come to pass in the time since she first awoke in the forest.

"I believe I should start even farther in the past," Merida said. She tipped her head to the side. "Actually, it is not in the past, but in the future. This is so confusing."

"I do have other business to tend to today," Freya prompted.

Merida quickly told her the story of how her parents met, ending with the man she'd seen being rescued the day before. Freya's mouth gaped, her jaw dropping more with every detail.

"What do you make of this?" Merida was almost afraid to ask once she was done. She prayed Freya had a logical answer.

"I think it is obvious," Freya said. "You spent the night in MacCameron Castle. You know who Elinor is."

"She is my . . . my mother," Merida said.

"Based on what you have told me, yes, I believe she is," Freya answered. "I also believe the two of you never should have met, at least not under these circumstances. Elinor *should* have happened upon the emissary from Clan DunBroch in the woods yesterday. That was her fate."

"I know." Merida groaned.

"But she met *you* instead," Freya continued. "And because she rescued *you*, I suspect it has disrupted what was supposed to have come to pass."

She returned her attention to the book in her lap, mumbling to herself as she skimmed the pages. It was disorienting, seeing this younger woman yet knowing somewhere inside of her resided the gray-haired wood-carving witch. But of all the people she had encountered since waking up in the woods, Freya seemed to be the only one who knew Merida's true identity. Appealing to her was Merida's only choice if she wanted things to return to normal.

Merida thought quickly back to the wisps, the witch's cottage, the split-second decision she'd made to use the spell for herself. "What would've happened if I'd given the cake to my mother instead?"

The witch tsked, wagging a finger at her, resembling her older form. "No, no. That's not how this works. No going back now. Metaphorically speaking, of course."

"I just wanted to change my fate—"

"Well, you have. You have changed your fate in unexpected ways. And I suspect not just your own, either."

An uneasy weight settled in the pit of Merida's stomach. "What do you mean?"

"We are all connected in some way, Merida. I am certain that the fate of many now hangs in the balance," Freya said.

She read more, her expression becoming more troubled by the moment.

Merida's heart thudded. "Can you help me fix it? Create another spell?"

"There is no easy way to do this," Freya said. "You cannot just magic-spell your way out of every problem. The less magic we introduce into this situation, the less chance we have of causing further disruption."

"So what do I do?"

"You have to figure out another way to bring your parents together."

"Oh, just that," Merida muttered. She thought about how suspicious young Elinor had been of Clan DunBroch in general, of her father's unconscious form being taken away by his clansmen. Finding a way for the two of them to meet on pleasant terms—let alone fall in love—seemed like a tall order.

"Even if I do find a way to get them together, what about me? How will I go back . . . to *my* time?"

Freya considered this, looking up to the ceiling as though the answer were written there. "Hmmm . . ." She glanced back at the book in her lap, flipping through the yellowed pages. "Uh-huh . . . uh-huh . . ."

She raised a finger. "The summer solstice. There is much power in that moment when the sun is at its highest. It opens pathways to the unknown. Get your parents back on track before then, and there should be an opening to send you home."

The book of spells disappeared. Freya rose and started to nudge Merida toward the secret door.

"You had better get moving. The solstice will coincide with the Highland Games in less than a fortnight, which will take most folks' attention. You get your parents to fall in love, and I will work on finding a spell to send you home."

Freya ushered her past the chamber filled with bear carvings, and then into the empty front room. Merida looked around for the older woman, but she was nowhere to be found.

"Wait!" Merida yelled before Freya could push her out the front door. She turned. "What happens if I cannot get my mum and dad to fall in love before the summer solstice . . . exactly?"

"You do not want to find out, Merida."

And then Freya shut the door.

CHAPTER TEN
Elinor

The fire that crackled in the library's hearth had doubled in size, making the room stuffier than usual. Elinor itched to leave, but she had been at her lessons for only a short time. There was no way Queen Catriona would release her from this private hell so soon.

Of course, her mother did not consider this hell, but rather the most important aspect of her daughter's life. And because Elinor's success reflected her mother's tutelage, the queen would not settle for anything less than perfection. She believed the future queen must be adept in all manner of languages, geography, and a dozen other things Elinor would never use if she were to be merely someone's wife.

"I do not understand why I must know how to speak

the old language of Northumbria," Elinor said. "It is hardly used anymore. Besides, I will never set foot on the soil in Strathclyde or Galloway or any of the other places where it was spoken. You and Father have made sure of that."

"Because you are a princess, and you must show that you are knowledgeable about the history and languages of all areas of this country, not just your own," her mother replied. "It does not matter that you will never go there."

Except the area that made up the ancient kingdom of Northumbria was exactly the place Elinor had in mind as she planned her escape. The vast lands that made up the southern tip of Scotland were known for their beauty, and the people were known for their intellect. Every book she had read in the past two years had come out of that area. Even after the Danes had tried to suppress the cultural life when they invaded in the previous century, the spirit of the scholars and the artists would not be denied. Elinor longed to explore it all.

Her mother continued to lay out the various lessons on Elinor's schedule for the day. Between her language lessons, music lessons, and instructions in how to conduct clan diplomacy, Elinor was not sure if she would have time to catch her breath.

But what she *really* needed to do, more than any lesson her mother had in store for her, was talk to MacCameron

Castle's newest patient. She had not had a chance to check in on Merida all morning, although she had been assured by Orla and Gavina that the girl was resting comfortably after being tended to by the physician.

Elinor had no doubt that the MacCameron physician had treated Merida's injury with the utmost care. She was sure to be healed and able to return to her home in no time. Which was why Elinor needed to see her as soon as possible.

"Are you listening to me?"

Elinor snapped to attention. "Of course, Mother," she said. "What were you saying?"

Her mother's lips thinned to the point of being non-existent. Elinor tried her best not to cower under her severe stare, but after a lifetime of being the recipient of such looks, adjusting her reaction to them was not easy.

Queen Catriona remained silent, her nose pointed up in the air.

"I am sorry," Elinor finally said, knowing she would not be allowed to leave this room without issuing the apology her mother's expression demanded.

She would do whatever was necessary to get her mother out of this room so that she could get to Merida. This young and brave Merida of DunBroch—who knew how to kill a hare with a bow and arrow, how to skin it and cook it—would teach Elinor everything she needed to learn in order for her to escape the prison that was her life.

She was a meticulous planner, but it wasn't until she observed Merida's makeshift camp in the woods that Elinor realized just how unprepared she was. She had calculated the amount of provisions she needed to pack, but what if she encountered a delay? She had no contingency if she were to run out of food. She had to be ready for anything if she wanted to make a successful escape.

"May I be excused?" Elinor asked her mother. "I would like to check on Merida before dinner."

"There are servants and a physician to check on that girl you brought here," her mother said. "You have more important things to tend to."

"Can I not have a short break, Mother? I would like to make sure she is doing well. I found her, after all. I feel as though she is my responsibility."

"Your responsibility is to your lessons and to your clan," the queen replied.

"Yes, ma'am," Elinor said with a slight nod.

A long, fraught silence stretched between them. Elinor knew it was yet another way for her mother to exert her control, the way she made her daughter sit under her intense scrutiny, daring her to move a single muscle. Elinor kept her entire body as rigid as possible.

"You never explained exactly *how* you and that girl happened to cross paths," her mother said.

Elinor went into more detail about her discovery of an injured Merida in the woods, embellishing some parts of the story and leaving out others.

The queen's eyes narrowed. "I had better not learn that you were doing anything untoward, Elinor."

"I would never consider it," Elinor said. "May I be excused?" she asked again.

More silence.

Finally, her mother said, "Go. But you will be tested on languages tomorrow. I expect an exemplary performance."

Elinor nodded again, then pushed away from the table. She maintained a steady gait as she exited the library, holding her head up in the regal manner in which she had been taught, knowing her mother was observing her every step.

The moment she crossed the threshold, Elinor picked up the pace, her excitement at the thought of making her plea to Merida spurring her forward. But that was not the only thing hastening her steps.

She was running out of time.

Her betrothal would be announced at the Highland Games. If she did not make her getaway before the announcement, it would only make it that much harder for her to escape.

Having the entirety of Clan MacCameron on her heels was one thing, but once she was officially betrothed to Lachlan, the eldest son of the chieftain of Clan Fraser, both clans would consider themselves responsible for her. And Clan Fraser would see it as an affront if she were to leave after a pledged union was announced to one of their own.

The potential implications of what could happen if her betrothal became official made Elinor's heart race. It was imperative that she leave before that happened.

She lifted the hem of her kirtle as she ran up the stairs to the row of guest chambers. The girl had been placed in the one farthest from the family quarters, a standard practice at the castle. Precautions were taken to ensure the safety of the king and queen, even from an injured slip of a girl who would be easily overcome by the many guards in the castle.

"Oh, there you are, Princess," she heard just as she approached the door to Merida's guest chamber. Elinor whirled around, her eyes bulging as Morag, her mother's longest-serving and most loyal maid, drew near.

Elinor had to remind herself that she had no reason to feel guilty. No one in the household knew what she planned to ask Merida.

"Yes, Morag?"

"Queen Catriona wanted me to remind you that you are

to wear the sapphire gown tonight, so you should not eat anything else before dinner."

Elinor did her best to keep her cynical reaction to herself.

It was not as if they were having company tonight. Would it be the end of creation if she attended a simple dinner with her family dressed in a regular kirtle and not a confining gown?

Her mother took great pleasure in constantly reminding Elinor of the privilege she enjoyed, being the daughter of the king and queen of their kingdom. But Elinor often wondered what life would be like if she had been born to someone else. She would be glad to feed the hens or muck the horse stalls if it meant dining in a loose-fitting gown.

Well, maybe not the horse stalls.

"Would you have Gavina ready the gown for tonight?" Elinor asked the maid.

The woman nodded, then continued down the corridor.

Elinor waited until she could no longer hear Morag's heavy footsteps or those of anyone else before entering Merida's chambers. She opened the door and her heart dropped.

The room was empty.

CHAPTER ELEVEN
Merida

After tying Angus's reins to the tree where he had spent the previous night, Merida used her fingernails to brush down his coat, whispering soothing promises she was unsure she could keep. Not after everything she had learned from the witch.

She rested her forehead against Angus's long nose.

"I'm sorry I ever ate that cake," she whispered.

No, she was sorry she'd ever approached the wood-carver's cottage.

Better yet, she was sorry she had ever left Castle DunBroch in such haste. If she had not run away like a spoiled child and had instead talked things over with her mother like a princess on the verge of adulthood, none of this would have happened.

"This is all my fault." Merida let out a hiccuping sob, but quickly stanched her cries. Tears would get her nowhere. She needed to be clearheaded if she was to figure out what to do.

"I will fix this, Angus," Merida said. "I must."

The horse neighed and nudged Merida with his nose.

"I will be back for you soon," she told him. "Now that I know we won't be leaving this place for some time, we must find somewhere more permanent for you."

She patted Angus, then gathered her skirts and started for the castle. During her earlier escape, she had noticed a door directly across from the gate where she had left. Once inside the castle wall, Merida walked swiftly across the bailey, trying not to draw attention to herself.

Some of the tension in her muscles ebbed when she reached the door unnoticed. She gently pushed and leaned forward to get a peek inside.

It was the chandlery, the room where all the candles used to illuminate the castle were made. Dozens upon dozens of them hung by their wicks from rods that ran the length of the room. Merida quickly traversed the small room. She closed her eyes and tried to picture the layout of the castle as best as she could recall from the short time she had been there. If she was not mistaken, the scullery should be next, and then the kitchens.

She exited the chandlery and entered the next room. A scullery maid stood at a shallow basin, scrubbing a large, dented copper pot. Before Merida could speak, another girl came through the door.

"Who goes there?" she asked. It was the girl who had come to the bedchamber to collect the chamber pot, the one with the ice-blue eyes. She had an elegant nose and was very, very pretty.

Merida's heartbeat escalated. "Uh . . . I am sorry. I got lost," she answered.

"You're the lass Orla was seeing about last night," the girl said.

"Yes. I am a guest of Princess Elinor," Merida said.

"A guest?" The girl sniffed. "That's a bit fancy, ain't it? From what I heard, the princess found you sleeping in the woods like a lost dog."

Merida was astonished that a maid would not only speak to a guest of the princess in such a way, but also repeat the gossip going around the kitchen between servants.

She held her head high. "If you will excuse me, I must return to my room," Merida said.

She made her way through the scullery and kitchens without further complications, but the moment Merida entered the chamber where she had spent the previous night, she was accosted by a furious Elinor.

"Where have you been!" the princess yelled.

Merida squelched a yelp. "My goodness," she said, clutching a hand to her chest. "You frightened me!"

"You cannot just go sneaking around, lass. One would think you would have learned that lesson after what happened to you," Elinor said.

"I . . . I wanted to check on Angus," Merida said. It was not a total untruth. She had tended to her horse after her sojourn to the village.

"I do not care how good you are with the bow and arrow, 'tis unwise for you to go off on your own," Elinor said. The princess paced before the hearth, gesturing with her hands in a way *Queen* Elinor would have told Merida was unladylike.

Merida could not help looking at the girl in a new light now that she knew for certain she was her mother. There were so many questions she wanted to ask that she knew she could not. This young Elinor could not know of her relation to the girl she had rescued only the day before. Merida had no idea how she would go about explaining it, even if she were inclined to do so.

"How is the horse?" Elinor asked. She finally stopped pacing.

"He is well, but is there a way we can bring him onto castle grounds?" Merida asked. "The longer he remains in the woods, the more in danger he is of being stolen."

"You are right," Elinor said. She chewed her bottom lip. "I shall talk to Ewan. He is the steward's son. He can take care of your horse while also keeping him out of sight of the others until we figure out an explanation for how you came to own such a fine steed."

"Maybe we can say he was a gift from my mother," Merida said. "And now that I am an orphan, he is the only thing of value I possess."

"*Are* you an orphan?" Elinor asked. She scrutinized Merida's face, her eyes roaming over every detail.

Would she notice something familiar, a feature she recognized in the face of the child she bore?

But she could not, because *this* Elinor had not borne her. *This* Elinor had borne no children at all. It was still difficult for Merida to wrap her head around it all.

Merida put a hand to her knot, deciding to play up her injury. "I fear my affliction is still causing some confusion."

She looked to Elinor and tried her best not to exhibit any of the worriment currently tormenting her. Try as she might, she could not suppress her trepidation. Elinor's answer to her next question could make the difference in whether Merida was even afforded the chance to bring her parents together.

"Do you suppose I can remain at MacCameron Castle for another night or two?" she finally asked.

Elinor's head snapped back. "You want to stay?"

"Please. Just until I am feeling more like myself," she said.

The sudden excitement dancing in Elinor's eyes came as a shock. The girl peered over her shoulder, toward the door. She crept over to it and peeked out, into the corridor, then closed the door. She put a finger to her lips and took Merida by the hand.

Merida frowned, but followed her mother—Princess Elinor—as she led her to the small bathing room that was connected to her chamber. Merida had taken note of the ingenious design when she first arrived.

"What are we doing in here?" Merida whispered.

"I have a proposition for you," Elinor said. She peered back into the room. Whatever she was about to ask Merida, it was clear she wanted no one to hear, not even the servants.

"I know that you are wanting to return to your homeland once you are well, but I would very much appreciate it if you would stay on at MacCameron Castle for some time. Possibly as long as a fortnight."

Merida's mouth dropped open. "*You* want *me* to stay?"

Elinor nodded vigorously.

Merida was unable to believe her good fortune. She had spent the entirety of her journey from the village trying to think of a way to get Princess Elinor to allow her to stay at MacCameron Castle. She had determined that just a few days would give her enough time to come up with a more feasible living arrangement that could keep her here until she could figure out a way to get her parents to fall in love.

But she would not have to go to the trouble of convincing Elinor to do anything. The princess was *asking* her to stay.

But . . . why?

"Why would you want me to stay on at MacCameron Castle?" Merida asked.

Elinor looked over her shoulder yet again. Then, with a smile tipping up the corner of her mouth, she said, "I want you to teach me your ways, Merida."

"My ways?"

"Of survival. You can start a fire, shoot and cook your own food, and defend yourself. I need to learn to do such things."

"But you are the princess. Why would you ever need to learn those skills?"

Merida recognized the irony in her question. She, too, was a princess.

But *her* lessons of survival had been more about

bonding with her father, not necessity. Princess Elinor had an entire kingdom filled with warriors who would willingly lay down their lives to protect her. Merida could not think of a single scenario where Elinor would need to use survival techniques.

Her eyes still twinkling, Elinor leaned in. In a whisper, she said, "Because the Highland Games will soon be upon us. And I plan to escape this castle and my fate before they begin."

CHAPTER TWELVE
Merida

Merida knew she must look like a fish gasping for breath the way her mouth hung open, but she could not close it. She just stood there, staring at the princess. She must have heard her wrong.

"Did you say you are planning your escape?" Merida asked when she was finally able to speak.

Elinor nodded excitedly.

"But . . . why?"

"*Why* I am leaving is not important. The only thing that matters is that I leave before the Highland Games begin," Elinor replied.

"What is so undesirable about the Highland Games?" Merida asked.

But then understanding dawned. Had she herself not just run away from DunBroch during the Highland Games? She knew better than most exactly what significance the games held to a princess of a certain age.

This must have been the year in which the firstborn sons from various clans would compete for her mother's hand, with her betrothal being announced shortly after. Apparently, like Merida, Princess Elinor did not agree with being handed out like a prize at a village fair.

Merida tried to summon a modicum of sympathy for MacCameron Castle's princess, but all she could feel in the moment was an overwhelming sense of resentment.

How many times had she been forced to listen to her mother go on and on about the importance of marriage and how it was a sacred duty she should embrace? Yet here Princess Elinor was, planning her big escape because she did not want to honor this archaic tradition. What about those stories of how marrying King Fergus was the best thing that had ever happened to her? To hear her parents talk about their romance, one would assume her mother had been delighted at the thought of becoming betrothed.

Merida's heart skipped as a thought suddenly occurred to her.

Was this the answer to her dilemma?

If her mother were to stay until the Highland Games,

and her father were to enter and win her hand, Merida would not have to go through the trouble of bringing them together.

Freya did not say that her parents must meet in the same way they originally had, just that they must fall in love. Her father winning the princess's hand would take care of the first part of that equation. She could only assume that love would eventually blossom between the two of them once they were together. It had happened once, hadn't it? Merida saw how her father lit up whenever her mother walked into a room, how the queen's eyes sparkled when he shared an anecdote. There were no two better suited for each other. And wouldn't an automatic betrothal help speed things up?

Merida could scarcely believe it, but it seemed the tradition she had despised with all her soul would be her saving grace.

Except that Elinor was determined not to go through with a betrothal at all.

"Is that what you were doing when you found me?" Merida now asked. "Were you trying to escape?"

"Shhh," Elinor said. She looked back at the door again, then answered Merida with a short nod. In a low whisper, she said, "And that is why you must help me, because I abandoned my plans in order to help you."

"But—"

Elinor reached out and covered Merida's mouth with her palm. She stuck her head in the air, listening. That was when Merida also heard it. There was shuffling on the other side of the door. Elinor put a finger to her own lips a moment before the door to the bathing room opened and the maid, Orla, entered.

"Princess," Orla said. "What are you doing in here?"

"I . . . uh . . . I wanted to check Merida's wound but was afraid to do so on the bed. I did not want to dirty the linens in case her injury was bleeding."

"Oh, you should leave that for the physician, Princess." Orla came farther into the small room, her eyes roaming over Merida. "How is that head?" she asked.

"'Tis better, I think," Merida said.

"But not healed completely," Elinor said through clenched teeth. She glared at Merida before turning to the maid. "I fear it is too dangerous for Merida to make the journey back to her home. In fact, I am not sure she even knows where her home is. She first claimed to be of Clan Argyll, and now she is saying she is from Lothian."

Merida was shocked at how easily the lies flowed from her mother's mouth.

"Do you not know your people, lass?" Orla asked.

"I . . ." Merida looked to Elinor, wondering why she

would choose clans that were so far away. But then she remembered what the princess had said about the fragility of the peace alliance. War and strife had ruled this land prior to the treaty between the clans; it was all many of these people had ever known. Merida understood why it might be difficult to forge trust between the clans—despite the peace accord—after so many years of fighting.

"I wish I could remember my people," Merida said, putting a hand to her head. "I cannot remember anything."

"You poor lass," Orla said.

"A head injury like hers may take days to recover from, even as much as a fortnight," Elinor said. "I believe she should remain at MacCameron Castle until she is well." She held her clasped hands to her chest. "I, for one, would not be able to live with myself if she were to suffer an even nastier injury because we turned her loose too soon."

Merida was stunned by Elinor's performance. Her mother had nearly convinced *her* that she was not well enough to travel.

"I understand, Princess." Orla nodded. "But, as you know, it is up to the king and queen whether or not she is allowed to remain here. Queen Catriona is not fond of guests."

"No, she is not," Elinor said. She bit her bottom lip, and

Merida could practically see the wheels turning in her head. A moment later she snapped to attention, her eyes widening as she looked from Orla to Merida and back again. "But what if Merida was to work here?"

"What?" Merida and Orla asked at the same time.

"The queen would be more inclined to have her stay if she were earning her keep, would she not?" Elinor turned to Orla. "What about in the kitchens? Hilda is with child and will deliver soon. Merida can take her place until she returns. I believe Mother would not object, don't you, Orla?"

"Well, I don't know, Princess. We *are* short one girl in the kitchens." The maid looked to Merida. "Can you cook?"

"I . . . I can clean," Merida said. "And chop. I chop turnips all the time."

She did not, but Merida figured if Elinor had no problem telling untruths so freely, she should be able to do so also.

Elinor nodded. "And this way, the physician can continue to care for her wound until all her faculties have returned."

"Maybe 'tis dangerous to have her in the kitchens if she does not have all her faculties about her," Orla said.

Elinor waved that off as if it was unimportant. "You

can instruct the staff to keep her away from the fire and the knives. As long as she is safe, but deemed useful, the queen will not demand she leave."

Orla looked skeptical, but after a moment, she lifted her shoulders in a helpless shrug. "Maybe she can work in the larder and Rhona can move into Hilda's place until she has that wee babe. I will suggest it to Duncan. He has control over the kitchens."

"Yes, please talk to Duncan. Let him know how important this is to the princess," Elinor said.

"Sorry, lass, but Duncan will not be thinking of you when he makes his decision. He will be thinking about what Queen Catriona will say."

Merida had yet to meet the queen, but from the tone of this discussion, she gathered her grandmother ran a very strict household.

She did not care what she had to do to convince the queen that she should stay. Merida would scrub pots and pans in the scullery, if necessary, as long as she was able to remain here until the start of the Highland Games.

Ensuring that her father was the suitor who won her mother's hand in whatever challenge the princess chose for the competition was another matter, but Merida would figure out how to deal with that later. All that mattered at the moment was that she had a plan.

The three of them filed out of the bathing room and back into the sleeping chamber. The moment Orla left the room, Elinor turned to Merida with a gleeful smile.

"This will be perfect," the princess said. "It will give us all the time we need for you to teach me everything you know."

"But how? If I am being hired to work, will I not have to . . . well . . . work?"

"I shall talk to some of the lasses in the kitchens and let them know that you are not to be tasked too hard. Maybe we can work it out so that you must work only in the morning! And once you are done with your duties, we can head to the forest, and you can train me."

The resemblance to her mother was a little disconcerting. Queen Elinor had a knack for conceiving meticulous plans at a moment's notice.

"I am not entirely sure this will work," Merida said. "What if your mother does not allow me to stay?"

Elinor chewed her bottom lip again, contemplating. "Then I'll hide you," she finally said. "What about the stables?"

"You want me to sleep with the horses?"

"It was just a suggestion," Elinor said. She waved that off. "But it will not matter, because I will talk to Duncan myself. He will convince the queen to let you work in the kitchens." She walked over to the bed and lifted a feather pillow. "Now, I must warn you that the servants' quarters are not as nicely appointed as these. I have not visited them in ages, but from what I remember they are very small. You shall have a room for yourself, however, and I will sneak in better linens for you."

She walked over to Merida and grabbed her hands. With an earnest smile, she said, "I will make your stay as comfortable as possible, I promise."

"You are willing to do all of this just so that I can teach you to start a fire?" Merida asked.

She wanted to remain at MacCameron Castle—*needed* to remain here—but still could not believe that Elinor would go to such lengths for these lessons.

"Yes," Elinor said. "And to fish, and hunt, and do all the other things one must do to survive several days' journey in the forest."

Merida stared at her for a moment before asking, "Where will you go?"

Elinor shook her head. "I shall not say. Even to you. It is too dangerous. Once the king learns of my escape, he will send for me. And if you know where I am headed, he will do all he can to retrieve the information from you."

"But what is to stop him from doing those things anyway? Won't he think I am not being truthful if I say I do not know where you have run off to?"

Elinor released a deep sigh. "This does not matter. When the time comes, we shall leave together. You for DunBroch and me for my new life. We can even travel the same path until you reach your home."

"So your plans will take you farther than DunBroch?"

"Of course," Elinor said. "All I am willing to share is that I plan to go far from this kingdom and the lands surrounding it. Any chieftain that owes fealty to the king is a danger to me. They will all inform the king if I am seen on their lands. That includes DunBroch."

The princess's earnestness was troubling. It was obvious to Merida that her mother had thought this through and was determined to stick to her plan.

Convincing Princess Elinor to give Fergus of DunBroch a chance to win her hand was going to be harder than Merida thought.

CHAPTER THIRTEEN
Merida

Merida deftly navigated Angus through the woods, heaving a sigh of relief as she galloped past the grouping of moss-covered boulders near where Elinor had found her. She was on the right track.

She knew she was taking a chance, sneaking out of MacCameron Castle so soon after her previous sojourn to find the witch, but learning of Elinor's plans meant it was imperative that she put her own into play.

She *had* to find her father. She needed to get her parents together before Elinor made good on her threat to escape. Locating Fergus was her first order of business. Though the clansmen who had rescued him from the forest floor had been several paces away, Merida had distinctly heard one of them mention a camp. There was no guarantee they were still there, but it was worth the effort to look.

She pulled on Angus's reins, slowing his pace. This was the area where she had spent the night in the woods.

"Which means . . ." Merida murmured.

She looked to the left. Her father's men had discovered him right over there. She brought Angus to a stop and climbed down. She would walk from this point forward.

One thing Merida had learned since the start of this nightmare was to be more cautious as she moved about. Although these were just like the woods she had frolicked around her entire life, they were different in so many ways. There was very little about this new existence she found herself in that was the same.

And if she wanted things to ever go back to the way they had been, she couldn't make any more mistakes. She did not have *time* to make mistakes. She must learn all she could about her father and then convince him to woo the princess of Clan MacCameron before the summer solstice.

"That should be easy enough," Merida groused.

She and Angus walked at least one hundred paces in the direction the men had taken Fergus. Just when she was ready to give up, Merida caught a glimpse of something pale brown peeking between the trees.

Could it be . . .

The wind blew and the brown thing flapped.

Yes, it was linen. She would have bet her next meal that it was from a tent. She had found the camp. Well, *a* camp.

As she walked ahead of Angus, she kept her eyes opened for the DunBroch tartan, and her ears opened for the sound of her clan's distinctive brogue. But as she moved closer, Merida was struck by how quiet things were. Had the camp been abandoned?

She tied Angus's reins around the slim trunk of a nearby tree so that she could investigate unencumbered. She squeezed through a narrow opening in the thicket of shrubbery surrounding the camp. They had picked a prime location. If not for the wind blowing the tree limbs apart, she would never have spotted that tent.

Using the shrubs as cover, Merida peered around the site. Pots were neatly stacked next to a firepit that still smoldered with embers. A cauldron hung on a rod above it, supported by two poles on either side of the firepit. Pallets covered with straw and bird feathers populated the enclosure, along with thick wool tarps.

This camp was still in use. If it had been abandoned, the men would not have left so many supplies for others to find.

A heavy thump snared Merida's attention. She looked to her right, and her back went ramrod straight.

There he was. Fergus.

He was more recognizable than her mother had been when Merida had first encountered her in the woods. She was still yards away from him and could only see him in profile, but from what Merida could make out, his beard did not have any gray hairs, and it was fuller. So was the hair on his head. The deep red glinted under the rays of the shining sun. His head was bandaged with a strip of linen.

Merida brought her hand up to the bump on her own head and realized her injury was in the exact spot of her father's. She had truly taken his place.

He stood before a large tree stump. On one side of him stood a pile of knobby logs. On the other side, a stack of evenly chopped wood. Fergus grabbed a thick log and set it in the center of the tree stump, then lifted one of the biggest axes Merida had ever seen and chopped the log right down the middle.

Her chest blossomed with pride. Her father was the strongest man she knew.

Merida started cautiously toward him, being careful not to make too much noise. He heard her anyway.

Fergus whipped around. "Who goes there?"

"Uh . . . hello," Merida called cautiously.

His eyes narrowed and his forehead creased with concern as he held the ax high, ready to attack.

"Who are you?" Fergus asked. "What are you doing here?"

Even his voice sounded the same, despite the sharpness of his tone. Merida was overwhelmed with emotion. She had to remind herself that she could not just blurt out that she was his daughter from decades in the future.

"I . . . uh . . . I am Merida," she said. She moved more quickly. As she drew nearer, Fergus's brow crinkled even more. He looked beyond her.

"Who is with you?" He tightened his grip on his ax. "A lass as young as you would not be in these woods alone."

"I am," she said. She pointed over her shoulder. "It is just me and my horse. He is fastened to a tree."

More frowning. "Did you lose your people?"

She had *found* her people. She had found him.

The urge to throw herself into his big, burly arms was almost too strong to fight. But her father had taught her at a very young age to be cautious of all strangers, even those who seemed harmless. He would never have given her advice that he would not also follow.

"I . . . uh . . . I did not lose my people in the way you may think," Merida answered. She stuck her hand out to him. "I am Merida of Dun . . . Dungaroo."

She inwardly cringed.

Dungaroo?

Fergus's brow rose, his skepticism apparent. "I'll ask you again, lass. What are you doing out in these woods alone?"

Merida paused for a moment. When she'd snuck out of MacCameron Castle that day, her goal had been to find the DunBroch camp. Now that she stood before her father, words escaped her.

Come now, Merida silently chastised herself.

She had a purpose. She could not afford to mess this up. There was too much at stake.

"I mean no harm, of course," Merida told him. "I was on a ride with my horse. His name is Angus." She paused, hoping Angus's name would ring a bell, but then she remembered that Angus was only six years old. He had yet to be born. And, unfortunately, she could not recall the name of the mare or stallion that had produced him.

"Uh, well, anyway," Merida continued. "I happened upon this camp and, well, decided to explore." She waved her hands, indicating their surroundings. Merida prayed her father was buying her story. Based on the way his brow furrowed, she was almost certain he was not. "I am still learning my way around these parts and got a bit turned around. That is how I found you."

The mistrust in Fergus's eyes deepened. Merida was not surprised by it. Any good warrior would be suspicious of a young lass traveling alone in the woods. It was a known decoy, to use a young lady who appeared lost and in distress to trick an unsuspecting soldier into letting down his guard. The longer she was out here alone, the more suspicious Fergus was likely to become.

She had achieved what she set out to accomplish: finding the camp and her father. But now she needed to find out what his plans were.

"Are you and your clansmen on your way to the Highland Games?" Merida asked. "I hear they are to take place in less than a fortnight. Is that why you are camped here?"

"I have more important things to worry about than tossing a caber, lass."

"Really?" She perked up. "What sort of things?"

Merida knew by the swift change in his countenance that she had gone too far. He went from mildly suspicious to downright hostile.

"It is of no concern to you," he said in a low voice. "You

need to run along. And do not disclose the location of this camp to anyone. I will know if you do."

"I will not," Merida said, backing away. "You have my word."

Her instincts told her that her father would never hurt her, but this man had not yet become her father. This man was a warrior.

Merida doubled back the way she had come and quickly mounted Angus. As she directed him back toward MacCameron Castle, questions began to bombard her.

What were he and his clansmen doing here? In all the times she had heard the story of how her parents met, Merida realized she had never been told exactly what had brought her father to the woods that fateful day—only that he was on a mission to deliver news from his chieftain to the king.

What news was he due to deliver? And why had he not delivered it yet? If he was well enough to chop firewood, it stood to reason that he was well enough to continue his journey to MacCameron Castle. Had his plans changed? Would he and his clansmen retreat?

They were all questions that only Fergus could answer, but if she had asked any of them just then, his suspicions would have grown even more. She raced toward MacCameron Castle, certain about only one thing: she must get her parents to meet as soon as possible. Because if the men of Clan DunBroch packed up this camp and moved, she would never find them.

And she would never get home.

CHAPTER FOURTEEN
Merida

The first thing that struck Merida was the chill that permeated the stagnant air inside MacCameron Castle's wet larder. From the moment she entered this frigid, dark room where she was to spend her mornings packing the meats and fish for the household, Merida had wondered how she was expected to do her job without freezing to death.

"You paying attention, lass?" Duncan Craig, the head of the kitchens, asked.

"Yes," Merida lied. But maybe she needed to pay attention. She knew nothing about preserving meats. The last thing she wanted to do was cause the entire household to become sick or, worse, poison her own mother with unpreserved mutton.

Duncan nodded and motioned for her to follow.

Merida could tell from the looks the other servants sent her way that having the head of the kitchens escort her on this tour was an anomaly. Some servants were curious, while others looked anxious, as if afraid of making a misstep while the boss was around.

What surprised Merida most—and unnerved her—was the jealousy she detected in a few of the stares. She did not pay much attention to household staff politics, but it made sense that any preferential treatment shown to her could be perceived as a threat to others, especially those servants who had worked at MacCameron Castle for years or who had aspirations of elevating their status on the staff. It was a complication she had not considered when Elinor first suggested this plan to keep her in the castle.

She, Duncan, and Duncan's younger sister, Sorcha, who had been tasked with assisting Merida during her first day in her new role, ended their tour in the dry larder, where the flour, meal, and breads were stored. Merida had not previously taken note of how much bigger MacCameron Castle was than DunBroch, but the sheer size of their kitchens told the story. It made her wonder how much land fell within MacCameron Kingdom and how many of the chieftains had pledged fealty to her grandfather. A grandfather she still had yet to meet.

She wondered if she would ever get the chance. Though Merida had been at MacCameron Castle for only two full days, she had noticed the stark difference in how her mother ran her household at DunBroch compared with her parents. Queen Elinor treated her staff like family, while the MacCamerons could not be bothered to share a brief greeting.

This entire castle was colder, and not just the temperature. It made Merida long for the warmth and gaiety she had foolishly taken for granted in her own home.

"Do you have any questions about the arrangement of the kitchens?" Duncan asked her now.

"Uh . . . no." Merida shook her head. "It is just like the—" She paused, hesitant to reveal anything about the kitchens back at home. She and Elinor still needed to discuss exactly what their story would be regarding Merida's background, but she knew she should not mention DunBroch. "It is just as I expected it would be," she finished. She wrapped her arms around her upper body. "Though I did not think it would be so cold."

"The food would sour if it were not this cold, which is why you must keep the doors closed at all times," Duncan said. "You sure you can handle this, lass?"

The intensity in his tone spoke to the seriousness with which he took his job.

"Yes." Merida vigorously nodded. "I can handle it."

"Of course she can handle it," Sorcha added. "She's a canny lass, this one. I can tell."

"You make sure to watch her," Duncan said to his sister. He returned his attention to Merida. "I know the princess wants you here, but if you cannot do the work, I cannot have you in my kitchens. It's as simple as that, lass."

"I can do the work," Merida assured him, even though she wasn't so sure she could.

Over the next hour, Merida made the trek to the underground icehouse three times to replenish the ice used to keep the food cold, and salted more than two dozen large herring. The backbreaking tasks made her appreciate the work the staff at Castle DunBroch conducted in order to get a hot meal on their plates every day.

She wiped her hands with a square of linen before scratching behind her ear. The area had been irritating her since her ride back from the DunBroch men's camp. She wished she could see the spot. It felt . . . hairy, as if something was growing there.

It had to have been one of the shrubs she had rubbed up against while hiding. She would have to be more careful.

"You're looking a bit weenach," Sorcha said. "Should I fetch the physician?"

"No, no," Merida said. "I'm not sick, I just . . . I don't like fish."

The younger girl let out a hearty peal of laughter. "Then you're working the wrong job, lass. The MacCameron loves his herring. You will see lots of it."

Just then, the door to the larder flew open and Aileen stormed inside, her blue eyes shooting daggers at Merida. The girl had taken a disliking to her, but Merida did not have the faintest idea why. Was it because Merida was a stranger?

"What is the cause for all this cackling?" Aileen asked. "Is that how you get work done, Sorcha? Do you think your brother would have something to say about you carrying on in such a way?"

Sorcha's smile instantly vanished. It was replaced by a somber frown.

"He would not like it," the younger girl answered. She looked to Merida. "Aileen is right. We should get back to work."

Aileen did not address Merida at all, except to scowl at her before turning on her heel and stomping out of the larder in the same stormy way she had entered.

It took every amount of control Merida possessed not to call out an angry retort to the girl's unnecessary nastiness. It would seem her mother's constant badgering for Merida to maintain her temper had not been for naught.

Instead of allowing the dour Aileen to put a damper on

what had been an otherwise agreeable—if tiring—morning, Merida chose to lighten the mood. She leaned across the marble dressing slab and whispered, "Who put bugs in her breeches?"

Sorcha's eyes widened in shock, though Merida could see her fighting not to smile.

"Aileen is Duncan's second-in-command," Sorcha explained. "She takes her job serious-like." Her shoulders lifted and fell with her deep sigh. "And she thinks I do not belong here in the kitchens. She thinks I got the job because I am Duncan's sister."

"Why should that matter?" Merida asked, scratching the back of her hand against her apron. "As long as you are good at it, you deserve to be here as much as she does."

Twin spots of red instantly blossomed on Sorcha's cheeks, but then she stood up straight. "You're right about that. And it is not as if you would ever see *her* in the larder. She thinks she is too good for such work."

"In my opinion, no meal would ever be prepared if not for the work done here in the larder, or the scullery, or the other parts of the kitchen lasses like Aileen think are beneath them."

Sorcha beamed. "You know, I like you, Merida. I'm glad you hit your head and landed here in the kitchens at MacCameron Castle."

Merida laughed. "Well, I am not happy about this bump on my head, but I am still happy to be here."

"Are you sure about that?" Sorcha asked, a cagey smile tipping up the corner of her mouth. Then she reached down and plopped a large herring onto the table. "Get to salting."

Merida and Sorcha kept things going in the wet larder until the midday meal. The family feasted on roasted herring, haggis, cabbage and kale sautéed with onions, boiled turnips, and oatcakes prepared by a slew of cooks. Merida's mouth watered at the thought of filling her belly with the savory dishes, but when she lined up with the rest of the kitchen staff to receive her meal, she was served a bowl of thick vegetable pottage along with a chunk of bread.

"Is this it?" Merida balked.

Sorcha shot her that wide-eyed look again.

A moment later, Merida heard the snide voice she was already coming to resent. "What did you think you would be eating, lass? Roasted pheasant?" Aileen asked.

Pheasant was one of her absolute favorites. But as a member of the staff, she guessed there would be no pheasant—no meat at all—in her future.

Was the kitchen staff at Castle DunBroch given meat with their meals, or were they fed only vegetable stews like this one? Merida had no idea. She was hit with a sudden sense of deep shame at how little she *did* know about their staff. It was something she must rectify when she returned home. After all, the staff's well-being would fall under her list of responsibilities as a member of the royal family.

"I was only inquiring about the bread," Merida answered. "I love bread."

"Well, I am sure if you ask the princess, she will make sure you get extra in the morn," Aileen said.

Merida swallowed down the acerbic retort she longed to level at the hateful girl. She had more important things to contend with than engaging in verbal sword fights with the likes of Aileen.

Like figuring out how to get her parents together.

"I shall enjoy the portion I have been given," Merida replied with a sweet smile.

Aileen's gaze was colder than the icehouse underneath them. "Feed your maws, then get back to work," she said. She looked directly at Merida. "The fishermen just brought in a load of fresh cod and herring. You make sure you salt them."

With a sigh, Merida returned to the wet larder, where a multitude of fish sat on a bed of ice. She reached for the first one and snatched her hand back.

"What is . . . ?" Merida's voice trailed off.

She stared at the backs of her hands, unsure what to make of the stubbly patches on her skin. It looked almost like . . . fur? She brought her hands closer, inspecting the fine hairs peppering her knuckles. They itched, just like that spot behind her ear.

What poisoned plant had she come across in the forest that could create such a rash? What sort of rash caused one to grow hair?

She did not want to bring any more attention to herself, but maybe she should call on the MacCamerons' physician again. Maybe he could make a salve to cure this peculiar ailment. And maybe he could tell her what had caused it so that she could avoid coming in contact with it again.

CHAPTER FIFTEEN
Elinor

Elinor used the wall to steady herself as she traveled down the narrow stone stairwell that led to the servants' quarters. It had been years since she'd ventured here, not since those days when she would sneak away to play with Gavina, Elspeth, Aileen, and the other children who lived within MacCameron Castle's curtain wall. Before they all grew up and were relegated to performing the roles they now held.

It had been a simpler time, when she could run carefree around the bailey, pretending to slay dragons and capture magical wisps. A time when she did not have to worry about betrothals, peace alliances, or any of the other duties she was now being forced to contend with as princess.

But she would not have to worry about these duties for

long. After Merida taught her how to survive the journey to Northumbria, she would have the freedom to study the region's fascinating artwork and listen to the poets who recited sonnets day in and day out. The freedom to spend her mornings tending to lost or injured animals, and her evenings singing folk songs with all the like-minded new friends she would meet. Her mother and father considered such things trifling—a waste of time for a future queen. But Elinor could not wait.

She descended the final step, then made her way down the dim corridor. The wall sconces were more widely spaced than those found on the upper floors. Only half of them held candles, and the few candles that *were* there had burned so low that they gave off only a feeble light. Why had they not been replaced? Elinor would have argued that it was more important for the servants to see down here, where they carried supplies for the household on a daily basis, than in the upstairs chambers.

She saw two maids at the end of the corridor. One leaned over and whispered something to the other, and they both giggled. When they spotted Elinor they stood up straight and performed a brief curtsy.

"Princess," the women mumbled simultaneously.

"Hello, Greta. Agnes," Elinor said, nodding to them both and injecting extra cheer into her voice. She hated that they thought they had to take on such a somber countenance in her presence. Such was the case with the king and queen. Her parents expected the servants to remain undemonstrative as they went about their duties. When she was with her parents, Elinor found herself treating the servants with the same reserve, too afraid to show any familiarity with the same people she had known and who had taken care of her for much of her life.

"Has either of you come across the new girl who started in the kitchens today?" Elinor asked. "She goes by the name Merida."

Agnes pointed toward the door. "She is by the wash, Princess."

Elinor nodded her thanks and smiled again before continuing through the passage that led to the washhouse. She found Merida standing before one of the huge copper washbasins, vigorously scrubbing her hands.

"Are you trying to rub your skin clean off your body?" Elinor asked.

Merida looked back over her shoulder. "If that is what it takes to rid myself of this dreadful fish smell, then I am willing to do it. The fish scales have also caused an itch on my hands and arms, and even behind my ear."

"Behind your ear? How did you get fish scales there?"

"I don't know, but it has been itching all day. I think I

am allergic to the wet larder." Merida submerged her arms up to the elbow, then picked up a piece of stained linen and started drying them.

Elinor reached around her and lifted the tin can filled with mutton fat and wood ash. She took a sniff. "Ugh. Are you sure this is not making the smell worse?" She set the tin back on the nearby table. "The one I have is perfumed with lilacs. I shall bring some for you when we get back from our first lesson. Let us get the horses and go into the woods so you can teach me to shoot."

Merida paused in the middle of drying her hands. She stared at Elinor, her eyes widened, as if she'd just had an epiphany.

"Of course," Merida whispered. "Of course! We must go into the woods for your lessons!"

"Where are your bow and arrows?"

"We will not need the bow and arrows today, except for protection."

Elinor frowned. She looked around to make sure they were alone before leaning in close.

"We had a deal," she said in a fierce whisper.

"I know," Merida said, keeping her own voice low. "I am to teach you how to survive on your own, and after observing you on our ride to the castle, I have decided our first lesson should be on how to properly gallop on your horse."

Elinor's immediate thought was to tell her that a princess did not gallop, but Merida was right. If she was going to make it halfway across the country, she would need to learn how to gallop. The dainty trot she usually took across the glen on Alistair's back would not cut it.

Elinor held her shoulders back and her head high. "Well, then, teach me to gallop."

Merida grinned. "I think you will make a most excellent student, Princess."

It took a promise of three oatcakes and milk sweetened with honey to convince Ewan to keep quiet about her and Merida taking the horses out of the stables. But in no time at all they were on the other side of the curtain wall and trotting toward the woods. They stopped just after clearing the tree line. The air was crisp, with the faint scent of rain imbuing it.

Elinor directed Alistair toward the right.

"Where are you going?" Merida said.

"If we are to gallop, it would be easier to do so across the open glen toward Kincardine."

"No. No, we should go this way." She pointed left, in the direction of the village of Clan Innes, where Elinor had first discovered her.

"Trust me. I am more familiar with these lands," Elinor reminded her. "This is the better route."

"But—" Merida looked mournfully toward the village. "I guess you are right," she said, before reluctantly turning her horse and coming to Elinor's side.

She peered over her shoulder again, and Elinor thought she would put up another argument to head toward Clan Innes. Instead, she sat up straighter on the horse and gave a firm nod.

"Now, the most important lesson in learning to gallop is positioning," Merida said. "This is the position you should maintain, but only after you have cantered for some time. Remember, you must build up to a gallop."

Elinor carefully studied Merida's every movement, leaning forward when she did and lifting her bottom slightly in the air.

"The horse will respond to the pressure you apply to his flank as you ride," Merida explained. "It is something you both must learn to sense in each other, because every horse is different."

"How did you learn to do this?" Elinor asked. "I have not heard of many lasses being taught to gallop."

A smile broke out across Merida's face. "My dad thinks a young lass should be taught the same skills as a lad."

"Your dad sounds like a fine gentleman. I think I would like him."

"I am counting on it," she said.

Elinor frowned. "What?"

"Nothing." Merida shook her head. "Let me show you how to hold the reins. It too is *very* important."

After insisting Elinor demonstrate that she understood the proper way to hold the reins, Merida finally started them out on a slow trot.

"I know how to go slowly," Elinor said after several minutes. "We are supposed to gallop."

"In due time," Merida stressed. She looked over at Elinor and released a sigh. "Fine. We shall canter for several furlongs, then we can gallop."

They clopped along at a steady pace for a few minutes, going as fast as Elinor had ever dared ride. The warnings she had been given were more about propriety than safety, but Elinor took care to heed them all the same.

The moment their horses cleared the trees and came upon the glen, Merida yelled, "Yah!" And she and her horse, Angus, shot forward.

Using Merida's instructions, Elinor sent Alistair into a powerful gallop across the expanse of land. Her heart thudded in time with the horse's hooves pounding into the ground. The trees that lined either side of the glen looked like green water rushing alongside her. The taste of sweet Scots pine stuck to her tongue as she rode with her mouth open, unable to contain her smile.

It was glorious.

"We should slow down," Merida called after several minutes of riding.

Elinor shook her head. She leaned forward, bracing her chin against Alistair's muscled neck. The power in his stride, the wind in her face—this was what freedom felt like.

"Princess Elinor, we must give the horses rest!" Merida called. "You are doing damage to him!"

That made her pause. The last thing she wanted to do was cause her beloved horse harm.

Except she had forgotten how to make him stop. She had been so transfixed by her ride that everything Merida had just taught her escaped her mind.

"How do I stop him?" she called out in a panic.

"Pull slightly on his reins. Not too fast; you do not want to startle him."

Elinor did as she was told, increasing the pressure as she pulled the leather reins toward her. Alistair slowly reduced his speed until they were once again at a canter. They rode a few minutes more before slowing down to a trot.

"That was amazing," Elinor said.

"Listen, Princess. I know there is much to enjoy about galloping, but understand that the horse cannot sustain such a swift pace for long stretches, especially a horse who is not used to it. I could see the strain in Alistair, even if you could not." Merida looked around. "I wonder if there is a creek nearby. Both horses need refreshing."

"There is," Elinor said. She pulled the reins. "Follow me."

They took a slow walk to the creek, making their way carefully over the trees that had fallen during a particularly nasty storm that had passed through a few weeks earlier.

"Be careful," Elinor warned Merida. "The soldiers do not ride this way, so there is no path."

"Are we still on MacCameron land?" Merida asked.

"Yes," Elinor said with a sigh. "We would have to gallop for a full day before we reached the border of MacCameron land."

Merida's eyes grew wide.

"'Tis true," Elinor assured her.

"It is hard to fathom having so much land under one king's rule. How did the MacCameron convince so many to pledge fealty to him?" Merida asked.

Elinor shrugged. "I wish I knew, but that information has not been shared with me."

"Maybe it will be once you become queen."

"Except I will not be queen," Elinor said. "I will leave this kingdom long before I can rule it."

Merida tipped her head to the side and stared until Elinor became uncomfortable.

"What?" Elinor asked with a hint of irritation in her voice.

"Many people would do anything for the power to rule your kingdom. It is rather strange to hear you denounce what is your right by birth."

"You are correct. It is my birthright, yet the land would be under my husband's rule, not mine."

"That is true," Merida replied. "It does not seem fair, does it?"

"Not at all," Elinor agreed. Not that she would remain here even if she *were* allowed to rule the land. Her mind was made up. She would be enjoying her first taste of freedom in the Lowlands before the summer solstice arrived.

She and Merida arrived at the creek, and both of their horses immediately began lapping up the cool water. Elinor rubbed Alistair's neck, whispering an apology for working him so hard, while secretly anticipating the next time they would be able to gallop.

"If you don't mind me asking, why are you so against the betrothal?" Merida asked. "Isn't it tradition?"

"Do not take this the wrong way, but you are not a princess. You do not know what it is like to be forced to marry against your will."

Merida stared at her for a moment before she erupted in laughter.

Elinor's mouth fell open. She was shocked as she watched the girl gasp for breaths. "Are you quite finished?"

"I am. I am sorry," Merida said.

"You find my predicament amusing?"

"It is not that, Princess Elinor," she said. Although the tears of mirth she wiped from the corners of her eyes said otherwise.

"Do not call me Princess Elinor," she said. "Just Elinor. Being a princess has brought me nothing but grief."

"Well," Merida said. "It has brought you lilac-scented soap, has it not?"

"You think that is worth giving up my freedom?"

"Forgive my tasteless joke. That is not what I am saying," Merida replied. "But after spending the morning in the larder, and the better part of the afternoon trying to wash the smell of fish from my hands, being a princess does not sound so bad. I have gained a new appreciation for the work servants and other laborers do around the castle."

"So this *is* the first time you have done such work, then? I am not sure why, but I sensed you were of noble blood from the first moment I met you."

Merida glanced at her before looking back at the creek. "My father is a guard in his chieftain's army," she answered.

"And your mother?"

Merida looked at her again, an odd smile lifting one

corner of her mouth. "My mother is rather obsessed with the nobility, if I am being honest. She speaks often about the duties those of royal blood must conduct."

"You should tell her that there is no need to be jealous or to strive to be a royal. The pressures are . . . immense."

As she looked out beyond the creek, at the horizon that stretched into the distance, Elinor wondered what would happen if she just kept going. If she sent Alistair into another powerful gallop and left this life behind.

But what would she find when she arrived in that new land?

She still was not sure what she was running toward; she knew only that she wanted to escape this marriage that was being forced upon her—to do more than what tradition or her future husband commanded she do. She wanted a say in how her life unfolded.

But would she find her purpose once she found her new home, or would she feel as lost and trapped as she did right now? The question pestered her.

Elinor shook her head. She did not have to cater to these worries at present, because she could not leave. Not yet. She would not make it as far as the border of MacCameron land before she starved or froze to death. She could not believe she had not been better prepared.

There was still time—not much, but things had not

yet become dire. She had a fortnight before the start of the Highland Games, and the announcement of her betrothal. She would learn all she could from Merida and leave just before the games commenced.

"Should we return to the castle?" Merida asked.

"No. Not yet," Elinor said. She was not ready to face the suffocating confines of the castle grounds just yet. "It is a gorgeous day. Let us explore more of the forest."

Merida shot her a curious smile. "I think I know just the place we should go. Follow me."

Elinor hesitated only for a moment before moving after her. "Only if you let me gallop."

CHAPTER SIXTEEN
Merida

Merida dropped her head into her outstretched hands and dragged her fingers down her face. "You have got to be kidding me," she muttered.

She frowned, rubbing her hands along the underside of her jaw. Why did it feel like . . . bristles? Merida pulled her hands back and studied her fingers.

"Is this correct?" Elinor called.

Merida returned her attention to Elinor and groaned. "No," she said.

Why had she agreed to start an archery lesson when it was obvious Elinor was not ready? She knew her mother was sheltered, and thus, Merida had kept her expectations low. But this was ridiculous. The princess did not know the first thing about archery.

"You must keep your shoulders squared," Merida said. "Stand up straight and concentrate."

"Maybe if you let me use a real arrow," Elinor complained.

Not a chance.

Within minutes of the start of their lesson, Merida had realized putting a deadly arrow in her mother's hand would be a mistake. Instead, she had scoured the forest floor for thin sticks to use in place of the arrows. And it was a good thing she had. Elinor had sent the sticks sailing through the air with abandon. Several had landed near Merida's toes.

"We have gone over this, Princess. You must perfect your stance before you can shoot with real arrows. You are slouching. That is why you have sent the sticks sailing everywhere but the target."

"I do not have time to perfect my stance," Elinor said. "Just teach me to kill a hare!"

"And then what?" Merida plopped her hands on her hips. "What will you do when you kill the hare? Do you know how to skin it? Do you know how to cook it?"

"You know I do not," Elinor groused.

"Exactly. Which is why you need to be patient and listen. My father taught me how to do all this, but he did not do it in a day. These things take time, Elinor."

"Surely your father did not teach you to cook!"

"He did," Merida replied.

Elinor huffed. "Well, maybe I should get your father to teach me how to shoot a bow and arrow."

Her idea exactly.

Merida knew she was taking a chance of angering Fergus by bringing Elinor here. He had given her a stern warning not to disclose the location of his camp to anyone, but she could not afford to wait for fate to bring her mother and father together again. Time was of the essence; they had to begin their courtship so they could fall in love before the solstice.

She would nudge fate this one time, and then she was done.

"Wait one minute," Elinor said. She pointed to the boulders. "Isn't this where I first found you?"

Merida tried to look surprised. "Why, it is, isn't it? I guess it is the one place that is most familiar to me. I would like to see a bit more of the forest, however," she added. "Why don't we explore on foot?"

The DunBroch camp was less than sixty paces away.

Elinor ignored her. Instead, she stooped low to examine the gathering of rocks and burnt twigs.

"Is this where you cooked the hare you killed?" Elinor

asked, her voice imbued with wonder. "I am not sure you understand just how remarkable it is that you were able to catch your own food, especially with that injury to your head. How long did it take you to learn to shoot with such accuracy?"

"Uh, not long," Merida said as she looked toward where the camp was located.

"I must learn how to do this," Elinor said. "Promise you will give me a real lesson, Merida."

"I will," she said. "But, Princess, why don't we . . ."

Just as Merida was about to make another plea to continue with their journey, a young man wearing DunBroch tartan emerged from the trees. Merida saw the moment Elinor noticed the man's plaid. The princess looked at her. She tightened the shawl around her head, a clear sign that she had no intentions of revealing that she was a DunBroch.

"What business do you lasses have here?" the man asked.

His heavy brogue instantly put Merida at ease, even though she knew she needed to be alert. This man did not know that she was a member of his clan.

"What are *you* doing here?" Elinor asked. "This is MacCameron land."

Merida jolted. She was taken aback by Elinor's swift change in demeanor. She had transformed into a noblewoman before Merida's eyes, lifting her chin in the air and commanding respect.

"Ah, Princess Elinor," the man said. He sketched a short bow, but the lack of warmth in his voice matched his expression. Merida had wondered if the fragile peace alliance would be enough to soften a DunBroch's view toward a MacCameron. Apparently not.

"I am on an outing with my new maid," Elinor replied. "We are exploring MacCameron Kingdom. I shall ask again, what are you doing here?"

"Are you traveling for the Highland Games?" Merida interjected. She looked to Elinor. "I suspect many of the kingdom's clansmen have begun their journey." She gestured to the bow draped over his chest. "Have you been practicing your archery? The princess has a keen interest in the sport. Perhaps you can provide a demonstration of your skill."

Elinor glanced at her, but Merida kept her focus on the soldier. His distrust was as virulent as Fergus's had been when Merida last visited this camp.

"My maid is correct," Elinor said. "I would very much enjoy it. I have heard Clan DunBroch is particularly talented with the bow and arrow. Is that so?"

Flattery was always a good idea, especially when dealing with the male species. Merida could tell by the way the soldier puffed out his chest that the princess had hit her mark. He began a monologue about the intense training the DunBroch warriors were required to undergo.

"Even with the peace alliance, we continue to perfect our skills," the soldier told them. "A threat can strike at any time."

Merida was aghast that the young man would openly share such information. Clearly, he did not think she or Elinor posed any risk, unlike Fergus the day before. Whether it was due to the princess's position as a royal or because they were female, Merida did not know, but it was a foolish assumption. Two young lasses could cause all manner of havoc to an opposing clan. She had heard her father caution his soldiers of that fact numerous times. Merida now wondered if his warnings had been born out of something that happened to Clan DunBroch in the past.

The clansman executed several successful shots with his bow, though they lacked the accuracy Merida would have displayed. She feigned excitement at the soldier's shooting but sensed that Elinor's praise was genuine.

Merida had seen enough. She had not brought the princess here to watch this man strut around like a rooster. She needed to find Fergus.

"Sir, would you have something for us to drink?"

Merida asked. "The princess and I have been traveling for quite some time. We are a bit parched."

"Uh . . . there is a creek nearby," the soldier said. He looked nervously in the direction of the camp. "But maybe you would prefer mead." He motioned for them to follow.

A few moments later they arrived at the camp where Merida had encountered Fergus. She scanned the area, searching for her father among the clansmen scattered about the area.

"What are you doing here, Gaufrid?" one of the men asked. "Why aren't you at your post?"

A half dozen men stopped what they were doing and looked their way. Merida wondered again why they had set up camp here. If her father's sole mission had been to speak to King Douglass on his chieftain's behalf, surely he would have continued on to MacCameron Castle by now.

"Because the Princess of MacCameron Kingdom requested a cup of mead," Gaufrid announced.

"Did she now?"

They all turned at the sound of Fergus's booming voice. Merida could barely contain her relief. Although that quickly turned to anxiety at the sight of his sardonic expression.

"The princess and her maid happened upon the camp," Gaufrid said to Fergus. "They are particularly interested in observing our archers at work." He puffed out his chest again. " 'Tis fitting, seeing as DunBroch archers are the best in the land."

"They just happened upon the camp?" Fergus asked, leveling a skeptical look at Merida. But when he spoke again, it was to Elinor. "Is Gaufrid speaking the truth, Princess? Have you come to observe us?"

Elinor tipped her nose in the air. Her demeanor had switched from simply aloof to pure ice in a matter of seconds. She managed to look down at Fergus, even though he was several inches taller than she.

"Your clan's prowess with the bow and arrow is well-known, but I am not sure I would say I'd come to observe you do anything, let alone shoot," she said.

"That is only because you have not seen my clansmen at work," Fergus replied. "You should see what the men of Clan DunBroch can do with the bow and arrow. You would have no choice but to admit we are the best."

Elinor scoffed. "I would never do such a thing."

"Oh, but I think you would," Fergus said. He angled toward her. "Even if you could only admit it to yourself."

Acrimony crackled in the air between them, so pungent Merida could almost smell it. But there was something else there. Something fiery and intense. It pulsed with life as the princess and the warrior stared each other down.

With his eyes still trained on Elinor, Fergus stuck thumb and forefinger in his mouth and produced a loud whistle. "Gather round, lads. Let us show the princess how the best archers in the kingdom got their reputation."

Fergus sauntered toward a flat rock that served as a mark on the ground. With a grin, he hefted the massive bow he carried and held it in position, then pulled an arrow from the quiver strapped across his back.

Merida had no idea why he was acting this way. It would only further antagonize Elinor.

He finally directed his gaze at something other than the princess, turning his attention to a target that was at least fifty paces away. Merida slowed her breathing as Fergus secured the tail end of the arrow to the string. She followed along with the steps he took, recalling the words he would preach to her during their hours and hours of practice.

Her father released the arrow and sent it sailing toward the target. It struck it dead center.

Merida burst into applause, earning a censuring look from Elinor. She immediately stopped, but internally, the cheers continued. Her father's skill with the bow and arrow was unmatched in both form and accuracy.

Additional soldiers gathered around to watch as Fergus put on a splendid display.

Merida leaned over to Elinor and whispered, "If you want to learn to shoot, you should pay close attention. Do you see how he holds his arms tight and his shoulders stiff? That will keep the arrow on its straight path." She glanced over at Elinor when she didn't get a response. "Why are you frowning? Are you not enjoying yourself?"

"Not particularly," Elinor answered.

"You are getting a lesson in archery from one of the best shooters I have ever seen."

"That one thinks he is better than everyone else."

"Because he *is* better," Merida pointed out. "He is excellent with the bow and arrow." She glanced at Elinor's profile.

She sniffed. "And he knows it. His confidence detracts from his looks."

Merida pounced on her admission. "So, you've noticed how handsome he is?"

Elinor shushed her, then straightened her shoulders as Fergus walked up to them.

"How was that, Princess?" he asked.

Once again, Elinor peered at him. "Satisfactory."

Fergus cocked a furry brow. "Only satisfactory? Well, what would it take to impress you, I wonder?"

"Is that your goal?"

He bent forward until they were eye to eye and, with

that easy grin, said, "My goal is to prove to you that the men of Clan DunBroch are the best archers in the land."

"If that is the case, you have failed," Elinor retorted.

His grin widened. "Well, I can't have you going back to MacCameron Castle thinking those clansmen of yours are better than DunBroch. The thought does not sit well with me, Princess." He snapped his fingers toward the group of young soldiers that stood on the periphery of the camp. "Patrick. Symon. Bring forth your bows. Let us see if you can impress the fair princess here."

Merida noticed the way Elinor stiffened as Fergus came to stand beside her. The tension between the pair was so palpable it hummed in the air.

Fergus's chest puffed out with pride as he watched his men hit target after target. Meanwhile, Elinor stood stoically, her face impassive.

Merida wanted to shake some sense into them both.

Why were they making this so difficult? Why could they not fall into each other's arms, recognize that they were meant for each other, and pledge their undying love? It would have made Merida's life so much easier.

Alas, her mother seemed determined to remain unimpressed, despite the men of Clan DunBroch putting on a splendid show. And her father appeared to be having a grand time antagonizing his guest.

Fergus turned to face Elinor and crossed his arms over his massive chest.

"How was that?" he asked. "Still just satisfactory?"

"DunBroch is not the only clan that can shoot a bow and arrow with precision," Elinor said. "It will take more than that to impress me."

"Is that so?" He took several steps back, unsheathed the sword at his hip, and brandished it. "We also excel at fencing. Would you care for a demonstration, Princess?"

Elinor glared at him. "I have seen quite enough, thank you."

"Are you sure?"

Merida wanted to scream.

She wished for him to woo the princess, not frustrate her. She had to do something before this got out of hand.

Merida looked up at the sky. There was a single fluffy white cloud floating overhead.

"Uh, Princess, it looks as if rain is on the way. Should we be heading back, you think?"

Elinor latched on to the excuse. "You are right. We shall be on our way." She turned to Fergus, haughtily tossing her hair over her shoulder as she did so. "I guess we will determine which clan is best at the Highland Games."

"I guess so," Fergus replied, his overconfident smile on full display. "See you there, Princess."

Merida wanted to bang her head against the nearest tree. The first meeting between these two could not have gone any worse.

Actually, it *could* have gone worse. Elinor could have taken the bow and shot Fergus with it, something Merida at one point feared she might do. At least there were no injuries.

The young soldier—Gaufrid—escorted Merida and Elinor back to their horses. They quickly mounted their steeds and started on their way.

"We must make haste," Elinor said, taking the lead. "I have my other lessons to tend to. The queen will question me if I am late."

"And Aileen will question if I am late salting the fish," Merida said.

Elinor's brow furrowed, probably at the distaste Merida had not been able to hide in her voice. "Is the larder not to your liking?" the princess asked.

" 'Tis fine," Merida said. "I shall handle it for as long as necessary."

They were forced to travel at a slower pace as they wound their way through the forest, dodging fallen branches and rotting tree stumps. Merida debated bringing up what had just happened back at the camp; she was intrigued by Elinor's strong reaction to Fergus.

"The DunBroch clansmen are very good with the bow and arrow," Merida volunteered.

"They are sufficient," Elinor replied. She looked over at Merida and rolled her eyes. "Fine, they are outstanding. I doubt anyone in Clan MacCameron will be able to best them at the Highland Games."

"Fergus is particularly skilled."

"Fergus is an oaf," Elinor quickly rebutted.

"But his competence is unquestionable." Merida decided to push a bit more. "I find him rather charming."

"Charming!" Elinor scoffed. "There is nothing charming about that lad." She stuck her nose up in the air. "And he smelled."

Merida choked out a laugh. "That is unfair. He and his men have been camped out in the forest. They all smelled."

"He smelled the worst."

Merida averted her face so that Elinor would not see the smirk she was trying desperately to hide.

"Well, I hope you did not allow the DunBroch's odor to distract you from his remarkable expertise. If you were kinder to him, he might be willing to teach you how to shoot."

"I do not need that DunBroch lad to teach me to shoot," Elinor said. "That is what *you* are to do, remember?" She straightened on her horse. "Enough about him. I do not want to think about Fergus and his face again."

Despite her words, Merida had a feeling the princess would have a hard time not thinking about Fergus. She would not have been so adamant in her disparagement of him had he not made an impression.

Merida tried telling herself that even a bad impression was better than none.

They reached the clearing and sent the horses on their second high-paced gallop of the day.

CHAPTER SEVENTEEN
Merida

Merida grabbed one of the hooks overhead and stuck a lean venison loin through it. She slid the slab of meat down the line and repeated the action with another. Sorcha had taken cubes of the fresh venison to the kitchens an hour earlier so that it could be added to a stew for that night's meal.

Merida debated whether to up her price for teaching the princess survival skills in the form of demanding dishes that contained meat. After eating vegetable pottage for the second day in a row, her body screamed for more sustenance.

Better to get her mind off food and focused on more important things, like orchestrating another meeting between Fergus and the princess. Their first encounter might not have gone quite as planned, but once those two realized they were perfect for each other, Merida could go back to her normal life.

The door to the wet larder swung open and Aileen marched in. "Come with me." She exited the room as quickly as she had entered.

Merida hesitated, unsure if she could trust Aileen. She reminded herself that she must not give anyone a reason to have her dismissed from this job. She wiped her hands with a square of linen before making sure her hair was secured under the shawl.

When she entered the kitchens, she found Sorcha and one of the scullery maids standing against the wall holding platters piled high with food. Both girls looked as frightened as mice.

"Three of the servers came down with the flux and had to take to their beds," Aileen announced. "You need to stand in. Have you ever served before?"

"I . . . no, not really," Merida said.

Aileen rolled her eyes. "Useless," she muttered. "You will carry the dishes to the tables and remove them when the king and queen have had their fill. You are not to be seen or heard, you hear me, lass?"

"Not to be seen?" Merida asked. "How can that be if I am to bring in and then clear the dishes?"

Aileen released an irritated sigh. "I mean that you are to be so quiet that they should barely notice you are even there." She shoved a loaf of warm bread wrapped in a cloth into Merida's arms. "Get in line."

Merida followed the other girls out of the kitchen, but not before stealthily lifting a small knife from the sideboard. She tucked it under the belt at her waist and hid it within the folds of her tunic. She would use it to scrape off the bristles that had formed on her jaw. Merida could not figure out what had caused the tiny black hairs to sprout.

She and the others entered the Great Hall, and Merida was immediately taken aback by the unexpected opulence of the space.

The Great Hall at Castle DunBroch was nicely appointed, but it was nothing compared to this. She looked up at the ceiling that soared above her with its thick, crisscrossing beams. Dozens of meticulously designed tapestries hung from the rafters. Like the others she had taken notice of in the castle, they seemed to tell a story, alternating between scenes of fierce battles and wholesome family celebrations.

Shields and suits of armor adorned the walls on either side. In the center of the back wall hung a remarkable display of claymores, battle-axes, and other weaponry. The candlelight gleamed against their shiny surfaces.

Merida was so focused on her surroundings that she did not notice Sorcha had stopped walking. The bread's crusty outer layer crackled underneath the towel as she slammed into the girl's back.

"Pay attention, lass," Sorcha whispered over her shoulder.

Suddenly, the bread, the tapestries, and everything else became a blur. Merida's entire focus homed in on the two people sitting at either end of the long wooden table.

Her grandparents.

The most she had ever seen of them was a tapestry that hung in the drawing room at Castle DunBroch. Merida had known that her mother and grandmother shared a likeness, but to see Queen Catriona in the flesh was jarring. It was as if she were looking at the face of the mother who had raised her. From their dark auburn hair to that patrician nose, the two women could have been identical twins born decades apart.

Merida finally took notice of the younger Elinor and her wide-eyed expression. It was clear that she had not expected to see Merida inside the Great Hall that night. If ever.

But Merida could not think about Elinor then. She was too curious about the king and queen.

"Do not stare," Sorcha whispered. "Remember, lass. Seen and not heard."

Merida tried to keep her head about her. She must behave as if she were a regular member of the household staff. She could not draw attention to herself.

She mimicked the other girls, gently placing her loaf of bread next to a bowl of turnips and promptly falling back in line. Taking her cues from Sorcha, Merida clasped her hands in front of her and stood mutely as the family ate their dinner.

"The tutor reported that you seemed absent-minded in your lessons today," King Douglass MacCameron pronounced.

It was the first time Merida had ever heard her grandfather's voice. She was mesmerized by the rich, deep cadence. But the more she heard him speak, the less captivating she found him; the words he spoke were appalling.

Merida clutched her hands into fists as she listened to the king reprimand Elinor for the grave offense of being caught looking out of the window during her Latin lesson. Merida did worse things before she even had a chance to break her fast most mornings.

She looked to Queen Catriona to see if she would intervene on her daughter's behalf, but the queen's expression was indifferent as she bit into a chunk of venison. It was such a disappointment to see the grandparents she had put on a pedestal in her fantasies treat their daughter—her mother—in this way. And at the dinner table, no less.

Merida could not help thinking about all the times she had thought her mother was being hard on her children—especially her eldest daughter. That was nothing compared to how Elinor's own parents treated her.

"You must understand how this makes me look, Elinor," her grandfather said. "Every misstep you make reflects badly on the kingdom. I will not stand for it!"

He slapped his flat palm against the table for emphasis, knocking over a goblet. Aileen, who had joined Merida and the other girls at their post next to the wall, ran to the king's side to wipe up the spilled ale. A smirk curved the corner of her mouth as she returned to stand against the wall.

She was enjoying this. Something about the princess being dressed down by her father amused Aileen. Merida wish she could take what remained in that goblet and toss it in Aileen's face.

As she stared helplessly at Elinor's bowed head, Merida began to understand more about why her mother was the way she was. King Douglass and Queen Catriona required perfection and deemed anything less unacceptable.

When asked a question, Elinor gave answers that were low and monosyllabic. She looked defeated. And embarrassed. Merida ached for her.

The dinner went on for another excruciating half hour, with the king lecturing his daughter about her responsibilities as a member of the royal family. It was obvious the king and queen believed carrying out one's duties was of utmost importance. But did they have to be so exacting?

After he finished the food on his plate, the king held up a hand. Both Elinor and Queen Catriona immediately set down their utensils, even though both still had several bites of food remaining. Aileen directed the girls to follow her, but Merida remained still, unable to believe that the two women at the table would stop eating their meal simply because the king had concluded his.

Aileen turned back to Merida with a blistering look, motioning for her to get to the table. Merida once again followed Sorcha's lead. She collected the square of cloth the bread had been wrapped in, along with a mostly empty platter that held a few carrots lingering in butter.

Aileen approached the king and asked, "Will you be having dessert tonight, King Douglass?"

The king nodded before taking a sip from his goblet. He then pronounced, "The chieftain of Clan Fraser and his eldest son will be joining us for dinner in two days." He settled his gaze directly on his daughter. "You are to be on your best behavior when your betrothed arrives, Elinor."

Merida dropped the platter she carried. She gasped as the porcelain shattered, and watched helplessly as carrots rolled onto the floor and under the table.

"What are you doing?" Aileen hissed at her.

"I am . . . I am sorry," Merida stuttered.

The king and queen looked at her with matching expressions of shock and censure. Elinor's eyes were wide with alarm.

"I am sorry," Merida said again. She looked at all three members of the royal family—her family—and tried to process the words she had just heard spoken by the king.

Elinor was already betrothed?

She scurried out of the Great Hall, running through the kitchens and out the door that led to the yard. Merida flattened her back against the castle's cold stone wall, sucking in slow, deep breaths in an effort to calm herself. It was not working.

She pushed away from the wall and paced back and forth, clutching her fabric-covered head in her hands.

Was it possible she had heard him wrong? Or that the king was mistaken?

Why would her grandfather tell Elinor that she was meeting her betrothed? The princess herself said the

Highland Games were not for a fortnight, so the competition for the princess's hand could not possibly have already taken place. So how could Elinor's betrothed be a guest at an upcoming dinner?

And why was he from Clan Fraser and not Clan DunBroch?

CHAPTER EIGHTEEN
Elinor

Elinor took small bites of the fig cake Sorcha had placed in front of her. She usually enjoyed a sweet at the end of the evening meal, but mention of her betrothed had soured her appetite for anything other than being dismissed from the table. Elinor knew her parents meant well—they were focused on how to best prepare her for taking over the kingdom—but she could not commit every waking hour to obsessing over her noble duties, especially her impending marriage.

"I would assume the girl who sent the platter crashing to the floor is the girl you rescued," her mother remarked.

"The girl she rescued? When did the girl you rescued become part of the kitchen staff?" her father asked.

"It is not important enough to trouble yourself with, Douglass."

For once, Elinor was grateful to her mother for intervening. She was not prepared to discuss Merida with her father. He should not even know that she was still at MacCameron Castle. She was not supposed to have entered the Great Hall at all.

"It would appear that I will need to speak with Duncan," the queen continued. "When I gave him permission to hire the girl, I thought she had experience in the kitchens."

"'Tis likely just nerves on her part, Ma," Elinor said. "I shall see about her."

The queen lifted her goblet to her lips and took a sip before slowly placing it back on the table. All the while her gaze was focused directly on her daughter.

Elinor took several more bites, waiting until she would finally be excused. Once her father finished his cake and granted those at the table permission to leave, Elinor went through the ritual of setting aside her utensils, daintily dabbing at both corners of her mouth, and rising with grace from her chair, as her mother had taught her.

She fought the urge to hasten her steps as she calmly walked the length of the Great Hall, but the moment she cleared the door, Elinor hurried to the kitchens. She rounded the corner and nearly collided with a maid carrying a stack of copper pots.

"Forgive me," Elinor called over her shoulder.

She navigated through the sea of people cleaning up the remnants of the night's dinner.

"Princess Elinor?"

She stopped and turned at the sound of Aileen's decidedly cool voice. She and Aileen had been friends when they were younger, but for the past few years Elinor had sensed a change in the girl's attitude. She was never hostile, for no one would dare be hostile to the princess of MacCameron Castle, but she did not behave as the friend Elinor once knew.

"Is there something we can do for you, Princess?" Aileen asked.

"I was hoping to speak with Mer—the new girl," Elinor said. "Is it the larder where she is working?"

Aileen's expression hardened. It was only for a moment, but Elinor noticed the shift.

"She *should* be in the larder, but this Merida does not seem to think she must follow the same rules as the rest of the staff. I guess she thinks she is special. Maybe someone told her she was."

Elinor straightened her spine. "I told the kitchens that

Merida is not to be taxed. She suffered a head injury just a few days ago. If you have anything to say about it, direct it to Duncan and he shall direct it to me."

Elinor would have to address the girl's attitude with Duncan, but she did not have time to worry about Aileen. She had to speak to Merida.

Except Elinor realized she had no idea where to find the wet larder. This was the farthest she had ever stepped into the kitchens.

She refused to ask Aileen for assistance. Instead, she approached a maid wearing a scullery cap, but when the young girl turned around and saw who was calling on her, she froze like she had seen a ghost.

"There is no need for nervousness," Elinor assured her. "I only want to know if—" Just then, Sorcha exited a room at the far end of the kitchens. "Sorcha," Elinor called. Duncan's sister would not cower. She pointed to the room the girl had just vacated. "Is Merida in there?"

"Yes, Princess," Sorcha answered with a short curtsy. "Though she is . . . well, you will see when you get in there."

If the queen had been around, she would have had something to say about Elinor's graceless dash to the larder. She entered the freezing room and found Merida sitting with her back against the wall. Her knees were drawn up to her chest and her head hung forward, braced against them.

"What is the matter here?" Elinor asked. "What happened back in the Great Hall?"

Merida lifted her head. "You are already betrothed?"

Elinor was confused by the unexpected question and the anguish in Merida's voice. "Why are you so upset about my betrothal? *I* am the one who is being forced to marry."

"But your betrothed—the king said he is of Clan Fraser? Why is he not of Clan DunBroch?"

"Clan DunBroch?" Elinor could not help herself; she burst into the most unladylike laughter. Her mother would have had an apoplexy if she had been standing there to witness it.

"I appreciate the lessons you are providing, lass, but thinking I would marry into your clan as payment is quite absurd." Elinor's eyes narrowed as understanding dawned. "Has this been your goal all along, to convince me to marry into Clan DunBroch? That is why you took me to their camp? Are you even injured, or has this been some sort of ruse?"

"That is far-fetched, Princess," Merida said. "Think about what you are saying. How would I have known that you would be in the forest the day you found me?"

She was right. Merida could not possibly have known

that Elinor had chosen that day to attempt her escape. And her injury had been tended to by the physician; he would have alerted Elinor if it had been feigned.

"It matters not," Elinor said. "And what is far-fetched is the thought of me marrying a DunBroch. 'Tis a union that would never happen."

"Why not?"

Elinor found her affront amusing. "Because the MacCamerons and the DunBrochs are sworn enemies. Wasn't it obvious back at that camp?"

"But there is a peace alliance between the clans."

"A *fragile* peace alliance," Elinor emphasized. "The MacCamerons and DunBrochs will always be enemies."

"Yet you brought me into your household?" Merida asked accusingly.

Elinor narrowed her eyes. "Should I have not?"

Merida released a frustrated sigh and pushed herself up from the floor. In a lowered voice, she said, "We should not discuss this here. I have only worked in these kitchens for a couple of days, but already I know that we should not say much around the other maids."

"You are right," Elinor said. "It is best we do not let anyone overhear us mentioning your clan's name."

Elinor turned to leave. She grabbed Merida by the hand, but then quickly let go.

"What is on your hand?" Elinor asked. "Why does it feel . . . hairy?"

"It is nothing." Merida tucked her hands against her stomach. "Just a rash. I think I came in contact with a poisoned plant. Do not bother about my hand." She looked over her shoulders. "Let us go. It is not just household gossip that worries me. I . . . I have an uneasy feeling about some who work in the kitchens."

Elinor led Merida through the door to the right of the scullery, near the washbasin. Several maids were out and about, emptying dirty water onto the ground. They all stopped at the sight of the princess. They looked back and forth between Elinor and Merida with confused expressions.

"As you were," Elinor instructed the maids. She peered over her shoulder and whispered to Merida, "Let us go to the south courtyard."

Elinor led the way, guiding Merida to the colonnade of rhododendron. Once she was sure they were alone, she turned to her.

"Now, what is your issue with my upcoming betrothal?" Elinor asked.

"I do not understand why you are already promised when the Highland Games are not for a fortnight," Merida answered. "Was there a competition prior to the games?"

"What does one have to do with the other?" Elinor

asked, wondering if maybe the girl's head injury was having lingering effects.

"How did you pick your betrothed, if not at the Highland Games? Did he not have to compete for your hand?"

"My betrothed has been chosen since shortly after my birth, Merida. 'Tis tradition that the eldest son—"

"Of each clan compete for your hand in marriage during the Highland Games!" Merida interjected. "Which means a member of Clan DunBroch would be eligible."

"No." Elinor shook her head. "I know nothing of this competition you speak of. Clansmen compete throughout the games, but my hand in marriage is certainly not a prize to be won. What kind of archaic nonsense is that?"

Merida's jaws went slack. She stared at Elinor, as if she could not understand the concept of a birthright betrothal.

"So you are really betrothed to this man? This man from Clan Fraser?"

"The betrothal will be officially announced at the Highland Games, as is tradition in the year the princess turns ten and nine. I am not sure why this comes as such a shock to you," Elinor said. "The same is done at Clan DunBroch, is it not?"

Merida shook her head. "No, that is not how it is done at all." She began to pace again, walking back and forth between the hedges and reminding Elinor of herself. She paced whenever she had to think hard about something. "If who you are to marry has already been decided, then I . . . I do not know what I am going to do."

"You make no sense, Merida," Elinor said. "Perhaps you should get some rest."

She stopped and stared at Elinor with wide, shocked eyes, as if Elinor had caught her off guard.

"Uh . . . you are right," Merida said. She put a hand to her head. "I am feeling unwell. I believe I will retire for the night."

"You should," Elinor said. "I fear your injury may be worse than we first thought. I shall ask the physician to visit you."

"No!" Merida shouted. "No, I just need rest. Please. Just rest and to not be disturbed for the rest of the night."

Elinor did her best to ignore the uneasy feeling in her gut as she nodded.

"As you wish."

CHAPTER NINETEEN
Merida

Merida sat on the edge of the thin, straw-filled mattress in the tiny room she had been assigned. There were no windows in the servants' quarters, so she could not tell if the sun had begun its morning ascent. She could only hope it had.

Merida tucked in the hair at her ears and tightened the cloth wrapped around her head, securing it with the pin Elinor had given her. She held her hands out in front of her face. More black hairs. She had plucked them before going to sleep the night before, and new ones had already popped up. She ran her thumb along her jaw and sighed at the feel of more stubble.

But she could not worry about a few stray hairs. She had more important matters to tend to.

She needed answers, and she was sure Freya was the only person who would be able to provide them.

At least Merida *hoped* Freya had answers to the myriad questions that had begun swirling in her head the moment she learned of Princess Elinor's impending betrothal. It had been hours since dinner, yet Merida was still overwhelmed with shock and disbelief. In all the times her parents had retold the story of their meeting and eventual marriage, not once had either mentioned that her mother had been betrothed to someone from another clan. The past night was the first Merida had even heard of Clan Fraser, yet her own mother had been promised to their chieftain's eldest son?

And what about the competition? Why was no one competing for the princess's hand in marriage at the Highland Games? It would appear that long-standing tradition Queen Elinor continually harped on had not had a very long history at all.

Had her mother been promised on that fated day when she found Fergus injured in the woods? She must have been. So how had their union come to pass?

Freya would know the answer. She *had* to.

Merida retrieved her bow and arrows from their hiding

spot under the bed. She lifted the straps over her head and across her chest, then pulled her kirtle over it all. If anyone looked too closely they would notice the lumps, but Merida was determined to once again make it off the castle grounds undetected.

As she approached her bedroom door, she took a moment to close her eyes and suck in several deep, calming breaths. She could not allow nerves to get the better of her, not with an undertaking as important as this one.

Once she was certain she could walk without her legs shaking, she said a short prayer and pushed the door open. Merida looked up and down the narrow corridor, grateful to find it deserted at this early hour. The only light came courtesy of a lone candle that burned halfway down the hallway.

Despite its emptiness, Merida proceeded with caution as she slipped out of her room and gently closed the door behind her. She was not certain of the hour, but if it was close to sunup—which she hoped it was—then the servants in charge of readying the staff for a long day of running the household would be out and about soon.

She kept her back close to the wall to avoid the candle casting her shadow. She could not be too careful, especially if someone like Aileen or one of the other maids who were becoming suspicious of her happened to enter the corridor.

Her heart pounded furiously, slamming against the

walls of her chest with each step. Merida did not breathe easily until she reached the short stairwell that would take her to the rear yard.

But she knew better than to let down her guard. Making it out of the castle was only the beginning. She next had to get across the yard, to the stables, and to Angus.

She had considered walking to the village where Freya and her mother's wood-carving shop was located, but it was at least a half day's journey to make it to and from the village on foot. Angus would get her there and back within an hour, provided she did not get lost.

Merida slipped out of the rear door and crouched low, grateful for the light fog that hung in the air. Combined with the predawn darkness, it helped provide her cover as she scrambled across the yard toward the stables. She knew she would curse that same fog if it slowed her down once she got Angus past the curtain wall, but that was a problem she would face if it came to pass.

She spotted Angus in his stall near the front of the stables. Merida looked around for a groom and saw the young boy, Ewan, sleeping against the outer wall. His head was thrown back and his mouth was wide open.

Merida crept around the side so as not to startle Angus. She prayed the horse would not neigh upon seeing her.

Her horse was smarter than she gave him credit for. It

was as if he sensed her need for stealth. He tipped his head in greeting, but remained quiet. Merida caught him by the reins and, as soundlessly as possible, walked Angus out of the stable.

The remainder of her escape from the castle grounds went smoothly, and she soon found herself traveling swiftly through the woods. Her apprehension began to abate as she made her way to the village, but her anxiety quickly spiked again at the thought of everything that could go wrong.

She would talk to Freya. Freya would know what to do.

Merida rode past the large downed tree that she remembered from her previous visit. A few minutes later, she brought Angus to a quick stop. Merida spotted a short figure dressed in a cloak and carrying a basket.

Freya.

She dismounted Angus and tied his reins around a slim tree trunk. As she got closer to the woman, she saw that her basket was filled with an assortment of mushrooms and vegetation.

Merida dismissed pleasantries and got right to the heart of the matter. "Why did you not tell me the princess was betrothed?" she asked.

Freya swung around. "Oh, Merida! I did not see you there."

"Did you not think it worth mentioning that Princess Elinor is promised to some lad from Clan Fraser?"

"Is she?" Freya frowned, then nodded. "Well, that would make sense. Clan Fraser's chieftain is the MacCameron's closest ally. Everyone knows that."

"I did not!"

Freya shrugged. "Now you do."

"Freya!" Merida screeched. "What does this mean?"

The witch picked up a fat mushroom and examined it from all angles. "Well, when one is promised, it means they are to be married in the future. In the *near* future. Although I do not think the princess's betrothal will be formally announced before the solstice. In the last few years, betrothal announcements have taken place at the Highland Games. Something of a grand opening of the games," she said, waving her hands in a flourish.

"I know what being promised means," Merida said. "I want to know what it means for Elinor and my father meeting and being married."

Freya finally stopped her foraging and turned to give Merida her full attention. "I would assume that if your mother were to marry into Clan Fraser, then she would not be allowed to marry your father."

"You assume?" Merida began to pace back and forth,

crunching the leaves that had fallen to the forest floor. She rubbed at her arms, which had started to itch again. "Does this mean that you do not *know* what will happen? You are guessing, just as I am?"

"I cannot predict the future, Merida."

"Yet you can change it," she accused.

"No, I cannot. What will it take for you to understand that I have limited control over what happens? And why are you scratching your skin so?"

"Because it itches," Merida said. She pushed up the sleeves of her kirtle and held out her arms. She blinked several times at the sight. Her arms were as hairy as her father's.

Freya set the basket on the ground and edged closer to Merida. She grabbed her hands and twisted Merida's arms back and forth.

"Have you always been this woolly?" Freya asked.

"No," Merida said, jerking her arms out of the witch's grip. "Do you think I am a sheep?" She ran her hands over the bristly strands. "I am not sure what is happening. The hairs started popping up on my knuckles and along my jaw. I think I may have brushed against a poisoned shrub."

Freya continued to stare at her arms for several more moments before lifting her eyes up to meet Merida's.

"I do not think a poisoned shrub caused this," she said.

Freya reached into a dark brown satchel that was the same color as her cloak and retrieved the bound book she had referenced a few days before. Finding a seat on a downed tree, she opened the book on her lap and began poring over the pages.

The woman's distress caused a sense of trepidation to bubble up in Merida's stomach.

"What is it?" Merida asked.

Freya looked up from the book. Merida wasn't sure what to make of the regretful look in her eyes. She pointed to the tattered linen pages. "I think I may have found the spell I created for your mother," she said.

"Finally," Merida said with a relieved laugh. Now that they knew the spell, they could figure out a way to reverse it. "Why do you look so alarmed?" Merida asked. "This is a good thing."

"No." Freya shook her head. "No, Merida, it is not."

CHAPTER TWENTY
Merida

Merida drew her head back, flinching from Freya's words.

"I thought finding the spell was the first step to getting me back home?"

"But this spell is . . . well . . ."

"Well, what?" Merida asked.

"It is turning you into a bear," Freya said.

Merida was sure she had heard incorrectly. She chuckled, and then the chuckle grew into a full-bellied laugh.

"How can you find humor in this?" Freya asked.

"Because—" Merida held her hand up, needing a minute to collect herself. "Because I thought you said that I was turning into a bear."

"That *is* what I said."

Merida's spine went rigid. "What do you mean I am turning into a bear?"

"It is the only thing that makes sense." Freya gestured to the spell book. "You came to me seeking a spell to change your mother, correct?"

"Yes, but not into an animal."

"The spell is based on the Legend of the Black Bear." Freya nervously twisted her gown in her hands. "Legend has it that the bear was once human—a young man—who had a difficult time seeing the world from any perspective but his own. The young man's family sought to find a way to make him more considerate of others so that he would stop trying to bully them into following his way.

"But the young man resisted. And instead of becoming more understanding, he became more stubborn, more brute. He had until the solstice to change his ways and mend the bond that had been broken between him and his family, but he chose not to, and he remained a bear for the rest of his days."

Merida's chest tightened. "Why would you give my mother such a spell? That is not what I asked for at all."

"Maybe you mentioned that your mother was being unreasonable and would not listen? And that you wanted her to see things from your perspective?"

Merida nodded slowly.

"Then that explains it. This is exactly the type of spell any good witch would choose in this situation." Freya hunched her shoulders. She wagged a finger at Merida. "And this is why one should never use a spell that is not meant for them."

"It does not explain anything," Merida said. She looked down at her arms. "And now I am turning into a bear!"

"Because your mother was a bear to put up with. The spell would have changed your fate by forcing your mother to change her ways. But you subverted those plans when you consumed the spell yourself." She pinched her forefinger and thumb together. "One small change—one tiny disruption—has the power to alter the course of history."

Merida released an exhausted sigh. "Why must you make it sound so dramatic? I did not change the course of history when I ate that cake."

Freya walked up to her and enclosed Merida's cheeks in her palms. "Oh, but haven't you? One person is all it takes." She held up a lone finger. "There are no insignificant people in this world, Merida. We all have our place and play our parts. One person's actions affect another, and another, and another. Think of it this way." She pointed to the ground. "If I were not here right now to tell you to move, the snake that is about to bite you would have a piece of your leg."

Merida yelped and jumped out of the way. She flattened

her hand to her chest in an attempt to slow the sudden rapid beating of her heart.

"See? Your life would have changed, just like that." Freya snapped her fingers. She picked up her basket of mushrooms and swung it toward the snake, shooing it away.

"Come." Freya grabbed Merida by the arm and tugged her over to the fallen tree trunk. She clasped her hands on her shoulders and encouraged her to sit. "You must be mindful of that injury to your head. Have no worries, there are no snakes here," Freya said. "Now, let us consider where things are. Your mother is promised to the eldest son of the Fraser chieftain, but you are proof that she was destined to marry the eldest son of Clan DunBroch."

"Yes. And together, she and my father have four children, me and my three brothers. The triplets."

"Triplets, you say? That is rare. Their union is a very special one indeed."

"Except there has not been a union, and according to you, there will not be one unless I can bring them together."

"That is correct," Freya said. "Because of where you were in that forest five days ago, Princess Elinor's and the lad from Clan DunBroch's lives changed from their original fates, along with the lives of everyone they would have eventually had an impact on. The longer your parents are apart, the more disruption it will cause. They are losing precious moments from their courtship."

Freya plopped down next to Merida on the fallen tree and placed her basket of mushrooms on the ground between them. "We must hasten things along," she continued, slapping her hands against her thighs. "We know your parents met and that they fell in love and had four children. Was there anything else significant that resulted from Princess Elinor discovering Fergus in the woods?"

"They also established a new kingdom together," Merida said. "I do not know much about the origins of the kingdom of DunBroch. It is a complicated story, and I must admit that I do not pay much attention to kingdom politics or history."

"The kingdom of DunBroch?" Freya asked, her brows arching in surprise. "Are you saying the MacCameron's kingdom fell? What about the new peace alliance? Did it collapse?"

"It must have," Merida said. "My father loves to tell the story of how he brought together the four clans that make up their kingdom to defeat the Vikings."

"Who are the Vikings, dear?"

"They were invaders," Merida explained. She jumped up from the log and began to pace as the words rushed out of her.

"This story I *do* know. The Vikings invaded from the north, by way of Moray. There were thousands of them, armed with lances and spears. According to my father, the clans were feuding with one another, but he convinced the chieftains that they must all band together if they were to defeat the invaders, because if they did not, the Vikings would take out each clan one by one."

"And then what happened?" Freya asked.

"My father and the other chieftains were victorious," she answered. "The Vikings retreated. And, because of that, they decided to name him king." Merida stopped short. She turned to Freya in confusion. "But what about my grandfather? *He* is the current king."

The furrow in Freya's brow deepened. "That is a good question," she said. "What were you told about King Douglass?"

"I have never known much about my grandparents. The few times I asked my mother about her clan, she would only say that the MacCamerons returned to their homeland in the south, but I never learned the story of why they left. Now that I have seen just how vast the MacCameron lands are, I am even more curious about why my grandfather relinquished all he had amassed."

"A powerful king does not simply relinquish his throne, Merida."

"You believe my grandfather was removed?" she asked.

"Did your father ever mention the MacCamerons when he told the story of bringing the neighboring clans together to fight the Vikings?'"

Merida shook her head. "He spoke of the Vikings who survived the battle and how they retreated following their defeat. My father was crowned king and my mother was crowned queen."

But where was her grandfather in all of this? What happened during the time between when King Douglass was removed from the throne and when her father, Fergus, was named king?

"My father never spoke of another clan that ruled after MacCameron Kingdom fell, so there must not have been much time at all between when my grandfather was removed from the throne and when my father was crowned king," Merida reasoned. "That means the Vikings must have arrived soon after . . ."

Merida's voice trailed off as more of the picture came into focus.

Freya put a hand to her mouth. Her eyes had gone wide with panic. "The MacCameron was not simply removed from the throne," she surmised.

He was killed.

Neither spoke the words, but then there was no need to. It was obvious what had happened. The Vikings had killed King Douglass, leaving room for Fergus to step in as ruler of a new kingdom.

A wave of unexpected sorrow overwhelmed Merida. Her brief encounter with her grandfather had not planted any seeds of affection in her for the man, but the thought of her mother suffering the loss of a parent—even a brusque, unfeeling parent—struck Merida as unbelievably sad.

A heavy feeling settled in the pit of her stomach as another thought occurred to her.

"I always wondered how my father was able to rally the chieftains of Clans MacGuffin, Dingwall, and Macintosh to fight with him against the Vikings. They are a strong-willed lot; they would not have simply followed his orders because they were asked to do so. There had to be something else to compel them to follow."

"Like the fact that he was the princess's betrothed," Freya said.

Merida nodded. It was the same conclusion she had come to.

"My father was already set to become king because of his upcoming marriage to my mother. That would explain how he convinced the other clans to join him." She looked at Freya. "If the clans had not banded together, there is no way they could have withstood the assault from the Vikings. Elinor and Fergus's marriage is the key to it all."

"Merida, do you understand what this means?" Freya asked.

Merida shook her head, even though the picture was becoming clearer.

"It was not only your fate that you changed when you consumed that spell, Merida. I think you may have changed the fate of your entire clan, along with the clans surrounding DunBroch."

Merida's jaw went slack as she stared at Freya, willing the witch's words to be untrue. But as more of the pieces of the puzzle fell into place, it became harder to deny the only possible conclusion.

"If I do not find a way to get my parents betrothed before the Vikings attack, my entire people will be in danger."

CHAPTER TWENTY-ONE
Merida

Merida was too stunned to speak. She plopped back down on the fallen tree trunk for fear that her suddenly weak limbs would not support her.

Her mind refused to accept the determination she had reached, but how could she refute it?

She had heard countless stories of how her father's bravery and ability to pull the clans together to defeat the Vikings had saved them all. But if Princess Elinor and Fergus did not marry—if Elinor married into Clan Fraser, instead—her father would not have the same influence over the clans. He would be seen as just another member of Clan DunBroch, not significant enough to inspire the other clans to follow his lead.

The Vikings would slaughter them all, clan by clan.

Merida still could not process her role in all of this. How could one tiny action on her part have such extreme consequences?

She did not have time to lament over her mistakes. She must commit all her energy to getting her parents together. She could not fail. The fate of her entire clan—of *many* clans—hung in the balance.

"I must make a plan," Merida said. She jumped up from the tree, but Freya grabbed her by the hand before she could take a step.

"Where are you going?"

"Nowhere," Merida said. "I need to move. It is the only way I can think clearly."

Freya grimaced. "You make me dizzy with all this back and forth, lass."

"I am sorry," Merida said as she trampled the ground underneath her feet. "How should I go about getting my parents together now that Elinor is already promised?" She stopped pacing as a thought occurred to her. "Maybe her betrothed can fall for another. It would be the easiest route, don't you think?"

"I am not sure there is a lass in all of Scotland who could convince a young man to break his betrothal to the princess."

Merida leveled a curious look at Freya. "Wouldn't that book you carry have a spell that could make that happen?"

"No more spells," Freya said.

She was right. The witch's spells had caused enough damage. Merida threw her head back in frustration and looked up at the sky. She was astounded that it could so closely resemble the sky she had spent hours gazing at while relaxing in the glen, when the reality she was currently living underneath it was so different from everything she knew.

"I wish I could talk to my mother about this. She is excellent when it comes to planning. But if I told Elinor how I really came to be in the forest, she would think me mad."

"Do not tell anyone how you came to be here, Merida," Freya warned. "People will label you a witch, or worse. And you will be cast out of the castle. I know what I am speaking of."

"I know you do," Merida said, recalling the attitudes she had encountered in the village when she had asked about the wood-carver. She wondered how long Freya and her mother had been labeled outcasts.

Maybe Merida could help. Once she was back in DunBroch, she could influence her mother and father to make a declaration of some sort. Or she could do so herself, once she was in a position to make decisions as a member of the royal family.

"Come on, girlie. Back to the matter at hand," Freya said.

"Yes." Merida nodded. One thing at a time. "I must get my parents on the path to falling in love before her betrothal is announced at the Highland Games."

"And before the solstice," Freya interjected. "Remember, the solstice is *your* best chance at returning home."

"Which means I have even less time to bring them together." Merida rubbed her temples to stave off the headache that was beginning to form.

Arranging another meeting between Elinor and Fergus would not be difficult now that she knew where the DunBroch clansmen were camped. The challenge lay in convincing Elinor not to spurn Fergus. It was hard to believe those two people who were so hostile to each other were the same people who had raised her. Her parents were nauseatingly in love.

"The one bright side to all of this is that the princess is not too keen on marrying her betrothed, either," Merida said.

"How do you know that?"

Merida was not sure she should share anything more about Elinor. The princess had impressed upon her how important it was that her intentions remain a secret. But Merida needed someone in whom she could trust and confide. Freya was her only ally outside of Elinor.

"Please do not share this with anyone, but when the princess found me in the woods, she was in the process of running away because she is against her betrothal."

Freya's eyes lit up. "Well, that works in your favor, does it not? If the princess disagrees with the Fraser lad as a match—"

"It is not just the Fraser lad. The princess does not want to marry *any*one," Merida said.

"Oh." Freya bit her bottom lip. "That is unfortunate. Understandable, but unfortunate. This may make it more difficult for you to bring her and your father together."

"You have no idea," Merida said. "Elinor does not trust Clan DunBroch due to the long feud between the clans. And she despises my father." Merida's shoulders slumped. "Convincing Princess Elinor that Fergus of DunBroch is trustworthy will be impossible."

"Not if Fergus shows her that he is," Freya said.

Merida swung around, her eyes widening. "Are you suggesting he court her?"

FATE BE CHANGED

"Well, that is how it is done when the match is not already made by virtue of one's birth," she said. "However, there is not enough time for a formal courtship, especially one between two young people from opposing clans. You will need to hurry things along, lass."

"You are right," Merida said.

But how was Merida to convince her mother that Fergus was trustworthy when she wasn't so sure *she* trusted him? Something about his presence in the forest continued to gnaw at her.

He was withholding something from her; she was certain of it. But another thing Merida was certain of was that her father was the most honorable man she knew. There had to be a good reason for his delay in seeing the king.

Her ultimate goal remained the same—to get her parents to fall in love.

"I must return to the castle and fetch the princess," Merida said. "I am to teach her how to start a fire." She shot Freya a knowing look. "Maybe I will solicit Fergus's help with today's lesson."

If the sparks she had witnessed between those two during the previous meeting were anything to go on, they should have no problem starting a fire. It was best she fan the flames in her favor before she ran out of time.

"And I shall return to my shop so that I can continue searching for a spell to send you back home," Freya vowed. "It is the only spell I will work on until the solstice arrives."

CHAPTER TWENTY-TWO
Merida

The revelations that came out of her visit with Freya had settled in the pit of Merida's stomach like a giant boulder, heavy and unyielding. She wished Freya were wrong, that the hairs that had sprouted along Merida's arms and jawline were due to some poisonous shrub, or maybe something she'd eaten. Anything but the result of a horrific spell.

A bear? How could that be? It was too terrifying to comprehend.

Even more harrowing? The idea that it would not matter if she became a bear, because if she could not get her parents to fall in love, she and everyone she loved might very well not exist once the Vikings invaded.

Merida let out a strangled cry.

She *had* to succeed. There was no other choice.

She nudged Angus's flank, hastening his stride as they made their way back to MacCameron Castle.

She still had not figured out how to get Elinor to return to the DunBroch camp without drawing suspicion. Maybe she should just drop all pretense and make the case for Fergus as the only acceptable suitor.

The princess would laugh in her face and then banish her from the castle.

Merida's back went ramrod straight as another thought occurred to her.

The one thing Elinor could not refute was that Fergus's survival skills were unmatched. If Merida could convince her that Fergus was better suited to teach her how to survive her trip to the Lowlands, she would not have to contrive these schemes to bring them together.

Of course, convincing Fergus to play the role of teacher was another matter entirely. But based on the teasing she had witnessed the previous day, Merida was not so sure he would turn down the opportunity to get underneath the princess's skin. There was something between them, although she was sure both would deny it.

Merida caught sight of the curtain wall surrounding MacCameron Castle through the trees. The path had become familiar over these past few days. Just then, something caught her attention from the corner of her eye. She immediately recognized the colors of the DunBroch tartan.

At first she thought one of the clansmen had snagged his plaid on a wayward branch, but as she moved in closer, she realized the plaid was attached to a person. Merida slid off Angus as quietly as possible. She removed her slippers and gingerly moved toward the figure. There was only one member of Clan DunBroch of such substantial size.

Had her father really left himself this exposed? He must have learned to be stealthier in his later years, because the man who had taught her how to conceal herself from the enemy would never have left himself so vulnerable.

Merida inched forward, leaned over Fergus's back, and whispered, "Do you see anything interesting?"

He jumped so high that he nearly hit his head on a low branch hanging above.

"Goodness, lass!" He slapped a meaty palm to his chest. "What are you doing here?"

"That is my question to you," Merida said. "Why are you creeping about these lands?" She looked around. "And where are your other clansmen? Are they surrounding the castle? Are you planning an attack?"

"You speak nonsense, lass."

"Do I?" Merida asked. "What other explanation is

there? You said you are not here for the Highland Games. So what are you doing here, Fergus?"

"It is no concern of yours. Now leave me be."

There was something he was not telling her, and she had just about had enough of it. The time for playing around had long passed. She did not want to do this, but he left her no choice.

Merida sucked in a fortifying breath, then said, "If you do not tell me what your purpose is here, I will tell the MacCameron guards where to find you."

For a moment, Merida thought she had miscalculated what Fergus's reaction would be to a direct threat. His nostrils flared and his face reddened. He took a step toward her before taking several steps back.

"Why can't you let me be, lass? I told you; this is of no concern to you."

"I do not believe you," Merida said. "You have been camped out in these woods for days, with no explanation for your actions. There is something afoot, isn't there?"

He glared at her, his jaw twitching. Several moments passed before he said, "Possibly."

Merida's stomach dropped. "What is it?"

"I do not know," he said. "That is why I am here, to figure it out. I believe there is a threat to the kingdom, but I have no proof yet."

"What sort of threat is there to my kingdom?"

Merida and Fergus both whipped around at the sound of Elinor's voice.

"Princess! What are you doing here?" Merida asked.

"We were to meet in the forest to make fire," Elinor answered. "But that is beside the point now." She marched up to Fergus. "What threat do you speak of?"

Fergus scrubbed a hand down his face and released an irritated sigh. "What is it with you two? Why are you always lurking in the woods?"

"You insufferable brute! Any lass would lurk in the woods if it concerned her kingdom." Elinor plopped her hands on both hips. "Now, I will ask you again, why do you believe we are in danger?"

"I am not at liberty to share," he said.

"Is it because you and your clan are the cause?" she challenged. "If there is a threat to MacCameron Kingdom, I would not be surprised if the DunBrochs are the ones behind it."

Fergus took a menacing step forward. His eyes glittered with fervent heat, but there was something else there, a latent passion simmering underneath the surface.

Merida's heart thumped wildly within her chest as she observed their fiery exchange.

"Are you forgetting that Clan DunBroch is part of this

kingdom, Princess?" Fergus replied in a deceptively calm voice.

"That means nothing," Elinor spat. Her contemptuous glare traveled from the top of Fergus's head to his grimy boots. "You are only part of this kingdom because of the peace alliance."

"Does that make me less of a citizen? It matters not how I became part of this kingdom; I do not want peril to befall it." Fergus's mouth twisted. "You may not care what happens to this place, but I do."

Elinor gasped, her eyes blazing with indignation.

"How dare you accuse me of not caring about my home, you redheaded lout!"

"So, you have noticed my nice red hair?" he taunted, flicking his fingers in the matted locks.

"You . . . you . . . boggin numpty!"

Merida's jaw dropped. Had her mother just called her father a foul-smelling fool?

"Does the king know that his prim princess has such a filthy mouth?" Fergus asked.

Elinor's cheeks were as red as a cardinal's feathers. She brushed her hands along the front of her kirtle, then stood up straight and stuck her chin in the air.

"It is what you deserved for suggesting I have no interest in what happens to my homeland. MacCameron Kingdom's well-being is at the center of everything I do. It is all I have been taught to care about since birth."

"Then you should not take issue with me seeking out this threat," Fergus said.

"If there is a threat to the kingdom, then *I* will uncover it."

"No."

Elinor's head snapped back. "No? Who do you think you are?"

"I will not have you interfering, Princess."

"And I do not take orders from you, sir."

"Soldier," he corrected her.

Elinor's chest puffed in and out with her shallow, aggressive breaths. She faced Fergus with daring boldness, undaunted by his size. Her fists were balled at her sides as if she was doing all she could to keep her hands off him.

Did she wish to choke him, or draw him closer to her? Merida could not be sure.

She watched in fascinated delight as the tension bubbled up between her parents. It was so intense she could feel it on her skin. Fergus's eyes teemed with a mixture of annoyance and attraction. And Elinor's outrage was layered with something else—an awareness. She would likely deny it, but it was potent and unmistakable.

Even so, it was probably best Merida put an end to this confrontation and get back to the matter at hand, ferreting out the cause for the alarm she saw in Fergus's eyes when he spoke of the kingdom.

"Maybe if you give us a hint about this threat, we can help," Merida said. "We all want the same thing: to ensure that nothing bad befalls MacCameron Kingdom."

Fergus looked back and forth between the two of them, his reluctance obvious. But then he sighed. "Perhaps you are right. It is possible that what does not make sense to me and my clansmen may make sense to you two."

He motioned for them to come near and turned his focus to Elinor. "Has King Douglass or his council seemed concerned about the upcoming Highland Games or the approaching summer solstice?"

"No." Elinor's forehead creased with her frown. "Well, there is always a concern when so many clans from varying parts of the kingdom converge on the castle, but I have noticed nothing out of the ordinary. Should they be concerned?"

Fergus hesitated. A nerve in his square jaw jumped. "Possibly," he said. He pulled at his quiver's strap, which lay flat across his broad chest, and revealed an ingenious pocket sewn into its underside. He untied the twine holding the pocket closed and retrieved a tiny square of parchment.

He handed the note to Elinor, asking, "Does this make sense to either of you? Maybe it is a children's rhyme from these parts?"

She read it out loud.

"'On the day the sun reaches the height faeries cherish, those under the roar's rule will perish.'"

She looked up at Fergus, her eyes wide with alarm. "'Those under the roar's rule will perish'? This does not sound like any children's tale I have ever heard," Elinor said.

"The height faeries cherish?" Merida asked. "What does that mean?"

"That part I believe we have figured out. My men and I think it refers to the summer solstice," Fergus answered. "It is the day the sun reaches its highest point."

"The summer solstice happens every year. It has never led to anything untoward, has it?"

"No, it has not," Elinor said. "The solstice is a time of celebration."

"Yet the rhyme foretells danger," Fergus said. "I am not certain, but I fear an attack by Mor'du is imminent. What beast has a bigger roar than that bear?"

Elinor pressed her palm against her chest. "But Mor'du has not been seen in ages. Some question whether the beast is even alive."

"And others believe that Mor'du is immortal," Fergus said.

"Which do you believe?" Merida asked.

A nerve twitched in his jaw as he stared beyond her, as if searching for the beast.

"I am not sure what to believe when it comes to that bear," Fergus said. He returned his attention to Merida, his eyes filled with worry. "What I do know is, if what is written on that parchment is connected to Mor'du, all within the kingdom are in danger, including the king."

Fear knotted in Merida's stomach. "Where did you find the note?"

"One of my men found it in the forest as we were making our way to MacCameron Castle. Someone must have dropped it."

"Well, why did you not bring it to the king?" Elinor asked.

Fergus stared at her with a cynical arch to his brow. "Let me see, why would a DunBroch hesitate to bring King MacCameron a note that threatens danger? Maybe because the king may react in the same way his daughter did and accuse the DunBroch of treason?"

"I did not go so far as to accuse you of treason," Elinor argued. She turned the note over. "This parchment is of good quality. It looks like one I have seen before."

"We have tracked it down to a parchmenter from Clan

Innes," he said. He pointed to a pale blue drawing of a boar's head. "That is his mark."

"We must bring this news to King Douglass," Merida said. "This proves that he may be in danger."

"This proves nothing," Fergus said, lifting the parchment from Elinor's fingers. "The king's council can say that I wrote this note myself." He looked to Elinor. "Do not be so bold as to suggest I did, Princess. I shall not defend my loyalty to the kingdom again."

"I was not going to suggest any such thing," she said. "But you must agree that we have to do something."

"*We* will not do anything," Fergus said. He folded the parchment and returned it to the secret pocket on his quiver's strap. "Me and my men will get to the bottom of this."

"This is *my* kingdom," Elinor said. "I will not stand idly by when my father and my people are at risk." Her insolent glare still directed at Fergus, Elinor said, "Forget today's lesson, Merida. I do not have time to learn fire making. I have a kingdom to save."

CHAPTER TWENTY-THREE
Elinor

Elinor paced the length of a fallen tree trunk, no doubt wearing down the leather soles of her slippers as she tried to come up with a plan. She, Merida, and Fergus had moved deeper into the forest, well east of MacCameron Castle. Her clan's soldiers sometimes trained in the glen south of the castle. She had to avoid them at all costs.

Questions would arise were she to be seen with a DunBroch, and as much as it pained her to admit it, she could use Fergus's help. Elinor had begrudgingly agreed with his assessment that they needed more proof before alerting the king of a potential threat to the kingdom. She had a feeling that he would make a good partner in this endeavor, despite herself.

Elinor closed her eyes and tried to think. Deciding how one should go about uncovering whether there was a threat to her kingdom, and potentially to her father's life, was a difficult task. The king had not been mentioned specifically, but if the kingdom was in danger—especially from Mor'du—it stood to reason that the king would be as well.

"Someone wrote that warning," Elinor said. "We do not know where they were taking it, but we can assume they were on the way to MacCameron Castle. But if they dropped it before reaching the castle, one would think that they would still relay such an important message to the king, wouldn't they?"

"Unless the message was not meant for King Douglass," Merida said. She stood next to Angus, brushing down the horse's coat with her fingers. "You said yourself that the peace alliance is still very fragile. If the kingdom was attacked by Mor'du while under King Douglass's rule, it would make an argument for removing him as king."

Elinor stopped her pacing long enough to study Merida.

"Why are you staring at me?" Merida asked.

"Because your observation is as competent as anything my father's council could have come up with."

"Really?"

Elinor nodded. "You seem to have an aptitude for dealing with such matters. Did you do so in your own clan?"

"No." Merida averted her gaze. Her voice held a tinge of guilt as she admitted, "I did not pay much attention to the inner workings of the kingdom."

"It is a pity," Elinor said. "You are good at it."

Merida briefly looked away again. "Well, should we start with the chieftains who were most against King Douglass's rule before the peace alliance?" she suggested.

"That would be the chieftain of DunBroch. I do not wish to bruise Fergus's delicate sensibilities by accusing his chieftain of being a traitor," Elinor said, rolling her eyes. She paused and looked around. "Where is Fergus?"

"He stepped away." Merida looked around as well. "He said he would only be gone a moment, but it has been quite some time."

Fury surged in Elinor's chest. Had he abandoned their agreement already? Was he off to uncover what the second part of the riddle meant on his own?

"I knew I could not trust him," Elinor said, fighting back a wave of disappointment. She should have known better than to place even the smallest bit of confidence in a DunBroch. In *any* man, for that matter. She had been foolish to think Fergus would be different, that he would be worthy of her trust.

"Ah!" Merida spoke with relieved enthusiasm. "There you are."

Elinor whipped around to find Fergus marching toward them. She was taken aback by the relief that swept through her.

He had unpinned his plaid from his shoulder and now cradled something within it. He stopped before Elinor.

"I ran across bushes of red currants." He held the plaid out to her. "I thought you might be hungry."

He scooped some into his meaty palm and offered them to her.

Elinor stared blankly at the fruit, stunned by his gesture. She had been given gold and fine silks; treasures fit for royalty. But this handful of berries was the most thoughtful gift she had ever received.

"Thank . . . thank you," Elinor said, picking a few of the berries from his palm. His skin was shockingly soft. She looked up at him. "This is very kind of you."

"You're welcome, Princess," Fergus replied.

Their gazes locked, and for several moments, Elinor could focus on nothing but the depths of his warm brown eyes. There was a kindness in them that surprised her. Had it always been there, and she had just never taken the time to notice?

"Uh, Princess?" Merida called.

Elinor jumped back, putting several feet between herself and Fergus. She resumed her pacing, popping several of the juicy, incredibly delicious currants into her mouth. She had taken only a small piece of bread to break her fast and was famished. She wondered if Fergus had taken note. Was he so observant of everyone, or just her?

She shook her head. She could not allow such thoughts to distract her.

"The obvious place to start is with the parchmenter from Clan Innes," Elinor said. "It is possible he keeps a record of those who have bought his parchment. Once we have the names, then we question every one of them until we find the one who wrote the message."

"Do you really think it will be so simple?" Fergus asked.

"Do you have a better idea?" Elinor asked.

"No," he admitted. "I, too, wanted to question the parchmenter. But we cannot show him the note. We cannot show it to anyone. If this is indeed a threat made toward the king, anyone may be behind it. Which means no one can be trusted."

Another possible culprit occurred to Elinor, and she was dumbfounded that she had not considered it sooner.

"What if this is the work of the guid folk?" Elinor asked. "Legend has it that they prowl about the forest, casting ruin on those they see fit. It is possible the king has done something to warrant such a fate."

Something like demanding his daughter be married to that blasted Lachlan Fraser.

"I do not believe in faeries, Princess," Fergus said.

Elinor took a step back, certain one of the mythical creatures would exact punishment on his person at this very moment.

"The note does mention the faeries," Merida pointed out. She had taken a seat on the fallen tree trunk.

"That is right," Elinor said. "The message said *on the day the sun reaches the height faeries cherish*."

Did he not realize it would be in their favor if the guid folk were behind this? Based on the legends of old, if she were to leave a token of some sort as a means of appeasing them, the guid folk might choose to reverse the fate of the person who had been cursed.

"This is not the work of faeries," Fergus said, joining Merida on the tree trunk. "And I can assure you that man or Mor'du are both more dangerous than any faerie creature you were warned about as a child."

"Well, if it is not the faeries, then we must figure out who it is as quickly as possible. The solstice is only days away." She turned to Fergus. "And we must do so without alerting the king. I fear you are right about how you would be perceived if you were to bring this to my father or his council."

She wedged herself between Merida and Fergus. "This is what we must do." Within seconds Elinor recognized the folly of her actions. Fergus's strong thigh brushed against hers and heat shot through her entire body.

Elinor sprang up from the tree trunk.

Fergus looked at her with an amused arch to his brow. "Is there a problem, Princess?"

She had to fight the urge to cover her face. Her blushing cheeks must have been as red as the currants.

She mustn't allow Fergus to affect her so. Or, at the very least, she mustn't allow him to *know* how much he affected her.

"This is what I propose." Elinor tried again. "We first seek out the parchmenter. Perhaps we can say we need parchment for some sort of announcement."

"Your betrothal?" Fergus asked.

"No!" Elinor took a moment to collect herself. She took a deep breath and said in a calmer tone, "No, my betrothal is of no consequence when it comes to this matter. In fact, I believe it is best I conceal my identity. I do not want word getting back to my father that the princess was seen in the village of Clan Innes. It will lead to questions."

"I doubt the parchmenter cares why one inquires about his parchment," Merida said. "As long as they have coin to pay for it."

"This is true," Elinor said. "We go to the parchmenter first, and if he is of no use, we move on to other merchants in the village. Perhaps someone saw something, but they do not realize it just yet."

"And what if that leads us nowhere?" Merida asked.

"We will figure out our next steps then. I would rather us be positive."

"And I would rather you both return to the castle and leave this to me," Fergus said.

"And as I have stated before, I do not care what you would rather," Elinor retorted. "Nothing matters more to me than making sure my kingdom is protected."

"Uh, Princess, what about your lessons?" Merida asked. "Are you saying they no longer matter?"

Her lessons. She had forgotten about today's lesson on fire making. What had seemed most consequential just this morning now paled in comparison to the task before her.

Or did it?

Elinor was torn. She knew the importance of continuing with her survival lessons. Every hour brought her closer to the games and the moment that her betrothal would be formally announced. But she could not even think of leaving MacCameron Castle if there was any hint that the kingdom was in peril. Never mind her own father.

What if she had already left? What if she had been well on her way to the Lowlands without any clue to the danger lurking around MacCameron Kingdom? Would it have been up to others like Fergus and his men to protect *her* family? This was her duty.

"We will find a way to continue the lessons, but right now we must head to the village of Clan Innes and ferret out this threat." She clamped her hands together. "And this is how we are going to do it."

CHAPTER TWENTY-FOUR
Elinor

Elinor reached under her hooded cloak to tug at the kertch covering her hair. She had donned both garments in hopes of disguising her face. Not that she expected many of the shopkeepers or villagers to recognize her. It had been years since she had visited this tiny village in her father's kingdom. Nevertheless, Elinor did not want to take any chances.

"I have changed my mind, Princess. I no longer agree with this plan," Fergus said underneath his breath. "Not after talking to my men."

While Merida and Elinor had returned to the castle for their disguises, Fergus had gone to his camp. Once there, his men told him they had overheard a lad mention that some chieftains were dissatisfied with the running of the kingdom and thought a new ruler was in order. It was exactly what Merida had posited earlier.

This new information did not change Elinor's approach.

"It is too late to change your mind," Elinor said. She struck his side with her elbow. "And do not call me princess. You will give us away."

"Fine, *dear*," he gritted out. "As your husband, I demand you return home."

Elinor cut her eyes at him. Why the sudden change? Earlier, he had been impressed by her plan. Elinor had suggested they come to the village under the guise of a married couple. Fergus was posing as a vicar from Gowrie, and she, his devoted wife.

As if *that* would ever happen.

"Spending the afternoon as your wife is not my idea of an enjoyable time, either," she said. "I pity the poor woman who will eventually be stuck with you."

She ignored the twinge of discontentment that fluttered in her stomach at the thought of Fergus married to another and directed her attention to the scene before them.

The village that housed this portion of Clan Innes was tiny but had a robust merchant area. The clan's red tartan could be seen hanging from store windows and wrapped about the torsos and shoulders of many who walked in and out of the shops.

Elinor smiled and nodded at a man who crossed in front of them on his way into the blacksmith's shop; then she turned to Fergus. "I am not going home until we speak with the parchmenter. Either you join me, or you go back to that dusty camp of yours. Now, which is it?"

"You are one vexing woman; do you know that?" Fergus pulled at the tight collar of his vestments. "Let us be done with this. I want out of these clothes."

"I don't know why. You look far better in them than anything else I have seen on you," she said before considering the implications of her words. She did not want to reveal that she gave any thought to his appearance whatsoever.

Fergus glanced at her, a rascally grin at the corner of his lips.

"Do not utter a word," Elinor said, her cheeks heating.

"Tell me, lass, do you prefer my green léine, or the brown one?" He winked. "I also have several in black back at Castle DunBroch. I can model them for you."

"Let us go," Elinor said, ignoring his laugh.

They started down the wide, dusty road that ran through the middle of the village. She immediately fell behind. She would have had a difficult time keeping up with his long strides even if the shoes she had pilfered from Orla's room were not too big for her. She'd had no choice. One look at any shoes she owned and the villagers would have known she was royalty.

"Slow down," Elinor said.

"Keep up," Fergus countered. "We don't have much time." He looked up at the sky. "You and your maid will need to head back before the sun begins its descent. Where is she, by the way?"

"Merida said she needed to visit the village woodcarver. Something about needing supplies for our lessons. She knows that she is to meet us in front of the butcher shop when the bell tolls for vespers," Elinor said, referring to the observance period for early evening prayer.

She leaned closer to Fergus and asked, "Now, where did your men say they heard whispers about this threat?"

"It was at the farrier's. They were tending to the horses when they overheard the lad."

Elinor pressed a hand to her stomach to stanch the instant panic that had settled there. Could the chieftains really be plotting to overthrow the king? It would not be the first time such an attack had been launched in her country's history.

Fergus halted. He turned to her, leaned forward until they were eye level, and in a low voice, said, "You must let me do the talking, lass."

"But I—"

"But nothing." He cut her off. "If you want these villagers to believe you are a vicar's wife, you cannot go around questioning their menfolk. It is just not done."

Elinor knew he was right, but that did not mean she had to like it. She begrudgingly nodded her agreement before motioning for him to continue.

She and Fergus visited the parchmenter, but to her disappointment, the man did not keep an account of those who purchased his wares, and he did not have any more of the particular parchment used for the message Fergus's man had found.

They next visited the farrier's shop, then the blacksmith's. Elinor had to admit that Fergus was skillful in his approach, inquiring about the men's satisfaction with the running of the kingdom with just enough detachment so as not to rouse suspicion. He came off as a simple country vicar interested in the goings-on of a village similar to his own.

Elinor smiled and nodded where appropriate. It was vexing to play the role of mute, obedient wife, but to her surprise, Fergus asked all the questions she'd instructed him to, and convincingly so. There was no denying that the two of them made a good team.

"Would you mind if we took a short break?" Elinor asked after visiting their fifth merchant of the day. She took a seat on a bench hewn out of a massive log. "I do not know how Orla can bear walking in these shoes all day."

"Do you need a drink?" Fergus asked. "I can fetch you mead or ale."

"I . . ." Elinor faltered at his thoughtfulness. It was the second time he had inquired about her needs that day. "Uh, thank you, but I do not need any."

She was just about to ask which merchant they should visit next when she looked across the road and noticed a boy picking through rubbish. She gasped when he dusted off a half-eaten apple and took a bite.

"No," she said, and started for him.

"What is it?" Fergus asked, pulling her back.

She gestured to the boy, who had ducked into the narrow passageway between the potter's and wool merchant's shops. "I just witnessed a child eating a discarded apple." She looked up at Fergus. "No one in this kingdom should be made to eat garbage. How is it even allowed?"

But as she said the words, Elinor realized that *she* had allowed it. She was part of the problem. This was *her* kingdom. As a member of the royal family, it was her duty to look in on the people who resided on MacCameron land, to make sure they were taken care of. Yet she had not visited this village since she was but a wee lass.

"Princess," Fergus whispered against her ear. "Do not fret. I shall find him."

Before she knew what he was about, Fergus took off in search of the boy. He returned with him moments later and headed straight for the baker. Elinor watched in awe as he purchased a thick loaf of bread and handed it to the boy, along with several coins.

Elinor's heart flipped within her chest. She was so overwhelmed with emotion that she could barely speak when Fergus returned to her side.

"Thank . . . thank you for doing that," she said.

"You are right, no one should have to eat garbage. In an ideal kingdom, there would be more than enough food for everyone."

She tilted her head to the side as she studied him. "What is your idea of an ideal kingdom?" Elinor asked.

Fergus shrugged his broad shoulders. "Simple. One where all citizens can live healthy, comfortable lives. And where there is a strong kinship between the clans." He glanced at her. "That is not to say that King Douglass is not a strong king. He was able to form a peace alliance between the clans after generations of fighting. He is doing the best he can, I suppose."

"Yes, he is," Elinor said, quick to defend her father. "But more could be done for the people of this kingdom," she had to admit. "My thoughts on an ideal kingdom very much align with yours."

"Do they now?" Fergus asked.

She nodded, her eyes focused on his strong jawline and firm lips.

"I shall make certain one of my clansmen returns in two days' time to check on the boy," Fergus said. "The bread and silver should keep him fed until then."

Elinor started to reach for him, then instinctively pulled back her hand. She folded both hands in her lap and gave him a short, regal nod. "It was a very kind gesture," she said.

"Even for a boggin numpty?" he said with a wry grin.

A heated flush crept across Elinor's cheeks. "I apologize for that," she said.

Fergus shrugged his massive shoulders. "I tend to smell from time to time." His expression turned serious. "But do not take me for a fool, Princess."

Her breath caught in her throat. She shook her head. "I do not," she said. "Your clansmen would not treat you with such deference if you were a fool."

Elinor tried to tear her attention away from his intense stare, but his gaze held her captive for several moments more. Finally, he said, "We must continue with our inquest. 'Tis getting late."

Elinor followed him into the potter's, then into the

alehouse. However, by the time the bells rang out from the tower of the small church, she and Fergus were still no closer to solving the riddle from the discarded parchment or uncovering any more information regarding disgruntled chieftains. They headed to the butcher shop, where they found Merida waiting.

Elinor frowned and pointed to her hands. "You were not wearing gloves when we arrived."

"Yes, I know," she said. "I bought them here in the village." She stuck her hands behind her back. "Let us be on our way. If I am not in the larder to ready the fish for tomorrow's meal, Aileen will have my hide."

The reminder about the next day's dinner instantly soured Elinor's mood. How she wished she could stay here. She would happily continue to play Fergus's pretend wife if it meant she would not have to face the man who was to be her real husband.

Assuming her role for the last time, Elinor tucked her arm in the crook of Fergus's and said, "Yes, let us be on our way."

CHAPTER TWENTY-FIVE
Merida

Fergus rode several paces in front of them, leading their tiny caravan back toward MacCameron Castle. As the maid, Merida rode behind the princess, essentially putting her body at risk if they were attacked from behind. The irony was not lost on her. If she were back in her own time, Merida had no doubts that her mother would readily stare down any attacker that dared to harm any of her children. And she would certainly protest Merida sacrificing her well-being.

Merida did not fear an attack. She had traveled across these lands several times already in the days since she had been here. There were too many other things to occupy her mind, like the claws that had suddenly grown on her fingers.

She had been standing in Freya's shop while the witch

worked on the spell that was to send her home. She'd swatted at a fly and torn a gash in Freya's curtain.

Freya had predicted that at this rate, Merida would be in full bear form within a fortnight. Which meant she would soon have characteristics that she could not hide.

She looked down at the gloves Freya had given her. Her claws were already poking through. Merida would need to find a rock or some instrument she could use to file down the sharp tips.

Elinor slowed in front of her and doubled back to come up alongside Merida.

"I am sorry, but we must stop," Elinor said.

"Princess, we must return to the castle," Merida said.

"That will take too long. I cannot wait." Elinor gave her a pointed look.

Ah. She needed to find a bush in the forest.

"I shall tell Fergus," Merida said, but when she started for him, Elinor stopped her.

"Do not tell him," Elinor said, her cheeks reddening.

Merida rolled her eyes, but inside she was bubbling up with excitement. Would the princess care what Fergus thought if she saw him only as a member of dreaded Clan DunBroch? No, she would not. Merida saw her modesty as a good sign.

She rode up to Fergus and told him that she needed to rest her horse. He did not question the fact that Angus had spent much of the afternoon resting while they visited the village of Clan Innes.

Once they had found a resting place, Elinor made her own excuses and quickly left them. Merida seized on the opportunity. She knew she would not get many more moments alone with Fergus.

The plan she had developed during their ride demanded she be up-front with him. Though it would require she tell him half-truths and a few outright lies, Merida felt there was just enough verity to it to make it believable. She was certain her plea would appeal to his sense of duty to Clan DunBroch.

She walked up to where he'd crouched over a patch of berries. "I have something to confess to you, Fergus," Merida opened.

He looked up at her, his brows spiked. "And what is that, lass?"

"Do you remember back in the forest when you asked about my people?

"You mean the imaginary Clan Dungaroo?"

Her mouth fell open. "How . . ."

"I am not stupid, lass," Fergus said. He stood, tossed a

couple of berries in his mouth, and pointed to her. "I know every clan from the North Channel to the Hebrides, and there is no Dungaroo."

"I know you are not stupid. You are one of the smartest people I know. You have to be," Merida quickly asserted. "Because you are a DunBroch." She whipped off the shawl covering her head. "So am I."

Fergus's eyes grew even wider underneath his bushy eyebrows. He studied her mass of fiery red hair with wary curiosity, his expressing growing more suspicious by the second.

"I am the son of the chieftain. I know every person in my clan. I know of no Merida of DunBroch."

Merida hated to lie to her own father, but there was no way she would ever convince him that she belonged to the same clan he had lived in his entire life. As a little girl, she had heard stories of the DunBrochs from the far west. Her father's clan had broken away during a famine and traveled to the Highlands in search of food and a better life.

"I am of the DunBrochs near Dunbarton," she said.

"Dunbarton? That is where my people originated," he said. His expression lightened for a moment, but then darkened once again. "You did not make the trip from Dunbarton on your own, lass. What are you up to?"

"I *did* come on my own," Merida insisted. "That part I

was not lying about. The rest of the clan is not happy with me for setting out on this journey, but I felt it my duty as a proud member of Clan DunBroch to reach out to our family here in the north."

"I find it hard to believe that our family to the west would allow a young lass like yourself to travel so far on your own."

"I am a bit strong-willed," Merida said. "And I know how to take care of myself. My clan has taught me well."

He grinned and nodded. "We DunBrochs do not believe in coddling. Everyone should be able to protect themselves if necessary."

"'Tis how I was able to make such a long journey on my own," she said. "I hope it has not all been for naught."

Merida clasped her hands together. It was time she make her big push to get these two together. She still had hopes that Fergus and Elinor would fall for each other, but she needed a backup plan to ensure they would marry.

A thread of uneasiness wound its way through Merida's head. The reason she was here was because her mother demanded Merida enter into a betrothal she did not want. Was she not doing the very same thing to Elinor?

This is different, Merida reminded herself.

They might not know it yet, but her mother and father were meant for each other. They shared a love unlike any other she had ever witnessed. It was not the same as her being forced to marry the lad from Clan Dingwall because he managed to shoot an arrow.

"You see, Fergus," Merida started, "I am on a mission as well. I want to build up Clan DunBroch. To make us stronger. I was hoping I could find someone from our clan here in the Highlands who would also be interested in strengthening the DunBrochs. That is why I was so excited when I ran across your camp."

Fergus crossed his arms over his broad chest. "What can a youngin like yourself have in mind for making Clan DunBroch stronger that others have not come up with?"

"Others believe the way of strengthening our clan is by using force, but I know there is a better way. A *smarter* way."

"And what way is that?"

She paused for a moment before answering. "Through marriage."

His eyes widened again.

Merida held her hands up. "Hear me out. Throughout history, an advantageous marriage has been the way many clans have made themselves stronger. Imagine what would become of a union between two of the most powerful clans in Scotland."

He huffed out a laugh. "You talk nonsense, lass."

"You find the thought of Clan DunBroch being a

powerful clan amusing?" Merida asked. "I thought you would want what is best for this clan."

"Strengthening DunBroch is always the most important thing to me," he said.

"So we have the same goals. I want to see our clan thrive. And I believe a match between you and Princess Elinor is the best way to accomplish that."

Fergus's mouth dropped open moments before he released a full-bellied laugh.

"You must have hit your head harder than I hit mine," he said. "Such a match could never be. Everyone knows the princess has been promised to the Frasers since birth."

"Promised, but not officially betrothed," Merida said.

He swatted at the air. "That is but words."

"The words matter," she stressed. "Think about our clan and what it would mean to have a union between a DunBroch and a MacCameron. It would make DunBroch stronger than anyone could ever imagine." She pointed at him. "And *you* would be the one to do it."

"And how am I to do that?"

"'Tis simple," Merida said with a shrug. "Make her fall in love with you."

Fergus looked at her strangely for a second before he erupted in more laughter. This time he laughed so hard that tears sprang up in the corners of his eyes.

Agitated, Merida plopped both her hands on her hips. "Why is that so funny?"

Fergus wiped at his eyes with the back of his hand. It took a moment before he could speak.

"What makes you think I can woo Princess Elinor?" Fergus asked. "For one thing, she is a MacCameron."

"So?"

"Our clans have been at odds for longer than we have both been alive. Even the DunBrochs who live in Dunbarton should know that. The clash with the MacCamerons began in the Lowlands, and it followed both clans up here."

"But there is a peace alliance now," Merida pointed out. "This is our chance to strengthen the clan by joining it to the most powerful clan in all of Scotland."

He shook his head, but Merida noted a spark of interest in his eyes. She pounced on it.

"You and the princess would make an excellent match. I know that you are fond of her, Fergus. I can see it."

He started to speak, but then shook his head.

"Do not try to deny it," Merida said.

He released an anguished breath. "I do not," he said. "But the princess hates me."

Merida slapped a gloved hand to her forehand. "How can you know so little about women?" she said. "Look, the princess does not hate you, and a union between the

DunBrochs and MacCamerons would produce the most significant kingdom the world has ever seen. How can you cede such authority to Clan Fraser without opposition?"

"Because the two are promised. That is how these things are done, lass. You cannot just go around changing tradition."

Merida's entire body froze as she was hit with a stunning realization.

Yes, we can *change it! Because someone* did *change it.*

As it stood, it was tradition for the promise of a betrothal to be arranged at birth, but at some point between now and her time, things had changed. She was all too aware of such a fate.

"I know what you must do to prove that you are more worthy of Princess Elinor than the Fraser," Merida said.

"And what is that?" Fergus asked.

She stared him right in the eyes and said, "Challenge the chieftain's son at the Highland Games for the princess's hand in marriage."

CHAPTER TWENTY-SIX
Elinor

At the start of every Highland Games, a musician of the queen's choosing pounded on a timbrel to welcome clansmen to the festivities. The *thump, thump, thump* of an open palm striking tautly pulled calfskin never failed to excite Elinor. The rapidly escalating beat of that drum was the way her heart now pounded as she traversed the woods on Alistair's back.

Her decision to leave the castle had been made so hastily that she had not had time to fully grasp what she was doing. Yet she persisted.

It all started when her lute practice was prematurely aborted after her instructor, Hextilda, popped the string on her instrument. Elinor had gone in search of Merida to see if she wanted to pursue the fire-making lesson, but Merida had been tied up in the kitchens, preparing for that evening's big dinner with the Fraser chieftain and Lachlan.

That was when Elinor decided to seek out another teacher.

She'd quickly made it out to the stables and mounted Alistair. Now she was halfway to the DunBroch camp.

She should turn back. Asking Fergus to teach her to make fire was insanity.

But she did not want to turn back. For reasons she did not even understand, she wanted to see him. She *had* to see him. And having Fergus assist her in making fire was the best excuse she could come up with.

She slowed Alistair when she was still some distance from the camp and dismounted him. Perhaps the walk would give her time to come to her senses.

"If you *had* any sense, you would go back to the castle," Elinor muttered.

She decided to do just that. But just as she was preparing to mount her horse, she heard, "Princess?"

She turned, her eyes widening as her heartbeat thudded triple time.

"Fergus!" Elinor squeaked. "I . . . hello!"

"What are you doing here, Princess?" He held a dagger in one hand and a large fish in the other.

Ignoring his question, Elinor frowned at his catch. "Did you kill the fish with a knife?"

Fergus looked down at the fish as if he had forgotten he held it. Then he burst into a deep, roaring laugh. "I am a fine hunter, but even I am not that good, Princess. The dagger is to clean the fish. I used my arrow and bow to kill it, just as your maid was teaching you to."

Elinor felt her face grow impossibly hot as embarrassment rushed through her. But Fergus had just given her the opening she needed.

"Yes, well . . . speaking of Merida and her lessons, that is actually the reason I am here." She suddenly felt shy and unsure of herself. She hated that feeling, but Fergus made her nervous. And . . . tingly.

"You see, yesterday Merida was to teach me to make fire, but it was interrupted by our sojourn to Clan Innes." She held up her hands. "That was more important. And even though we did not make much progress in ferreting out the potential threat to the kingdom, it is very good that we went. But I would still like to learn to make fire. And . . ." She toed a crescent-shaped rock, squeezing her hands so tightly that her nails dug into her palms. "Well . . ."

"Yes, Princess?"

She looked up. "I was hoping *you* would teach me."

His russet eyebrows arched into twin peaks over his striking eyes. But then those eyes narrowed, and Elinor's nervousness multiplied tenfold under his scrutiny.

"Why is your maid teaching you to fish and build a fire?" Fergus asked.

She was prepared for this question. "Because they are important skills for any lass to possess. When I learned that Merida's father taught her how to do such things, I thought it was admirable."

"The DunBrochs believe in preparing their children for anything," he said.

Elinor's mouth fell open. "You know she is of Clan DunBroch?"

"Of course," Fergus said. "I can spot my own. She is of the DunBroch of Dunbarton in the Lowlands."

The Lowlands?

Elinor tried not to let her face register the shock she felt. Merida had led her to believe she was of the Clan DunBroch that belonged to her father's kingdom. Elinor had figured that it was the girl's disguise that had prevented her fellow clansmen from recognizing her when they first encountered Fergus's camp, not that she was from an entirely different branch of the clan. One that lived in the Lowlands. Where she knew Elinor was heading.

Why had Merida not shared that she was from the same place Elinor wished to live? Why had she chosen not to be truthful?

"But you and your maid are not the same," Fergus continued, recapturing Elinor's attention. "You are of noble blood. I cannot think of a single occasion when you would need to catch your own fish or build your own fire."

Elinor shrugged. "Nor will I ever use the old language of Northumbria, but I have had to learn it."

His smile was quick and devastatingly charming. "Fair enough, Princess. You have made your point."

"So you will teach me?" Elinor asked. Her chest tightened with anticipation.

He stared into her eyes. When he spoke, his normally gruff voice was soft, almost reverent.

"You are the princess of the kingdom to which I have pledged my fealty. Who am I to deny anything you ask of me?" A rueful grin danced on his mouth. "Though I did deny you when you insisted on helping figure out what is behind that riddle, didn't I? But that was for your own safety."

"It is a good thing I did not listen to you." She stuck her nose in the air. "I proved to be very useful."

"Yes, you did. It seems we make a surprisingly good team, Princess."

He smiled again and Elinor smiled back, both staring at each other with matching mischievous grins. The air grew thick with a sensation she could not name. It was rich and warm and comforting, like being wrapped in a soft pelt as she sat in front of the fire on a winter evening.

Elinor was the first to break eye contact. She shook her head and took several steps back.

Fergus did the same, putting some distance between them. He cleared his throat and held up the fish.

"Follow me. I must bring my catch to the camp, and then I shall teach you to make fire."

He sheathed his dagger and captured Alistair's reins in his free hand, then led both Elinor and the horse to their camp.

Her steps faltered as they came upon the site. It had been stripped down to only the essentials: two tents, a small firepit, and a lone pot.

"There were more of you, were there not?" Elinor asked.

"I sent the other men back to DunBroch to gather the clan for the Highland Games. They shall return in a few days' time." He nodded toward the three soldiers engaged in various tasks around the camp. "I kept my best men with me so that we can dig deeper into this threat against the kingdom. If Mor'du crawls out of his cave, we will deal with him rightly."

"And if it is not Mor'du? If the threat is from one of the chieftains?"

Fergus did not hesitate. "Then we will defend our king."

His answer was absolute. And to think she had questioned his loyalty. Elinor felt a pang of guilt for ever having done so.

Fergus motioned for one of the men to come near. He handed him the fish.

"Tavish, cook this, will you? The princess has requested my assistance in an important matter." He turned to Elinor. "Tavish will need the firepit to prepare dinner, but I know someplace else we can go to practice your fire making."

He took her to the stream near the camp. Fergus gathered several sturdy sticks and set them in front of her. Elinor listened intently as he provided instructions; she wanted to impress him with her quick learning skills. Why it mattered so much to her if Fergus was impressed, she did not know, and she did not want to take the time to explore these strange feelings.

But, alas, she was impressing no one, because making fire was not as easy as it looked.

"Are you sure I am using the proper wood?" she asked after what felt like an eternity of trying to get the twigs alight.

"I am sure," Fergus said. He stood with his arms

crossed over his chest, observing her in the same way he had watched his men practice archery that day she and Merida happened upon their camp.

"No, no. You've got the wrong angle," Fergus said. He came up alongside her and knelt on one knee. He repositioned the twigs, securing the end of one into the groove of the other, which lay flat on the ground. "You will get better friction this way."

Elinor adjusted, then attempted to light a spark.

"You must work faster," Fergus said. He moved behind her. Wrapping his arms around her, he demonstrated. "Like this."

No part of his body touched hers, but she could feel the heat radiating from him. Elinor forgot about the lesson. She closed her eyes and soaked in the sense of warmth being so near Fergus provided.

Elinor felt him stiffen. Another beat passed before he hastily moved away from her.

"I didn't mean to . . . Forgive me, Princess," he said. "I did not mean to crowd you."

Elinor remembered where she was and stood. She knew she should throw a fit of indignation, but she could not bring herself to do so.

"It is quite all right. You were only trying to assist me.

'Tis fine." She ran her hands along the front of her kirtle and then gave him a firm nod. "But perhaps we should conclude the lesson for today."

"Yes, I think that is best," Fergus said.

"What do we have here?"

Elinor gasped and turned at the deceptively cheerful voice that came from her right.

Lachlan Fraser.

Elinor had not set eyes on the Fraser chieftain's eldest son since she was six and ten, but she immediately felt the same distaste for him that she had three years before.

Lachlan dismounted the handsome white Percheron he rode in on, tossing the horse's reins over its back. He stopped within three feet of Fergus and crossed his arms.

"You are a DunBroch," Lachlan said. "I can tell by that offensive hair."

Fergus's mouth curved in a wry smile. "Not everyone can be born with such gorgeous locks as your own."

Lachlan turned to Elinor. "Is the DunBroch bothering you?" He looked around. "And where are your MacCameron escorts? Surely they did not abandon you."

"No," Elinor said. "I was out riding and happened upon Fer—the DunBroch warrior."

Lachlan pointed to the sticks. "What is this?"

"The princess was interested in how one makes fire."

"Ah, you should have come to your future betrothed," Lachlan said. "I am quite good at building a fire."

He pulled a small steel hook from the satchel draped across his torso, along with a dagger. He gathered several more sticks and added them to the two Elinor had practiced with, struck the dagger against the piece of steel, and within moments had a spark.

"There you are," Lachlan said. He flicked the silver tool back into his bag. "Does Clan DunBroch not use firesteels? You are quite like the cavemen of old, are you?"

Elinor noticed the way Fergus's jaw tightened. She sensed that his patience was running thin and did not want a brawl to break out. Although she was certain Lachlan would be no match for Fergus DunBroch.

"It is getting rather late," Elinor interjected. "I think it is time I take my leave."

"Yes, I believe that is best," Lachlan said, his eyes still on Fergus. "I should go, as well. I have a few duties to attend to before tonight's meal at MacCameron Castle." He turned to her. "I shall see you at dinner tonight, Elinor."

Elinor recoiled at his use of her given name. She had not granted him permission to do so, but that meant nothing to this arrogant lout.

She turned to Fergus. His good humor had vanished.

It had been replaced with a stony expression that made her feel as cold as his smile had made her feel warm.

"Thank you for your time," Elinor told him.

A hint of the earlier levity returned to his eyes as he responded with a respectful nod. "You are very welcome, Princess."

Elinor quickly mounted Alistair and set out for home. It wasn't until she was almost to the castle that a terrifying thought occurred to her. What would Lachlan say to her parents tonight about finding her alone in the forest with Fergus?

CHAPTER TWENTY-SEVEN
Elinor

Elinor sat silently while Gavina gathered three strands of her hair and twisted them into a long, thick braid. The girl then draped the braid across the crown of Elinor's head and used a pin emblazoned with the MacCameron crest to secure it behind her ear.

She usually enjoyed Gavina's ministrations. The maid had a knack for turning Elinor's limp hair into a work of art. But the bit of pampering did nothing to boost Elinor's mood. Not when she absolutely detested the reason for all this adornment.

"Are you excited about tonight, Princess?" Gavina asked as she pulled several auburn ringlets down to frame Elinor's face. Her voice was bright with the enthusiasm of someone who had viewed Elinor's situation only with romanticized notions. As a young servant, Gavina undoubtedly saw Elinor's impending betrothal as something to envy, instead of something to dread.

"I am . . ." Elinor could not think of an appropriate word that would not give away her true feelings. "Somewhat nervous," she finally settled on.

"I bet you are. I would be, too," Gavina said. "The fella you're promised to is quite handsome. He's gonna make a fine husband, don't you think?"

Elinor tried to summon a smile, but her lips refused to complete the action. After her run-in with Lachlan this afternoon, the thought of sitting at the table with him, wondering if he would bring up Fergus, caused a dizzying panic.

She'd considered feigning some sort of ailment that would prevent her from joining them—a stomachache, maybe. But a mere stomachache would not be enough in Queen Catriona's eyes. She would expect Elinor to suffer through it.

Indeed, this entire night was bound to be one that brought much suffering to her, even if Lachlan did not mention the fire incident. Yet Gavina thought Elinor should feel excited? How could she possibly be excited to dine with a man she barely knew, but who would have control over her life in just a few months' time?

He will not *control your life. You will be gone long before that comes to pass.*

Despite her fierce determination, her stomach tightened with a sickening feeling. She would not allow herself to imagine an existence where she lived as the matriarch of Clan Fraser or any of the other surrounding clans. She was a MacCameron, and a MacCameron she would remain until *she* decided if she wanted to marry.

And if she *did* marry, it would never be to Lachlan Fraser.

Elinor had met the lad only a few other times over the past nineteen years, and what she had seen of him she detested. He was an arrogant, entitled boor of a man who walked around as if he was a gift to the earth.

What made it worse was the way the rest of the lasses fawned over him. Gavina's giddiness was nothing compared to some of the others'. Elinor would never understand what anyone found appealing about that arrogant man. She would rather marry a goat. Or Fergus DunBroch.

What? No, you would not *rather marry Fergus!*

Elinor pressed a hand against her stomach to stave off the strange feeling that began to flutter around it. She would confess that Fergus was not the brute she had first thought him to be, but neither was he her idea of an ideal mate. No one was.

"There you are, Princess," Gavina said, beaming. She held up a looking glass and turned it to face Elinor.

As much as she appreciated Gavina's way with a brush and rouge, this time Elinor wished the girl were not so talented. She did not want to stand out. In fact, she hoped if she made herself seem homely—dour, even—that maybe Lachlan would object to their upcoming betrothal.

Though Elinor was not naive enough to believe that a slight change in her appearance would dissuade the Fraser from this union that had been promised since their birth. Because it was less about what either she or Lachlan wanted, and more about the alliance between their two clans. Both she and her future betrothed were but pawns in this chess game between the leaders of Clan MacCameron and Clan Fraser.

Knowing that Lachlan had as little say in his future as she had in hers did not soften Elinor's feelings toward the man. When all was said and done, he would benefit from their marriage much more than she would. As the man in their union, Lachlan would control everything.

Including her.

Elinor took the looking glass from Gavina's hands and peered at her face once more. She pinched her cheeks and smoothed her brows.

"It does not matter what I think about my future

betrothed," she finally said, answering Gavina's earlier inquiry. "What is promised is promised."

It did not matter. She would be gone before a wedding could take place. Once she, Merida, and Fergus figured out what was behind the threat to MacCameron Kingdom, that was. She would not leave while her kingdom was in peril. But ultimately she *would* leave. She had to.

She set the looking glass on the table and pushed herself up from the chair.

"'Tis time for dinner," Elinor said.

Let the charade begin.

Elinor's heart pounded against the walls of her chest as she made the long journey down the corridor, but when she entered the Great Hall, she did so with all the regal bearing her title demanded. The train of her ice-blue silk gown trailed several feet behind as she walked slowly toward the table where the chieftain of Clan Fraser and Lachlan were already seated, along with her father. Her mother would make her entrance last, as had become custom during any formal dinner. Queen Catriona believed that every eye in the room must be set on her, and the only way to ensure that was to be the last one to arrive.

The men all stood as Elinor approached the table.

"Good evening."

Both her father and the chieftain nodded their greeting.

"Good evening, Princess," Lachlan said with a deep bow.

Elinor's breath caught in her throat as she waited to see if he would mention their run-in that afternoon. But he did not. When the underbutler moved to show Elinor to her seat, Lachlan held him off.

"May I?" he asked, gesturing to her hand. She offered it to him and struggled not to flinch at his touch.

He guided her to the opposite side of the table, to the chair that faced his. He pulled the chair out for her, then pushed it back once she was seated.

Lachlan's fingers lingered longer than what would have been deemed appropriate as he slowly released her hand, brushing her wrist in a soft caress. Elinor's eyes shot to his, but he did not answer for his forwardness. He only smiled that oily smile that so many of the lasses in the kingdom thought was charming.

He returned to the opposite side of the table, but the moment he reclaimed his seat, he looked toward the front of the Great Hall and rose again. She followed his gaze.

Queen Catriona had arrived.

All at the table followed Lachlan's lead, rising as the queen made her way to them. The gold thread sewn into the hem of her dark green gown sparkled underneath the hundreds of candles burning in the chandeliers above them. Elinor had to admit that her mother excelled at making a grand entrance. She had tried to teach her daughter, but some things were innate. Commanding the attention of everyone with her mere presence was a gift her mother had likely possessed since birth.

Pleasantries were exchanged between the queen and the two men from the visiting clan before everyone was once again seated.

As dinner was served, King Douglass and the chieftain dived right into a conversation about the various issues facing their clans. Elinor normally detested such talk, but the longer they discussed these matters, the longer she would not have to worry about any other uncomfortable subjects being brought up.

She took small bites of the mutton stew and freshly baked bread that had been served so that, if she was called upon, she would not be able to respond. After all, Queen Catriona would be horrified if her daughter were to speak with a mouth full of food.

Her plan worked brilliantly for nearly half the meal, but as the second course of turnips, roasted hare, and kale was served, Lachlan spoke.

"Princess Elinor," he said when there was a lull in the conversation at the table. Terror struck Elinor's soul. Would he mention that he had seen her with Fergus?

"I hear that you are well versed in the lute. What are some of your favorite songs to play?"

Elinor was so taken aback that she did not know how to answer. She looked around the table. All eyes were on her.

She cleared her throat.

"I enjoy the Scottish folk songs that were brought to this region from Carrick," she finally answered.

"Lowlander songs?" Lachlan said with no small amount of disdain. "You come from a rich heritage of Highlanders, yet you enjoy the screeching sounds from Carrick?" He tsked. "I must warn you, I will not abide such music in my home."

Without thinking, Elinor shot him a menacing look.

This time it was the queen who cleared her throat.

"My family is originally from Carrick," the queen said. "I am the one who taught the princess the songs of the Lowlanders. My people also have a rich heritage."

The silence that came over the Great Hall was deafening.

"Well," Lachlan began after an excruciatingly awkward stretch of moments. "That makes all the difference, Queen Catriona. I shall be happy to hear the princess's skill with the lute." He smiled, but Elinor noticed the way his hand tightened around the stem of his goblet.

A layer of tension hovered over the room following the exchange between the queen and Elinor's future betrothed. Several dishes were served from the kitchen, but Elinor did not even bother with pretending to eat.

Just as the maids arrived to clear the table of the course before dessert, Lachlan pushed his chair back and stood. "Will you excuse me?"

The underbutler rushed to his side.

"No need to follow," Lachlan told him. "Just point me to the privy chamber."

Elinor welcomed the short reprieve. Even when Lachlan was not paying attention to her, she still found herself on edge.

She was surprised by the queen's defense. During all their lessons, her mother was always quick to point out that once she was married she was to defer to her husband in all matters, but apparently that wasn't the case when it came to the music of her people.

Elinor glanced over at her mother and smiled, but the smile was not returned. She was not sure what she had done now, but it was obvious the queen was not happy with her performance.

She released a sigh of resignation.

It was time she accepted that she would never please her mother, no matter how hard she tried.

It only strengthened Elinor's resolve. If she was going to be a disappointment, she should give Queen Catriona something to *truly* be disappointed in. Like running away from what everyone thought was her duty by birthright.

They had to uncover whatever was behind this threat to the kingdom. The time was drawing near when she would have to make a break for it. She could not hold off for much longer.

CHAPTER TWENTY-EIGHT
Merida

"Bring this to the larder."

Merida expelled a shallow *"oof"* as one of the bakers dropped a sack of flour into her arms. The bag slammed into her chest, knocking the wind from her lungs.

"Hurry it up," Rhona said. "Once you're done here, you're needed in the scullery."

"But I am not a scullery maid," Merida said. She could not scrub dishes in the scullery wearing gloves, and removing them was not an option. Even after she had filed down her claws, they were still far too noticeable.

Rhona shrugged her broad shoulders. "'Tis where the boss says you are to be."

The boss. Aileen.

The girl had better be grateful that Merida was no longer in the business of relying on spells, because if she had been, she would have gotten Freya to turn Aileen into the toad she was.

Or a bear! *She* fit that description far better than Merida did.

Aileen seemed to take pleasure in making Merida's life miserable. For the life of her, she could not figure out why. She had not done a single thing to warrant the girl's nasty wrath.

Just get through this dinner service.

Despite the grueling, nonstop work—and after a tongue-lashing from Aileen, of course—Merida's mind was never far from the Great Hall and what was currently taking place there.

Ever since the chieftain of Clan Fraser and his son had arrived, the lasses throughout the kitchens had been in a tizzy over the handsome Lachlan Fraser. Merida had not set eyes on her mother's promised mate, but she doubted he was worth the uproar.

She took solace in the fact that Elinor did not seem taken with the Fraser lad. In fact, she seemed to loathe him. In contrast, Merida suspected Elinor's feelings for Fergus grew fonder every moment the two were together.

She should not be surprised. Her mother loved her

father. It was the purest love Merida had ever witnessed.

She just needed them both to recognize they were perfect for each other—quickly.

She hefted the flour more securely against her chest as she hauled it out of the kitchen. The sound of a voice speaking in a hushed tone caused Merida to halt her footsteps just before rounding the corner on her way to the dry larder. There was nothing unusual about hearing whispers—the lasses who worked in the kitchens shared gossip day and night. But this voice was male. The only man Merida had seen around these parts was Duncan, and he never whispered.

She tried to ignore the strain in her arms from the heavy sack as she inched nearer to the corner. She stretched her head as close as possible. That was when she heard the female voice.

Was that . . . Aileen?

Merida frowned. If there was one thing Aileen did not do, it was whisper. She always wanted people to know exactly when she was around. The woman thrived on exerting her power over everyone who worked under her.

Footsteps suddenly began moving toward her. She froze.

Before Merida could figure out what to do, Aileen and the mysterious man appeared. Merida's eyes grew wide with surprise and bewilderment as she realized that, based on his attire and his countenance, this must have been Lachlan Fraser.

What was Elinor's betrothed doing in the kitchens?

She noticed the strange look that passed between Lachlan and Aileen before the girl turned to Merida and snapped, "What are you doing here?"

Merida quickly changed her expression to one of indifference.

"I am . . . uh . . . returning the flour to the dry larder," she answered. "Rhona's orders."

Merida chanced another glance at the Fraser's eldest son. He was the complete opposite of her father. Where Fergus was big, and burly, and lovable, this man was slim and seemed cold. He and her mother would never suit.

Lachlan awkwardly cleared his throat and turned to Aileen. "How do I return to the Great Hall? I feel like a fool for getting lost."

"I'll show you," Aileen answered. She shot Merida another foul look before guiding Lachlan back up the corridor they had come from.

Lachlan had gotten lost. That explained it. He had probably been on his way to the privy chamber when it happened.

Merida was not surprised. She had found herself lost

on more than one occasion in the few days she had been in this massive castle.

And yet . . .

There was not a privy chamber for guests anywhere near this area. The chieftain's son would have had to get really turned around to find himself all the way in the kitchens.

And why had she heard him whispering to Aileen? If he had been lost, would he not have just asked for directions and been on his way? The two had stood there in the shadows for several minutes before they encountered Merida.

She tried to shake off the uneasy feeling traveling down her spine. There was no cause for suspicion here. She was being foolish.

But Merida also knew better than to dismiss her instincts. Another thing her father had instilled in her was to always trust that feeling in her gut. He insisted that would save her when everything else failed.

So what was her gut trying to tell her this time?

Merida hated to think that anything untoward could be going on between those two, but it would make sense. Could Aileen and Lachlan be engaged in some sort of dalliance? Would the girl be so bold as to do such a thing to the princess of her kingdom?

Merida did not like Aileen one bit, but to levy such

a charge against her was extreme. And yet something seemed off about Aileen and Lachlan's supposedly random encounter.

There was more to this, and she was going to figure it out.

Merida continued to the dry larder. She deposited the sack of flour and helped Sorcha store away the other items that had been used to make that night's desserts. For a moment she considered mentioning the encounter with the princess's future betrothed, but the girl would likely think her daft if she shared what were likely unwarranted suspicions.

"You *are* being daft," Merida whispered to herself.

"What's that you say?" Sorcha called.

"Nothing," Merida quickly replied. "Are the dinner preparations complete?"

"Yeah," Sorcha answered. She leaned closer. "You just missed your favorite person. Aileen was in here a minute ago, preparing the king's dessert. She will not allow anyone else to bake his fig cake because she knows it is his favorite, and she likes it when he praises her for her recipe."

Unfortunately, Merida had not missed Aileen.

"Well, if all is done here, I shall head to the scullery," she told Sorcha.

"The scullery? What you going there for?"

She hunched her shoulders. "'Tis where I am needed."

Or where she had been banished to by Aileen.

She left Sorcha in the dry larder and made her way to the scullery. Fortunately, there was enough distance between the washbasins to keep her hands out of sight of the other girls gathered here.

Merida removed her gloves and set out to wash the dishes. Her pointy nails were visible, but not as long as earlier in the day. Still, she would need to file them down as soon as she was able to get away. She seemed to spend all her time filing the claws and shaving the prickly bristles that continued to pop up on her jaw and neck. Hair had begun to sprout all over her body, but she had time to rid herself only of that which could be seen by others.

As much as she tried to tell herself she did not mind, after only ten minutes of scrubbing with the hot water and harsh lye soap on her already raw, plucked hands, Merida was ready to do just about anything to end her time in the scullery.

As she carried an armful of spoons and ladles to a basin, she slipped on the wet floor, earning giggles from the girls at the other washbasins.

"What did you do to Aileen for her to send you here?" the one name Isla asked.

"I took a breath," Merida said.

Isla looked at her strangely before she burst out laughing. "Don't," the other girl said. "She'll come running."

Everyone knew who the girl was referring to. It had become obvious to Merida that the only people who did not despise Aileen were the people who were trying to get into her good graces. Merida did not pay much attention to staff politics, but she had seen enough of what went on at Castle DunBroch to know how these things worked, and she wanted no part of it. She would stand at this washbasin and scrub pots until her fingers fell off before she gave Aileen the satisfaction.

Merida added more soap to the murky water before carting the last of the utensils to the wash basin. She had just lowered the last knife into the water when she heard, "What are you doing in here?"

Merida whipped around to find Elinor standing near the door to the scullery. No one had ever looked more out of place than the princess, standing there in her ice-blue gown amid the stacks of dirty dishes, pots, and cooking utensils.

"I was sent here," Merida answered.

"By whom? Duncan?"

Merida shook her head.

Elinor's forehead dipped in a frown, but then her lips thinned.

"Come with me," she said before lifting the hem of her gown and marching out of the scullery. Merida looked at the other girls, who watched them with shocked expressions. Something told her that they had seen the princess more in the past two days than they had in the past two years.

Merida quickly dried her hands and arms with a rough square of linen and slipped on her gloves before following behind Elinor.

"Why are *you* doing in the kitchens?" she asked Elinor as she walked just behind her. "I would have thought the meal would still be going on."

"Father had to retire early," Elinor answered. "He fell ill at the end of the meal. Thank goodness the Fraser and his son decided to take their leave once my father withdrew to his chamber."

They arrived in the main cooking area. As had been the case during Elinor's previous trip to the kitchens, much of the staff stared with a mixture of curiosity and apprehension.

"Princess," Aileen drawled as she rounded the massive cauldron. She tossed the towel she had been using to wipe her hands over her shoulder. "You're in the kitchens again? We may have to strap an apron on you soon."

Everyone in the kitchen went silent as they waited for Elinor's reply.

"I am only here to get Merida," she said.

Aileen's brow rose. "Oh? And what do you need her for this time?"

"That is not your concern," Elinor said.

"Well, I will have to tell Duncan something when he asks why the lass he hired to work in the kitchens is not working. Again," she tacked on.

"I said she is none of your concern," Elinor repeated. "You do not have to worry about Merida anymore. She has been promoted."

Merida's eyes widened to the size of the dinner plates stacked on a nearby table. "I have?" she asked.

"Yes. You will work as my personal maid," Elinor said.

There were several gasps from those in the kitchen. Merida glanced around and took in the shock in some of the faces. She saw outright malice in the eyes of a couple of the girls. In Aileen's, she saw barely leashed rage.

Elinor turned to her.

"Follow me, Merida."

CHAPTER TWENTY-NINE
Merida

Merida was aware of the hostile stares following her as she carried the tray of hot tea and oatcakes down the corridor toward Elinor's room. She was not sure what the princess had been thinking with this latest move, but the minuscule amount of acceptance Merida had earned from the staff had been lost with the promotion. No one thought she deserved it. Well, except for Sorcha. She was the only person in the kitchens who would even speak to Merida when she went to get Elinor's tea.

As for the other servants throughout the household, they too apparently thought it was unfair that someone who had worked in the castle for only a few days would be elevated to the princess's maid. Orla, who had been kind to her when she initially arrived, had grown cold and stand-offish. When Merida mentioned it to Sorcha, the girl told her it was likely because Orla's second daughter, Bridget, had been next in line to work as the princess's personal maid. Merida had usurped her position.

Elinor seemed oblivious to the chaos her decision had caused among the castle's staff. Her focus was on the deal she and Merida had made and on working with Fergus to ferret out the threat. They were to retreat to the woods after the princess's lute lessons for an afternoon of fishing and hunting practice, then meet up with Fergus so that they could figure out the next part in their plan.

Merida arrived at the princess's bedchamber and, using her elbow and shoulder to push the door open, backed her way into the room.

"I am sorry that took so long. I hope your tea isn't as cold as some of the attitudes in the kitchens," Merida said as she entered the room.

She turned to find Elinor staring at her with a panicked expression. Standing next to her was Queen Catriona. Displeasure teemed in her grandmother's dark brown eyes, sending a chill down Merida's spine.

"Oh . . . oh, I'm sorry," Merida said. She bowed her head and dipped into a curtsy. "Good morning, Queen Catriona."

The queen ignored her as she turned her attention to her daughter.

"I assured Orla she must be mistaken when she inquired about your new maid," the queen said. "Who gave you permission to make changes to the staff?"

To her credit, Elinor did not cower under her mother's blistering stare.

"I thought you would be pleased that I would take such initiative. 'Tis the type of decision I will be required to make once I am running my own household, is it not?"

The queen did not look pleased by her daughter's answer. Yet when she spoke, Merida was certain she heard a hint of admiration in her voice.

"The next time you feel the urge to make such decisions on your own, ignore it. This is *my* household. I am to be consulted about staff issues, no matter how insignificant."

The emphasis placed on the last word left no room for interpretation. Merida was the equivalent of horse dung in the queen's eyes.

"Yes, Mother," Elinor answered with a deferential nod.

Merida did not dare move a single muscle as Queen Catriona's cold gaze settled on her. The weight of the tray she held multiplied with each second that passed, but she maintained her control.

Several excruciating moments ticked by before the

queen lifted her nose in the air and walked past her without saying a word. Merida held her breath, afraid to make a sound until the woman cleared the room.

Once alone with Elinor, she released the breath she had been holding and set the tea tray on a nearby table.

"Forgive me for saying so, Princess, but your mother is the most frightening person I have ever encountered," Merida said.

"You should have met my grandmother," Elinor replied with a giggle. "She made my mother seem like a sweet wee lamb."

Merida shuddered at the thought. She had no idea she had come from a line of such terrifying women. She recalled that horrible argument the morning of the Highland Games and realized just how lucky she was that her mother treated her with respect, even when they disagreed on matters.

"I know what you are thinking," Elinor said.

"What?"

"That there is no reason for the queen to be so aloof."

"Well, there isn't," Merida said. "I have yet to see her smile."

"I know my mother can be rather unfeeling, but I understand why she is that way. She was raised to believe that to effectively rule, one must garner the respect of their subjects. She does not abide informal relationships with the staff because she believes that familiarity breeds disrespect." Elinor shrugged. "I may not agree with everything she does, but I can appreciate her perspective. It is not easy being queen. Ensuring there is peace within the kingdom is a difficult task."

"It does sound like an overwhelming responsibility," Merida said. It was the same responsibility she had run away from, one her own mother handled with such grace.

"But just imagine the satisfaction one feels when their kingdom thrives," Elinor said. She leaned over and whispered to Merida, "Personally, I would rule differently. I believe one can get their subjects to respect them while still being open and inviting."

Merida nodded. "Yes, it can be done. I have seen it."

She had seen *her* do it. As queen, Elinor had taken all the favorable things she had learned from Queen Catriona's rule and combined them with her own humility and sense of obligation to the people of DunBroch Kingdom.

Not for the first time, Merida thought that if she had met her mother under different circumstances, they likely would have been friends. They *were* friends.

Yet, as much as she enjoyed having Princess Elinor as an unlikely friend, it would never be enough. She wanted to go back to having her as a mother.

CHAPTER THIRTY
Elinor

Elinor stood before the open wardrobe in her bedchamber, scanning the dozens of gowns her mother had insisted she needed for the upcoming Highland Games and the pageantry that surrounded them. She had spent hours with the dressmaker. Recalling the constant fittings over the past few weeks still gave Elinor nightmares.

"If you do not mind my asking, Princess, why would one ever need this many gowns?" Merida asked from just over Elinor's shoulder.

"For the games," she answered. When the girl did not respond, Elinor peered at her over her shoulder and clarified, "The Highland Games."

"But you are not participating in the games."

"Of course I am not, but there are many events—dinners and meetings with dignitaries from surrounding kingdoms."

"And you need a different gown for each?"

Elinor shrugged. "'Tis what Queen Catriona demands."

"It sounds exhausting," Merida said. She cut to Elinor's right and moved to stand before the wardrobe. "I guess I should not complain when my mum tries to dress me in a gown," she commented, running her gloved fingers along the yellow silk one Elinor had worn to the previous year's Hogmanay celebration. Elinor had no idea why the girl insisted on wearing those gloves.

Merida returned her attention to Elinor. "My mother only requires that I dress in formal attire a few times per year."

"You are very lucky to have a mum who does not expect you to wear these confining garments constantly," Elinor said. She pulled a dark blue one from the wardrobe and held it in front of her. "But it is a small concession in the grand scheme of things. Besides, many of the lasses in the kingdom can only dream of owning such a fine gown. I have more than I know what to do with."

"But isn't it tiring?" Merida asked.

"Wearing gowns?"

"Being the princess. And all the duties that comes with it."

"It is," Elinor said with a sigh. "But it is who I am."

"But it is not *only* who you are," Merida pointed out.

For a brief moment, Elinor could only stare at her in astonishment.

She knew that she was more than merely the Princess of MacCameron Kingdom, but this was the first time she had ever heard anyone else voice that sentiment. From the day she was born, her title had defined every single moment of her life. Everything she did, she did in service to the king and the kingdom he ruled. She had no say in the matter, even though she always thought she should.

And now here was this strange girl, who caught and killed her own dinner and galloped on her horse like a carefree lad, recognizing that Elinor should have a say in her own life.

She returned the gown to the wardrobe, then turned to face Merida. "So, who do you think I am, if not the princess?" Elinor asked.

"I said you are not *only* the princess."

"Well, what else am I?"

Merida took her by the hand and sat her at the vanity. "'Tis not a question for me to answer. Who do *you* want to be? What are your dreams?"

"You know what my dream is," Elinor whispered. "To leave this castle, and this kingdom."

"But what will you do when you leave? Have you thought about that?" Merida asked.

"Of course I have." She had spent countless hours thinking about it. "I want to learn more about the world around me. The Scots to the south are much more enlightened. Musicians travel from as far as Rome to study and perform there, and their museums are filled with art from all over the continent. I want to see it all."

"Then what?" Merida asked. "You cannot spend all your time visiting museums. There must be something of substance you plan to do."

"I am still pondering that part," Elinor answered with a sigh.

She had thought about what she could do to support herself, and the list was very short indeed. She would not have the safety and security that came with being the king's daughter. Her status as princess would mean nothing to the people of the Lowlands.

Elinor considered bringing up what Fergus had said about Merida coming from the Lowlands, but decided against it. She hoped the girl would share the truth about her origins with her in due time.

"I can sew rather well," Elinor said. Maybe those

countless hours she spent working on the MacCameron tapestries had not been for naught. "I am sure I can find work as an embroiderer."

"You do not sound very excited about it," Merida remarked. "Why seek this freedom if you cannot do something that makes you happy? What lights a fire in here?" She pressed two fingers to the center of her chest. "And here." She tapped those same two fingers to her head. "What makes a tingle race down your spine when you think about it?"

"Aiding the villagers who are in need," Elinor answered without hesitation.

"Really?" Merida asked.

"Yes." She smiled as a memory emerged; one she had forgotten. "When I was a young lass, maybe about seven or eight, my mother's maid—the one she had before Orla— would sometimes take me with her to the village. Whenever there was a large gathering at the castle, she would take the leftover food to the church. I loved helping to feed the villagers who did not have a means for providing for themselves. Nessa—my mother's maid—said I had a natural ability to make people feel loved."

Elinor thought about that young boy from the village who had needed to rummage through garbage to find food.

Nessa would have been aghast to learn that people in their kingdom were in such need, and that no one in the royal family had sent aid.

"It is true, you know," Merida said. "You make people feel that way, even when they are not being very lovable to you."

Elinor was touched by her words, but there was something disconcerting about hearing them from someone she had known for less than a fortnight.

"You know, Merida, there have been moments since I found you in the forest that it has felt as if I've known you for much longer than these few short days. It seems as if I know you better than people I have lived with my entire life," Elinor said. "It is very strange, don't you think?"

Merida broke eye contact, looking from the vanity, to the window, to the tapestry hanging on the wall. When she returned her attention to her, Elinor noted her discomfort.

Merida hunched her shoulders and said, "I do not think it is strange at all. Sometimes you simply connect with people." She squeezed Elinor's hand and sent her a sly grin. "Speaking of, do I sense a connection between you and Fergus DunBroch?"

"Absolutely not!" Elinor said with more vehemence than was warranted, but she did not want anyone—even

Merida—to know that she did, in fact, feel a connection with Fergus. The feeling was still too new to her. She needed time to explore it for herself before she shared it with anyone.

"Well, what do you think of him?" Merida asked.

"That he is ridiculous."

"He is not!" Merida protested.

"He most certainly is; the way he saunters around as if he owns the world."

"Well, from what I hear, his father is the chieftain, so he will own DunBroch soon enough."

Elinor looked her up and down and sniffed. "You are biased, being a DunBroch and all."

She turned to the mirror and made an effort to ignore the knowing smirk tipping up the corners of Merida's lips, but that proved to be as futile as her attempts to forget about that big, burly, conceited Fergus. Thoughts of him had consumed her since leaving him after their fire-making lesson.

It was frustrating, infuriating, and . . . confusing. She should not feel anything whatsoever for Fergus.

The man was a DunBroch, for goodness' sake! The clan had been a fierce rival of the MacCamerons for centuries. This peace alliance was too new—too fragile—to negate years of such intense hatred between their clans.

Even if Fergus had not been a DunBroch, she should not be entertaining thoughts of some warrior.

She had found his skill with a bow and arrow and his ability to make fire impressive, and the surprising care with which he'd treated that young boy was to be admired, but it was not enough to alter how she should feel toward him. Men like Fergus believed that their prowess on the battlefield was all that was needed to get through life. What rankled Elinor the most was that they were right. If a man could shoot an arrow or wield a claymore, he need not accomplish anything else. He would be praised for the rest of his days.

Well, although she appreciated that had he been willing to teach her a few survival skills, she would not feed Fergus's ego any more. She was sure the lasses at DunBroch did quite enough of that.

A streak of jealousy raced through her at the thought of those other lasses, but Elinor quickly suppressed it.

She tried to stave off the image of his smile, but it popped into her mind uninvited. The way his red mustache curved up with his grin sent excited tingles skittering along her skin. Elinor cursed both the tingles and the man who had caused them.

"'Tis no matter what I think of Fergus DunBroch," she told Merida. In a lowered voice, she said, "What matters is that, if there is truly a threat to MacCameron Kingdom, Fergus is willing to help uncover it. I wish we could go back to that village today and search for more clues."

"Why can't we?"

"Because the queen has ordered that I am to spend the rest of the day preparing my speech for the start of the Highland Games. I am to deliver it for the first time." She looked at Merida and laughed. "I am a bit nervous, but I have been preparing for weeks."

"You seem so excited. Won't you miss such duties when you are gone?" Merida asked her. Her earnest expression was disarming. "Are you sure you have thought your plans through, Princess? You will be giving up so much by leaving. You're giving up everything you've ever known."

Elinor's throat grew tight as she digested Merida's warning, but it was not as if she had not considered all of this.

"Yes, I have thought it through," Elinor said. "It is worth giving up all of it for the one thing that I will gain. My freedom. Do you not understand, Merida?" she implored. "My life is not my own, but it will be when I travel to the Lowlands. I will be free to make my own choices and not have everything I do dictated by my mother and father, or by my position. I will gladly give this up if it means I can be free."

CHAPTER THIRTY-ONE
Merida

The splash of cold water struck Merida in the face, dampening the cloth that was wrapped around her head, along with the front of her kirtle.

"Princess!" Merida screeched.

"I just wanted to make sure you were awake," Elinor said before bursting into giggles.

Merida rolled her eyes but could not help laughing herself. It was rare to see the princess's playful side. It evoked memories of how jovial her mother had once been, back when Merida was still a wee girl.

Queen Elinor had become more and more serious over the years, especially as Merida neared marrying age. Her mother spent so much of her time preparing Merida for her eventual reign as queen that she seemed to have forgotten what it was like to just enjoy being with her daughter. Maybe, once Merida returned home, they could get back to enjoying the relationship they once shared.

If she ever returned home.

You will.

In another act of defiance, instead of practicing her speech for the Highland Games, as Queen Catriona had ordered, Elinor had decided to keep up with the day's planned survival lesson. Merida had hoped that she would change her mind about escaping before her betrothal was announced at the Highland Games, but her mother was still determined to leave.

Ironically, the one thing that would likely keep her here was the one thing that scared Merida the most—this mysterious threat to the kingdom. Elinor pledged she would not leave until the matter was handled and MacCameron Kingdom was no longer in danger.

More water splattered onto Merida's face.

"Really, Princess," she lamented.

"I am sorry. That was the last time, I promise," Elinor said between peals of laughter.

"Are you paying attention?" Merida asked. "This is

supposed to be a lesson, remember. You must focus. This is not a time for leisure. It takes work."

"I know, but it is so very hard to think about work in the midst of all this beauty," Elinor said with a dreamy sigh. She tipped her head back and smiled up at the clear blue sky, the picture of contentment.

She sat upon a rock with her knees against her chest, her arms wrapped around them. Earlier, when Merida had suggested she remove her slippers and dip her toes in the water, her mother had looked at her as if she were speaking a foreign tongue. That was when Merida had learned that in her nineteen years, Princess Elinor had never been allowed to swim in any of the pristine lakes that speckled MacCameron Kingdom.

Her mother lived a privileged existence, but also a tragic one. Over the past week, Merida had learned just how little joy Elinor MacCameron had experienced in her life.

"Did your father teach you to kill fish with the bow and arrow, as well?" Elinor asked.

"He did," Merida answered. "He taught me everything I know."

"I cannot imagine my father doing such a thing."

"Having met him, I cannot imagine your father teaching you to hunt and fish either, Princess."

"Not just teaching me; I cannot imagine him hunting or fishing at all."

"How could that be? I thought every young Scottish lad learned to hunt. 'Tis a rite of passage."

"Oh, I am sure he hunted for sport in his youth, but he became king very early in his life," Elinor said with a shrug. "He was but eighteen years old when he and my mother were betrothed, and my grandfather, the queen's father, was killed soon after. King Douglass ascended to the throne and has been tended to by servants and his army ever since."

"My father still hunts, even though—" Merida stopped herself just in time. She had not revealed to Elinor that her father was the king of DunBroch Kingdom. "Even though he is high up in his clan's army," she finished.

"Your father is a rare one, indeed," Elinor said. "I would like to meet him one day. I want to applaud him for bucking tradition and teaching his daughter the skills she needs to survive."

"I think I can arrange that," Merida said, trying her best not to laugh. She stooped down and scooped up a handful of water, sending it flying toward the princess. "Now get over here and let me show you how this is done."

She was gloveless this afternoon, having filed down her

claws just before leaving the castle. However, she had used ribbon to secure the sleeves of her léine at her wrists to prevent the hair on her arms from sticking out. It was at least two inches long and now covered much of her legs as well. Merida feared she had only a few days left before she could no longer hide what was happening to her. It was paramount that she remedy things here as soon as possible.

Elinor pushed herself up from the rock and, holding her plain brown kirtle up above her ankles, tiptoed over to Merida. They stood on the edge of the shallow creek, which teemed with salmon and herring.

Merida handed Elinor the bow and arrow and instructed her on how to home in on her target.

"Once you have a certain fish in your sights, you must follow it. Do not just aim at the water and hope you strike one."

Elinor nodded and lifted the bow.

"No, no," Merida said. "You must keep the bow close to your chest. It affords you better control, remember?" She put her arms around the princess and caught hold of the bow. "You should hold it like this."

"Maybe I can help."

Both Merida and Elinor yelped and spun around at the same time.

Fergus stood several yards away, casually leaning an elbow against a tree near where their horses were tied. The fact that neither Angus nor Alistair had alerted them to his presence demonstrated how comfortable both horses already felt with him.

"Fergus," Elinor greeted with a curt nod.

"Princess," Fergus said, bending over with a full bow.

"We did not expect to see you until later in the evening," Elinor said.

Fergus looked to his left and then to his right. "I do not see a sign that says 'No DunBrochs allowed.'"

Merida noticed Elinor's mouth twitching, but she managed to rein in her grin. She stuck her regal nose in the air and, with a cheeky smirk, said, "Well, maybe there should be one."

"Oh, but I do not think so, Princess. You see, according to the peace alliance, I am allowed to explore these lands at my leisure." Fergus arched a brow. "Or was the MacCameron being untruthful when he offered those terms to the various clans in the kingdom?"

His tone was playful, and to Merida's utter delight, so was Elinor's.

"These lands are vast," Elinor said. "I am just surprised that you would end up here of all places."

"Everyone knows this creek has the most fish," Fergus said. "Stay here a bit longer and you're bound to see the feisty lads from Clan MacNair. They love the herring and whiting." Fergus nodded at the bow in her hand. "Besides, your maid told me where to find you."

Elinor turned to her. "You did?"

"She did," Fergus said. He pushed away from the tree and sauntered toward them, his arms still crossed over his massive chest. "Learning to fish, eh?"

"Just a short lesson," Merida said. "We were coming to your camp once we are done so that we can return to Clan Innes."

He shook his head. "We should not return to the village just yet."

"Why not?" Elinor asked.

"One of my men was just there. He said several of the shop owners mentioned the vicar and his wife who visited the other day, asking questions of everyone. We do not want them to become suspicious." He looked to Elinor. "I think I would rather help you learn to fish today, Princess. Some say I am an even better fisherman than archer."

He positioned himself next to Elinor, retrieved an arrow from his ever-present quiver, and used the bow to send it sailing into the creek. He struck a fat salmon on the first try.

"How did you do that?" Elinor asked. She didn't even try to hide the admiration in her voice, which told Merida just how impressed she was by Fergus's skill.

"It is all in the flick of the wrist," Fergus said. "Here, I will show you." He rounded Elinor, stopping just behind her and capturing her left wrist in his hand. Before she could put up a protest, he said, "I just want to show you how to hold the bow."

Elinor's shoulders lost some of their stiffness. She gripped the bow's handle. "Is this correct?" she asked.

Fergus peered down at her and, in a voice so soft Merida could barely hear it, said, "It is perfect."

Merida brought her hand to her chest. It felt as if her heart had grown to twice its size. She was torn between slipping away so they could be alone and drawing closer so that she would not miss another word.

He reached behind him and pulled another arrow from the quiver, then slipped it into Elinor's right hand. His massive size enveloped her.

"Nice and steady," Fergus said as he guided Elinor's hand back. "Now, shoot!"

Elinor released the arrow, sending it flying into the water. Her delighted squeal told Merida that she had hit her target, even though Merida could not see it.

Elinor bounced up and down like a wee lass who'd been

awarded a sweet cake. She turned to Fergus and threw her arms around him.

Merida's breath caught in her throat. But before she could get too excited, Elinor pulled away, taking several steps back.

"Uh, thank you. That will be all," Elinor said.

"But we are not done with the lesson," Fergus said.

"Yes, we are," she said. Her voice was back to being prim and proper.

Merida slapped her palm to her forehead. She wanted to scream!

And her mother wondered where she had gotten her stubborn streak from. It was nothing but pigheadedness preventing Elinor from seeing how perfect she and Fergus were for each other.

"If that is what you want. I guess I should get to my fishing," Fergus said. "But I must warn you, Princess. I like to take a swim in the creek before I fish." He put his hand on the brooch that pinned his plaid in place.

"Don't you dare!" Elinor warned. She looked to Merida. Her cheeks were as red as raspberries. "Let us go before this scoundrel disrobes right here in front of us."

The princess stuck her chin in the air, spun on her heel, and started marching toward the horses. Merida followed closely behind. She looked back at Fergus and shot him a disapproving glare. It did nothing to wipe the grin from his face.

As they approached the trees where they had tied the horses, Angus and Alistair suddenly went into an uproar, neighing wildly and stomping their hooves.

"Now they decide to make noise," Merida muttered under her breath.

But then she stopped short at the sound of rustling. A second later, dozens of birds took flight from a nearby tree, as if they had been spooked by something.

Merida put a hand on Elinor's arm. "Wait," she said.

Elinor looked back at her. "What?"

Merida put a finger to her lips. She peered through the trees, past where the horses had, fortunately, calmed down.

"I thought I heard something," she said.

"'Tis probably that arrogant DunBroch splashing in the creek," Elinor replied.

Merida looked over at the princess and noticed the red hue was still staining her cheeks. That blush was rather telling, but Merida knew better than to mention it.

"He only wanted to vex you."

"Well, it worked. He is the most vexing man alive."

"He just taught you to fish," Merida pointed out.

"I thanked him, didn't I?" she replied, as if that was sufficient.

With that, she gathered her skirt in her hand and continued stomping toward the horses.

Merida looked up at the sky and released an exhausted sigh. Just when she thought they were making progress.

CHAPTER THIRTY-TWO
Elinor

Elinor guided Alistair through the patchwork of fallen limbs and uprooted tree trunks that peppered the forest floor on the north side of MacCameron Castle. She rarely traveled this way. Another twenty miles toward the sea lay the edge of her family's kingdom, which her father had declared forbidden territory for both Elinor and her mother.

However, she had spotted soldiers from Clan MacCameron engaged in combat exercises in the clearing where they usually entered, making this roundabout approach necessary. Elinor did not want to chance running into any of her father's men.

Merida had suggested they visit the lake on the far side of the glen to continue their fishing lesson, but that would have put them much too close to Clan Fraser's land. Instead, Elinor decided they should return to MacCameron Castle for tea. It was not as if she would be able to concentrate on fishing after her run-in with Fergus DunBroch, anyway.

She hated to admit how unsettled she was by his mere presence, but there was no denying that he left her flustered. He was confounding.

The people of this kingdom tended to show her an undue amount of respect simply because she was the king's daughter. Fergus DunBroch did not seem to care that she was the princess. He appeared to take much pleasure in taunting her. It was infuriating.

And just a tad bit enjoyable.

She had hugged him!

Elinor was aghast that she had not been able to control her emotions. The man was insufferable, and . . .

"Are you sure we are going the right way, Princess?" Merida asked from a few yards behind her.

"Yes," Elinor called over her shoulder. "There is a hidden entrance in the curtain wall. It is a secret escape route in case of an attack from the south. It shall put us on the rear side of the stables."

She slowed Alistair to a walk as they approached the thirty-foot stone wall that surrounded MacCameron Castle.

"Look for a black stone near the base of the curtain wall," Elinor said. "The secret entrance is a few paces past it."

They traveled another ten yards or so before Merida said, "Over there."

"Yes, this is it," Elinor said. She slid off Alistair's back and called for Merida to help her. "It is tricky to enter from the outside," she said. "We must push three of the stones inward at the same time. It will release the hidden locking mechanism."

"How do you know how to do this?" Merida asked.

"Aileen's brother, Gregory, showed us when we were younger. He was several years older than we were, but he would humor us when we went into the stables to play."

"Aileen was your playmate?" Merida asked.

Elinor nodded. "Not just Aileen. I used to play games around the bailey with many of the servants' young children. Mother put a stop to it once she learned of it."

"Because she does not believe the royal family should befriend the staff," Merida said, remembering what Elinor had told her.

Elinor shrugged. "I disagree with the way both my mother and father rule. I shall never reign as queen, but if I did, I would treat my clansmen differently. I would respect them and not look down on them."

"'Tis a shame that you are so determined to leave,"

FARRAH ROCHON

Merida said. "I believe this kingdom would thrive with you as its queen."

Elinor had to avert her gaze for fear that the girl would see something in her eyes that Elinor did not want her to see. She swallowed past the lump of emotion suddenly welling in her throat.

"Well, we shall never know," Elinor said. "I am sure the clans will vote on a suitable replacement to rule the kingdom once the MacCameron's rule is over." She pointed at the curtain wall. "Let us move along. I am in need of hot tea." She swiped at her face and felt the rough, gritty dirt on her skin. "And a warm bath," she added.

Elinor pointed to the stone lowest to the ground. "You push here. I shall push the other two."

Merida flattened her palm against the stone.

Elinor gasped. "What is going on with your fingernails?" They were sharp points.

Merida quickly pulled her hand away and shoved it within the folds of her kirtle.

"'Tis nothing," she said. "I shaped them that way to better scratch my back." She gestured to the wall. "Let us get inside."

Elinor frowned, wondering how she reached her back and why she would ever do such a thing to her nails when there were more convenient methods for relieving an itch.

She did not have time to worry about Merida's strange grooming habits.

Together, the two of them pushed the three stones aside and, with not as much effort as she had expected, managed to shove the secret door open wide enough to get themselves and their horses inside.

"If I remember correctly, 'tis easier to close from this side," Elinor said. They pushed the door back in place, then started for the entrance to the stables. She could hear the horses in the pen on the opposite side of the wooden structure. This was about the time the groomsmen took them out for their evening exercise. It should make it that much easier for her and Merida to slip Angus and Alistair inside.

They rounded the side of the building and were met with a bevy of activity. Some of the same groomsmen she would have expected to have been out in the pen with the horses were dipping in and out of the stalls as if searching for something.

"Psst . . . Princess."

Elinor turned and spotted Ewan. The young groom looked terrified.

"Ewan, what is going on?" Elinor asked as she handed him Alistair's reins.

Ewan looked over her shoulder, his eyes widening in alarm.

Elinor turned and gasped. "Father! What . . . what are you doing in the stables?"

"Where have you been?" King Douglass demanded.

Elinor was still so shocked to see him that she could barely think of a response. He looked out of place, dressed in clothes much too formal for the stables.

"I . . . I went riding with Merida," Elinor finally answered. "We were—"

"Do you understand how dangerous it is for you to be out in these woods without protection, Elinor? What if you had been hurt, or worse, kidnapped?" His eyes narrowed. "And what is this I hear about you cavorting with the son of Clan DunBroch's chieftain at the creek? The one they call Fergus."

Elinor felt the blood draining from her face even as her cheeks became burning hot. Had Lachlan told him about their encounter after all? But if he had, would her father not have confronted her the day before?

"I was . . . we were not . . . cavorting," she said. She turned to Merida, who stood a few feet away. The shock Elinor felt was reflected in the girl's eyes.

"Who have you spoken to?" Elinor asked her father.

"'Tis no matter how I got the information. I want to know if it is true!"

Elinor frowned. Her father had mentioned the creek where she and Merida had been that day but had said nothing of the small clearing where she and Fergus had practiced making fire the day before. How would Lachlan have known?

"Well?" her father prompted.

"I . . . he . . . he happened upon the creek where Merida and I were taking in the nice weather. I did not know he would be there. He did not know we would be there, either. It was all happenstance."

A muscle in the king's jaw jumped as his gaze traveled from the top of her head to the tips of her boots.

"I was told that you spoke at length to the DunBroch. And that you stood close to him, too close to be deemed proper."

Elinor's face flamed with shame, even though she had nothing to feel guilty about. There was nothing inappropriate about her run-in with Fergus. Who could have reported such things about her to the king?

A terrifying thought suddenly occurred, striking true fear in her as it put her plans of escape in jeopardy.

"Are you having me followed, Father?" Elinor asked.

"Do not question me!" the king bellowed. "This is my kingdom. I do not have to explain my actions to you."

Elinor flinched. She was mortified as she glanced to her right and noticed how many people were witnessing her father unleash his wrath on her.

She bowed and murmured, "I am sorry."

"I am only trying to keep you safe, Elinor."

"Fergus DunBroch will not hurt me," she said. She wished she could take the words back the moment she said them.

The king stared down his nose at her, his displeasure a palpable thing that hovered in the air around them.

"Must I remind you that you are to be betrothed to Lachlan Fraser in a matter of days?" King Douglass asked. "This union will be the most important in a generation. I shall not have you gallivanting across these lands like a commoner and putting yourself in a position to be compromised. You are the future queen, and you will behave as such from this moment forward. Do you understand me, Elinor?"

"Yes, Father." It was difficult to get the words past the lump in her throat.

As she stood underneath the glare of her father's blistering disapproval, Elinor could see her plans for escape fading like the sun's rays on a cold winter day. She knew her father well enough to know what his next move would be. She was bound to be under even greater scrutiny after this incident.

And if he was having her followed?

Evasion would not be simply unlikely; it would be impossible.

The king turned to the groom at his side. "Is this the girl? The new servant?" he asked the man.

Elinor realized he was talking about Merida. Thank goodness she had reminded the girl to bind her hair again.

The groom nodded. "'Tis so, according to Orla."

King Douglass looked to Merida. "You are no longer the princess's maid."

Elinor exhaled a swift breath. Her father's withering glare warned off the words she was about to speak.

"You are to have no dealings with the princess," King Douglass continued.

With that, he dismissed them both, walking past them without another word.

CHAPTER THIRTY-THREE
Merida

Merida shrugged off the hands that were jabbing her shoulder and twisted around on the straw mattress. She'd had a difficult time falling asleep. She would not be awakened so early.

"Boys, leave me be," she said. She had warned her brothers more than once about disturbing her sleep.

Her brothers?

Merida sat up straight. "Boys?"

"Shhh . . . not so loud."

No, not the boys. *Elinor.*

A confounding mix of disappointment and relief swept through her. Although she would have given just about anything to see Harris, Hubert, and Hamish at that moment, she welcomed Elinor's presence.

The irony was not lost on Merida. She found herself snarled in this predicament because she had wanted to get as far away from *Queen* Elinor as possible. Why did it take meeting her as a princess, and under these circumstances, for Merida to realize how special her mother was? She would never take their relationship for granted again.

"What are you doing here, Princess?" Merida asked her.

"Rise." A balled-up garment of some sort landed against her chest. "And then get dressed."

"But it is the middle of the night."

"Yes," Elinor said. She gestured to the garment. "Put on that kirtle."

Merida sat up. She pulled the counterpane up to her chin to hide the hair poking out the neckline of her night-gown. When she had undressed for bed, she discovered that nearly all her body was covered. With Elinor's having spotted her claws earlier that evening, Merida would not be able to explain away the overgrowth of hair.

"Princess, did you not hear your father today? You should not even be here. If word gets back to him that you and I spoke, it will cause all sorts of trouble."

"I do not care," Elinor said.

But Merida could tell that she did. She could see it in the way the princess's chin quivered with worry. She was afraid of being caught by her father's men. Merida did not want to imagine the king's wrath if he learned that his daughter defied him just after he had forbidden her from leaving the castle.

Merida knew she should have mentioned this earlier, when she had first suspected there was someone in the woods. She had tried to convince herself that she was being foolish, or that she was mistaken. But she now knew that she had not been.

"There is something you should know," Merida said. She was grateful for the dim candlelight. She hoped it inhibited Elinor from seeing the guilt in her eyes. "I had a feeling we were being followed today."

"What?" Elinor asked. "Why did you not tell me?"

"Because I was not sure. But do you remember how spooked the horses were when we were leaving the creek? I heard rustling just as we were approaching them. I thought it was an animal of some sort, but now . . ."

"So my father *did* send someone to spy on me," Elinor said.

"Yes, which is why it would be foolish for us to go out at this time of the night."

"On the contrary," Elinor said. "'Tis the perfect time to go. Father would never expect me to leave the castle in the middle of the night."

The candlelight danced across her face. Merida could see how tight her jaw was, as if she could barely contain her anger.

"But why do you want to go riding in the middle of the night?"

"We are not going riding for the sake of riding, Merida. We are going back to that village to investigate the threat against the kingdom."

"Princess, are you mad? Didn't you hear what Fergus said? You cannot return as a vicar's wife, and you certainly cannot go as yourself. Word would get back to your father before the sun comes up."

"I am not going as a vicar's wife," she said. "And I am not fetching Fergus this time, either. *We* are going, Merida." She reached into a satchel that Merida had not even noticed she had and retrieved two white garments. She held them up, and Merida recognized the coif and veil. "As nuns!"

She really had gone mad.

"And then, after we hunt down this threat to the kingdom, we shall go to the DunBroch camp to show Fergus that we were able to do so on our own."

"Princess, think about what you are doing. The king will not accept such behavior from you."

"Well, he should expect such from me from now on," Elinor said in a fierce whisper. "I have been a dutiful daughter my entire life. Nothing I have done warrants him sending his men to spy on me."

Merida wanted to point out that the princess had been running away from home the day they met, but decided against it.

"I cannot talk you out of doing this, can I?" Merida asked.

Elinor shook her head. Excitement danced in her eyes.

With a sigh, Merida retrieved the kirtle.

"Give me a few moments to get dressed," she said. "I shall meet you at the stables."

The muted purple of the predawn sky peeked through the branches overhead, providing just enough light to make this ill-advised journey not as harrowing as it could have been if it had been as early as Merida had first assumed. That she had convinced Elinor to stay on the well-traveled path through the forest, and not branch out into parts unknown, also made it less dangerous.

At least she hoped they were not in danger. Merida was not naive enough to think that they were ever completely safe in these woods. Hazards lurked everywhere, and at all times.

She had considered attempting once more to talk the princess out of this, but the more she thought about it, the more Merida realized that Elinor needed this. After nineteen years of being under her father's thumb, she deserved to experience the freedom that accompanied this small act of rebellion.

Merida knew firsthand how cathartic it could be.

Of course, if they were caught, the princess was at risk of having her movements more restricted than ever before.

"Princess, I doubt anyone will share information with two nuns," Merida said. "I think we should turn back."

"I disagree," Elinor said. "People trust nuns."

Her mother's stubbornness as a queen paled in comparison to how stubborn she was as a young princess.

"The longer we are away, the better chance your father has of discovering that you left the castle," Merida said. "Please, think this through, Princess."

Elinor brought Alistair to an abrupt halt. Merida pulled on Angus's reins to slow him down. She doubled back to the princess, who was waiting for her.

"Do you not understand, Merida?" Elinor asked. "My father has left me no choice. He and my mother have made me a prisoner of that castle without my even realizing it." She bit her trembling lip. "Do you know how upsetting it is to discover that someone has been following your every move? I have no idea how long this has been going on. Has there been someone watching when I am reading in my favorite place in the garden? What lengths has my father gone to in his efforts to protect me?"

Her voice escalated with each word she spoke. She looked at Merida with tears in her eyes.

"I have always known that my life is not my own—that it is dictated by my title. But I thought I had some semblance of privacy. Instead, I find out that I have been spied on by my own father for all of my life!"

"Princess, I do not believe your father has been spying on you your entire life," Merida said. "Do you not think that your father's men would have told him that I have been teaching you archery if they had seen us? Or that we had visited the DunBroch camp? Surely, if you were being followed all this time, King Douglass would have had something to say about you venturing to Clan Innes's village posing as Fergus's wife?"

For a moment, it appeared as if Merida's words were starting to sink in, but then Elinor shook her head.

"'Tis no matter *when* my father started his spying." She looked at Merida and stubbornly stuck her chin up in the air. "If I am to be accused of cavorting with Fergus DunBroch, maybe I should really do so."

"No." Merida shook her head. "Princess, you cannot."

As much as she wanted to see her parents together, it could not happen in this way. Elinor did not seem to grasp the peril she was putting herself in by engaging in this level of defiance.

Another thought occurred to her.

"Be truthful with me, Elinor," Merida said. "Are you doing this to defy the king, or is it just an excuse to see Fergus? I have seen the way you look at him."

Instead of the adamant denial Merida had expected, her mother simply smiled. "'Tis no matter," she repeated.

"Yes, it is," Merida said, excitement rippling through her. Was it finally happening? Was her mother truly falling in love with her father?

"You see, I think Fergus likes you, too," Merida continued. "I know that you are promised to Lachlan Fraser, but Clan DunBroch is just as important to the kingdom. Could your father reject a union between you and Fergus if he is who you truly want?"

Elinor's expression brightened, but then immediately sobered. She shook her head.

"You still do not understand, Merida. This is not about what I want. It does not matter how I feel about Fergus

DunBroch. It does not matter how I feel about my father, or Lachlan, or any other warrior in this kingdom. In the end, it is still someone else controlling my life. I will never be free if I am someone's wife."

Her words settled like a rock in the pit of Merida's stomach. They made her question everything she thought she had known about her parents, and the plans she had for them right then.

What if she and her mother were more alike than Merida had thought?

What if her mother had truly never wanted to marry anyone at all?

CHAPTER THIRTY-FOUR
Merida

Merida let out a low groan as she hefted a gigantic clay pot out of the washbasin and set it on the floor. She took back every foul thing she ever said about working in the wet larder. She would gladly go back there. Even salting smelly fish was better than this backbreaking work, which was made even more difficult by having to hide all this fur and these claws.

Merida had been relieved when one of Fergus's men had intercepted her and Elinor on their ride to Clan Innes, but it had taken away her opportunity to see Freya again. In addition to trying to come up with a spell to send her home, the witch was also seeking one that would reverse Merida's transformation into a bear. Or, at the very least, slow down its progression.

She had shared her first attempt with Merida when she had visited while Elinor and Fergus were posing as husband and wife, but Freya's tincture had had very little effect so far. Merida could feel her own humanity slipping away with each day that passed.

Still, it was probably for the best that they were prevented from going to the village. Merida had no doubts that she and Elinor would have been exposed if they had gone through with the princess's misguided scheme to pose as nuns from Perth. As the DunBroch clansman had pointed out, no nuns would be away from their nunnery so soon after Whitsunday. The villagers would have surely become suspicious.

Merida was still troubled by the potential threat that lingered over the kingdom, but she was even more concerned about the princess's attempting to uncover it on her own.

They had made their way back to the castle, and Merida went straight to the kitchens. She had been directed to return to her old post by order of the king himself. Except this time, instead of Duncan, Aileen was put in charge of Merida's permanent assignment. And, of course, she had chosen the scullery.

Based on the gossip Merida had heard being passed about—which had not been whispered, but instead spoken loud enough for the entire kitchen to hear—the only reason she had not been thrown out of the castle was that King Douglass had found it somewhere in his heart to let her remain. But Sorcha had given her the full story. She'd shared that one of the king's advisers had cautioned him that it was too close to the start of the Highland Games for him to release a young girl to the forest on her own.

Several of the clans at the southern tip of the kingdom were already making their way toward MacCameron Castle. While she would not have to worry so much about a fellow Scot from this kingdom harming her, she would be vulnerable to the vagabonds and thieves who lurked around the forest during this time of the year, seeking to rob those heading to the games. Merida had no idea which adviser had spoken to the king on her behalf, but she was grateful. It had bought her more time at MacCameron Castle.

During their previous trip to the village, Freya had assured her that she needed only a few more days to work on the spell that would send Merida back home. But what home would she be returning to?

Merida thought about the despondency in Elinor's voice that morning. *I will never be free if I am someone's wife.*

It was the entire reason Merida and her mother had

butted heads: because others wanted to make the decision about her future.

Why had she automatically assumed that her own mother had willingly walked into her union with her father? Maybe Elinor had felt forced to do so. Even if it *had* been love at first sight, or if she had grown to love Fergus over time, Merida now realized that Elinor never really had a say in her future.

But maybe she could now.

A heavy weight settled in the pit of Merida's stomach.

She needed to speak to Freya, although she suspected she already knew what the witch would tell her if she asked the question that had been niggling at her all day.

"What are you doing just standing around?"

Merida whipped around to find one of the scullery maids, Elspeth, waltzing into the room with an armful of dirty bowls. The girl had not liked Merida from the very first day she had arrived to work in the larder, and her disdain had only seemed to grow now that Merida was working in the scullery.

She walked past Merida, clipping her with her elbow.

"Sorry. I did not see you," Elspeth said over her shoulder.

Merida ignored her apology and reached for another clay pot. A second later, Elspeth bumped her in the middle of her back, causing her to drop the pot in the basin and splash water across her frock.

"Hey!" Merida yelled. Her limbs tensed and a flash of heat flushed through her body.

"Oh! Did you move, lass? I did not see you there again," Elspeth said.

"What ails you?" Merida ground out.

"You ail me," the girl spat, all pretense of innocence gone.

Merida just stared at her for a moment, dumbfounded by her admission. She clenched her fists, struggling to maintain her calm.

"What did I ever do to you?" she asked.

The girl set the bowls on the table next to the basin and then plopped her hands on her hips. The malevolence in her expression made Merida's blood run cold.

"Wanna know why I don't like you, lass? 'Tis because I don't trust you. No one does. You show up here from outta nowhere, walking around like you're better than everybody else. You chum up to the princess and have her treating you all special-like. But now look at you." She huffed and peered down her pointy nose at Merida. "You're no different than any of us. Covered in dirty, smelly dishwater."

It took everything Merida had within her not to declare

herself the princess of the kingdom of DunBroch. She knew if she did, Elspeth would only laugh at her, and that made the rage within her flare to life.

The intensity of her fury frightened her; the tenuous hold she had on her emotions was both confusing and disturbing. She did not understand what was happening to her.

"You know nothing about me," Merida told her.

The girl looked her up and down. "You're right about that, lass. No one seems to know anything about you. Except that you came here on a fancy horse and that you've got some sort of sorcery up your sleeve."

"Sorcery?" Merida scoffed. "That is ridiculous."

"Why else would Princess Elinor pick you to be her new maid when everybody knows it should have been Bridget? You must have put a spell on her."

Merida turned away from the girl. Her words were too close to what Merida had originally intended for her mother. When she thought about that first time she'd met Freya, and how she had willingly traded her necklace for a spell to change the queen, it made Merida sick to her stomach. She would have given anything to have that day back.

"Why are you still here?" Elspeth asked. "That bump on your head is healed. You should be gone back to where you came from."

If everything went according to what Merida and Freya had devised, Elspeth would get her wish. But she would not give the girl the satisfaction of knowing that.

"Apparently, King Douglass would like me to remain in his employ," she said instead. "I shall stay on at MacCameron Castle for as long as the king and queen would like me to be here."

The look the girl leveled at her could have scorched the fur growing on Merida's skin. Elspeth pointed to the waning fire underneath the pot of water that was constantly boiled for cleaning.

"Do your job and get more peat for the fire," Elspeth said before stomping out of the room.

Merida yearned to lash out at the sour-faced lass. The urge to do so hummed through her entire being.

Merida sucked in several deep breaths.

Until that point, her transformation had been limited to her body, but now Merida felt it in her soul. She was changing into someone—or *something*—she no longer recognized. And that was far scarier than the sudden appearance of the fur and claws.

Merida *had* to speak to Freya. They must find a way to slow the progression of that spell before it was too late.

But that was not the only reason she needed to speak to Freya as soon as possible. She was the only person who could provide the answers Merida sought. At least she hoped Freya held the answers. If the witch did not know the consequences of Elinor's choosing not to marry, Merida was unsure what she would do.

Another maid, Alesone, came into the washroom. Merida braced herself for another attack, but Alesone's small smile reminded her that not all those in the kitchen hated her. The girl had never been particularly friendly, but she was not overtly nasty like Elspeth, Aileen, and some of the others.

Alesone used a pail to scoop water into the bucket used for mopping the floors.

"The water is a bit tepid," the girl said. "You should get more peat."

"I was just about to," Merida said.

She noticed the girl looking at her hands and quickly shoved them behind her back. The more she filed down these claws, the faster they seemed to grow.

Goodness, but she hoped Freya would be successful in finding that spell, at least.

She grabbed one of the burlap sacks that was used to haul peat from the storage, then headed for the door that led outside. Because peat was used in all areas of the castle—from the kitchens to the fireplaces in each bedchamber—the room that housed it was centrally located. Merida was grateful she had yet to experience having to haul the heavy bags during the rain. She had been told that one had to carry the peat underneath one's kirtle to prevent it from getting wet.

Just as she rounded the structure, she noticed shadows stretching across the ground. A second later, she heard voices. Merida stopped short.

It could not be Aileen again, could it?

But she instantly recognized the girl's nasal tone. Though unlike the previous time she had happened upon Aileen engaged in a whispered conversation with some lad, the other voice did not sound like Elinor's betrothed. They also were not whispering. Whoever the other voice belonged to was a lad with a brogue even thicker than Merida's father's.

"It has to be tonight," the man with the thick brogue said.

"No. 'Tis too soon." This from Aileen. "'Tis better to wait until the other clans are here. That has always been the plan."

"What about the princess?"

Merida's back went ramrod straight at the sound of a third voice, another she did not recognize.

"Are you sure she was with a DunBroch?" the mysterious new voice asked.

"I saw it myself. The big one they call Fergus. They were at the creek. And there was another lass with her, the one with the bandage on her head."

Merida barely managed to hold in her gasp.

"Lachlan suspected something was not right," the man continued. "'Tis why he had me follow the princess after he and the Fraser were here the other night."

Lachlan. It was the princess's betrothed who had set a spy on their trails, not King Douglass.

"Sneaking around with a filthy DunBroch," Aileen said, the word dripping with disgust. "She should be hanged."

Merida clenched her fists so tightly that her claws nearly pierced her skin. She strived to tamp down the fury bubbling up inside her before it caused her to do something irrational.

"Do not say that, Aileen."

"It is true," the girl said.

"I do not understand why you hate the princess so much. You and Elinor used to be the best of friends when you were both wee lasses."

"Not anymore."

"What should I tell Lachlan?" the other man asked, his voice anxious.

"Tell him I will take care of it," Aileen said.

"That is not enough. Lachlan will want to know more."

"He does not need to know any more," Aileen countered. "We stick to the original plan. Now get going."

Merida flattened herself against the castle wall, but the person must have gone in the opposite direction.

"What are you gonna do, Aileen?" the other man asked.

"'Tis no concern of yours. Now go. You need to get back to the stables, Gregory."

Gregory? Where had she heard that name?

Merida waited with her back against the hard stone for several more minutes before she chanced peeking around the corner. They were gone.

She rolled up the burlap sack and stuffed it behind a stone near the castle wall. She did not have time to worry about the dwindling fire in the scullery. She needed to speak to the princess.

The chieftain of Clan Fraser and his son were due to return to the castle that night for another dinner. Merida could not let Elinor dine with her future betrothed without letting her know that he was the one who had sent someone to follow them.

Merida had suspected Lachlan Fraser was not to be trusted from the moment she had first discovered him with Aileen outside the larder. After this latest revelation, there were no lingering doubts. He and Aileen were embroiled in some sort of dalliance, and he was likely having Elinor followed to make sure she did not find out.

Merida raced up the front stairs, the ones she was not supposed to use as a member of the kitchen staff. She could not be concerned with Queen Catriona's barbaric rules. She had to reach Elinor.

But when Merida opened the door to her bedchamber, the princess was nowhere to be found. Instead, she faced a young girl who shared Orla's strong facial features. This must have been Bridget.

"Where might I find the princess?" Merida asked. "I must speak to her."

She braced herself for more of the nastiness she had encountered from Elspeth in the scullery, but she did not sense any malice coming from Bridget.

"The princess just left for dinner," the girl answered.

No.

"Why?" Bridget asked.

Merida tore out of the room without further explanation. She ran down the corridor, dodging servants left and right. Relief soared through her when she spotted Elinor's deep brown hair at the end of the long hallway.

"Princess!" Merida called just as Elinor was preparing to descend the staircase.

The princess whipped around. The flash of delight that lit up her eyes quickly turned to concern.

"You should not be here," Elinor said in a low voice. "I do not care what Father does to me, but I do not want to make you a target of his ire again."

"Do not worry about me," Merida said. "I need to tell you about—"

Just then, a loud crash and yell came from the area of the Great Hall.

Merida and Elinor looked at each other, then took off.

CHAPTER THIRTY-FIVE
Elinor

Elinor's heart thumped wildly as she hastened down the corridor toward the commotion. A million scenarios traveled through her mind as she realized the threat to the kingdom had come to pass. What was it? An attack by a neighboring clan gone rogue? A bear breaking into the castle? The animals were not normally seen much at this time of the year, but the legend of Mor'du claimed that the beast was notorious for wreaking havoc anytime he saw fit.

But it was neither Mor'du nor a rival clan. And the commotion had not come from the Great Hall. Instead, she saw several servants rushing to her father's private parlor.

Elinor stopped in the parlor's entryway to find her father slumped against the side of his second-in-command,

Gawin. The king's most loyal deputy held him up by his arms. A host of servants and men from her father's council stood nearby, all looking shell-shocked.

Elinor entered the room, trying to make sense of what had taken place.

On the floor lay the suit of armor that usually stood just behind the thick oak table where the king conducted his work. The armor was broken into a half dozen pieces. Its iron legs had scattered several feet away, one on either side of her father's worktable. The torso had landed closer, near the feet of the men crowded around him. Most frightening, the battle-ax lay exactly where her father's head would have been if he had been sitting at the table.

Elinor's blood ran cold at the sight of the sharpened ax wedged firmly in the block of wood. The thought of how close the king had come to possibly being beheaded sent tremors racing along her skin.

"What happened?" she finally asked, looking around at the men who surrounded the king.

"'Tis very peculiar, Princess," Gawin said. "The armor has been standing here for years with no issue. There is no reason for it to fall like this."

"Father, have you been harmed?" Elinor asked.

"No, I am fine," King Douglass said. But then she saw it. He *had* been injured. There was blood on his sleeve.

"Get the physician," Elinor said to one of the servants.

She knew her father was shaken when he did not object to her call for the physician, or her taking him by the arm and leading him to a nearby chair.

"And someone call the queen. She'll want to know what has happened," Elinor said to no one in particular. She did not look up to see who had gone to fetch her mother.

"'Tis nothing," King Douglass said.

"'Tis not so," Elinor replied. "You could have been killed."

His severe stare told Elinor that she had gone too far in suggesting he could have been felled by an inanimate object.

"I am just concerned, father," Elinor said. "I never want you to come to any harm." She looked to Gawin. Her father's second-in-command had been by his side as long as Elinor had been alive. "Get Helga in here. Find out if someone from the staff disrupted the suit of armor. Maybe it happened when someone was cleaning it."

That was the only explanation Elinor could come up with. It made no sense that the armor, which had stood in that exact position since she was a little girl, would suddenly come tumbling down.

"We must make sure the other suits of armor around the castle are secure as well," Elinor finished.

Half the men who had been standing around her father

dispersed, while the others began to gather the disjointed pieces of armor. Elinor remained at her father's side until the physician arrived. Her mother followed soon after.

"Whose doing is this?" Queen Catriona asked the moment she entered the room.

"'Tis no one's doing," Elinor said. "It was an accident."

"How bad is the injury?" the queen directed to the physician.

"You would think it would be worse," he answered. "King Douglass, you are one lucky man. Once I sew you up, your wound should heal in a matter of days." The physician winked. "'Tis a good thing you're not taking part in the games. I believe the DunBroch and the Macpherson would best you at the caber toss this year if you were."

He bade farewell when no one laughed at his jest.

Elinor put a hand to her head, overcome with relief that her father's injury was not serious. She would speak to Helga herself about the other suits of armor around the castle. They should inspect the weapons displayed in the Great Hall, as well. There were items all about the castle that were used as adornments but that could prove to be deadly. Maybe they should hang more tapestries and fewer weapons of war on the walls.

Satisfied that her father was being taken care of, Elinor left the study. She found Merida standing just outside the door. The girl's face was ashen, her expression panic-stricken.

"You look as if you have seen a ghost," Elinor said. "What is the matter?"

"How . . . how is the king?" Merida asked.

Elinor expelled a tired but relieved breath. "He shall heal nicely, according to the physician. It could have been much worse had he been sitting behind his desk. The castle staff must inspect every suit of armor on display to make sure they are secure. We cannot allow another accident such as this to come to pass."

"Princess?" Merida said. The shake in her voice sent a tremor down Elinor's spine.

"What is it?" A cold knot formed in her stomach at the fear she saw in the girl's eyes. Something was not right. "Is it about the king?"

Merida nodded. She glanced to her left and then to her right, her teeth sunk into her bottom lip.

She pointed to the MacCameron coat of arms on the wall behind Elinor, then leaned forward and whispered, "I do not think this was an accident."

CHAPTER THIRTY-SIX
Merida

All the pieces began to click into place for Merida as she stood outside the king's private chamber, waiting for word from Elinor about what had happened to King Douglass. As she paced back and forth along the corridor, Merida had glanced over at the shield bearing Clan MacCameron's coat of arms.

That was when she noticed it.

In the center of the family's crest, just underneath two crossed daggers, stood a mighty lion.

"On the day the sun reaches the height faeries cherish, those under the roar's rule will perish."

Under the roar's rule.

The lion—the head of Clan MacCameron—was the one

who roared and the one who ruled. Could it be that the puzzling words written on that parchment Fergus's men had found referred to King Douglass?

It was a feeble explanation, but not implausible.

And the more Merida considered the threat, the more she wondered about the secret meeting she had happened upon between Aileen and the others. One of them had mentioned King Douglass. Was it possible that the threat was not from another clan, but from right here in this very castle?

"Why would you think this was not an accident?" Elinor asked.

Although something in her gut told her she was on the right course, Merida hesitated to say any more. She could not be certain that the conversation she had overheard between Aileen, Gregory, and the spy sent by Lachlan had anything to do with this incident with the king. It would be unwise—dangerous, even—to level such a serious accusation without any proof.

Besides, who would believer her? Her standing among the castle staff was already on shaky ground, with those like Elspeth raising suspicions about why she was still there. And she had garnered the ire of the king himself after her last outing with Elinor, being banished to the kitchens. Who would take her word against two loyal servants who had spent their entire lives in service to King Douglass?

No, she could not tell Elinor what she had overheard. Not without being certain that those three were behind what had happened to the king.

"Merida?" Elinor said. "I asked why you would think that it was not an accident. What else could it have been?"

"Of course you are right," Merida said. "Do not mind me. I am just . . . just tired."

The princess stared at her with a mixture of confusion and suspicion. She tilted her head to the side, her eyes narrowing as she studied Merida's face.

Merida's anxiety grew with each second that passed. As much as she loathed the scullery, she yearned to escape to it. Anything to avoid the challenging look the princess had leveled her way.

"I do not think so," Elinor said after some time. "I believe there is something you are not telling me. What is it, Merida? What do you know about Father's accident?"

It would have been dangerous to accuse Aileen and the others of attempting to harm the king, but she could still tell the princess what she had overhead and allow her to draw her own conclusions. Elinor must understand that her future betrothed was not to be trusted.

"I do not know anything about the king's accident," Merida started. "But you are right, Princess. There is something I have withheld from you. It is about Lach—"

"What are *you* doing here?"

They both turned at the sound of Queen Catriona's caustic voice.

"Mother!" Elinor squeaked, clearly caught off guard by the queen. Merida had not heard her leave the king's parlor, either.

"How . . . how is Father?" Elinor asked.

The queen ignored her. She homed in on Merida.

"You were warned to stay in the kitchens," Queen Catriona said as she advanced. "It is because of you that the princess was seen in a compromising position with a DunBroch."

Elinor gasped. "I have not been compromised by the DunBroch."

"Silence!" the queen snapped. "Not another word." She turned her attention back to Merida. "Have you any idea the scandal it would cause if news that the Princess of MacCameron Kingdom was seen with a DunBroch were to make its way around the villages?"

"I thought there was a peace alliance?" Elinor asked.

Queen Catriona blasted her daughter with a blistering stare.

Merida's heart jumped into her throat.

Why would Elinor openly challenge her mother this way? She must have known how the queen would react.

But it was clear that Elinor no longer cared about her mother's reaction.

"You are not to be near the princess for the rest of your time here," the queen said. "If I learn that you have disobeyed my orders, I will have you tossed out of the castle. I do not care what dangers may be out in the forest. And once the Highland Games have concluded, you are to leave this castle and never return." She stared down at Merida and, in a voice that brooked no argument, asked, "Have I made myself clear?"

Merida swallowed and nodded. "Yes, Queen Catriona." She looked to the princess. "Elinor?"

"Yes, Mother," Elinor answered.

Satisfied, the queen nodded brusquely and said, "Have Bridget ready the green velvet gown for tonight's dinner. The Fraser and your future betrothed will be here soon."

Merida nearly growled at the mention of Lachlan Fraser. To know that her mother was only days away from being betrothed to such a scoundrel made her blood run cold.

Thank goodness the union would not take place until after the reading of the marriage banns, which was done on each of the three Sundays prior to the wedding. Still, an official betrothal would make it that much more difficult for Elinor to pry herself from Lachlan.

They both stood there and watched as Queen Catriona took her leave.

Elinor started to walk away, but Merida caught her arm. She was willing to risk the queen's ire if it meant warning Elinor about Lachlan Fraser.

But the princess was having none of it. She glanced quickly at Merida and then to her mother, shaking her head.

"Elinor," the queen called, not bothering to look back.

The princess wrenched her arm free from Merida, but before she could walk away, Merida imparted a final warning.

"Be careful," she whispered.

CHAPTER THIRTY-SEVEN
Merida

The kitchens at MacCameron Castle buzzed with energy as the staff went about the preparations for the evening's feast. No one had mentioned it, but they all knew the significance of this gathering—this night. It was the final informal courting dinner before their princess's betrothal was officially announced. The girls who worked with Merida in the scullery could not contain their excitement. It was a constant stream of whispers and giggles and contented sighs.

Merida did not share their enthusiasm.

Her stomach felt as if it were tied into a million knots. She was unsure what to expect of tonight's meal. Was the king in danger? If someone employed in the castle was indeed behind the parlor accident, did they intend to finish the job that the suit of armor had failed to do?

The knots in her stomach tightened.

It wasn't until after Elinor had left her in the corridor—once Merida had returned to the kitchens and noticed Sorcha carrying a bag of flour from the dry larder—that another thought hit her. The dessert that had been served at the end of the last meal the Frasers attended! She recalled how Aileen had made King Douglass a special cake, and how the king had fallen ill soon after.

Had that been the first attempt on his life?

It was unfathomable, yet . . . it was clear that Aileen was involved in whatever was going on here. And that whatever it was, it was nothing good.

Another intense flash of fury swelled within her chest.

Merida wrapped her arms around her torso, as if she could shield herself from the wave of panic and uncontrollable rage that had begun to crash over her. She feared that what she had hoped was only a foolish notion was, in fact, a very real threat. The king was indeed in danger.

She could no longer disregard that unnerving feeling that had crept up when she stumbled upon Aileen and Lachlan. Or when she had overheard the maid speaking with the man who had been sent by Lachlan to spy on the princess, and with Gregory.

It had taken her a while to recall where she had heard his name, but finally it came to her that Gregory was Aileen's brother. Elinor had mention that Aileen's brother was the one who had taught them how to use the secret entrance to get into the bailey.

Even the way Aileen looked at the princess, with thinly veiled contempt, should have been a clue that the girl had been up to something.

But these were all just suspicions, of course. Merida found herself in the same position she had been in all along: that of an outsider attempting to level serious charges against two longtime members of MacCameron Castle's staff. If she imparted everything she knew and suspected to the princess, would Elinor even believe her?

It was a chance she had to take. If something were to happen to the king, Merida would never forgive herself.

And what if it did not stop with the king? What if Elinor and Queen Catriona were also in danger?

Merida glanced at the girls at the washbasin. She figured she could slip out of the scullery without any of them noticing. They were too busy chatting and laughing and not paying any attention to her. But before she could leave, Sorcha bounded into the room with a huge smile on her face.

" 'Tis time to go," she said.

The other girls let out a loud squeal, set down the dishes they had been drying, and scurried out of the room.

"Go where?" Merida asked with caution.

"Did no one tell you? We all have to act as servers tonight."

Oh, goodness. Not again. The last time she served the royal family their meal, she had made a mess of things. And that was before she had to hide the hair and claws that continued to grow, no matter how much she tried to stop them.

"Why so?" Merida asked.

"Because half the kitchen staff is getting the food ready for the Highland Games. 'Tis tradition that the king and queen provide a hearty meal for the clans that attend the games."

"Where are they preparing the meals for the games? I should like to help." It was preferable to the Great Hall.

Sorcha was shaking her head. "Do not worry, lass. You will get to help with that, too. It takes a lot to feed hundreds of hungry warriors. But not yet. You're needed in the Great Hall. Let us go."

Merida hesitated a moment, wondering if it was too late to feign a sudden stomach ailment. But Sorcha was already on her way out of the scullery.

"'Tis no use," Merida said with a sigh.

There was at least one upside to serving the royal family at dinner tonight. She would be able to keep an eye on Lachlan Fraser. She just hoped she could keep control of herself. If there was anyone who could trigger the sudden powerful fury that had begun surging within her, it was her mother's future betrothed.

By the time Merida arrived in the kitchen, platters of roasted pheasant, venison stew, and pickled herring were making their way out to the Great Hall.

"Where have you been?" Aileen snapped.

Merida jumped. "I—"

She could not form words as she stared at the woman who was possibly in the process of committing treason against MacCameron Kingdom. What could cause a person to turn against their own?

Aileen shoved a bowl of roasted beets into Merida's hands. "Take that out."

As she entered the Great Hall, Merida noticed that those seated at the table were in the same positions they had occupied several nights ago. However, there were three additional guests. A young girl who looked to be two or three years younger than Merida's sixteen years and a young man about her age sat on opposite ends of Lachlan. Merida could tell by their strong jawlines and tawny hair that the three were related. They must have been his siblings. It stood to reason that the demure woman to the chieftain's right was his wife.

Their presence was yet another indication of the importance of this meal. A sign that these two families were on the precipice of being tied together.

A marriage to this man could *not* be her mother's fate.

Merida felt Queen Catriona's eyes on her as she followed the other girls to the table. For once, she *wished* the queen would question her presence so that she could tell her it was at Aileen's bidding that she had been called to serve. But the queen remained silent, her regal nose lifted as she tracked Merida's steps, then settled on her gloves.

Merida set the beets on the table and soundlessly retreated, returning to the kitchen to bring out another dish. One by one, they would clear the plates as those enjoying their dinner finished each course.

Merida's stomach growled with pangs as she watched the MacCamerons and Frasers feast. She was not even particularly hungry, having already eaten her dinner of boiled carrots, turnips, and venison scraps—the meat a welcome surprise. But she was hungry for the scene taking place before her. She had taken the joys of sharing a meal with her family for granted. Not for the first time, an overwhelming sense of homesickness stole over her.

But this time, Merida was not so sure she *would* get home. If there would be a home to get to, even.

She closed her eyes, shutting out thoughts of what would become of her life—of her entire existence—if she posed the question that had been swirling in her head to Elinor.

Despite her growing affection for Fergus, if given the choice, would she truly choose not to marry anyone at all?

Merida's eyes shot open when she heard Lachlan's low voice informing the table that he needed to be excused. She studied him as he rose from his seat.

"I shall return in a moment," Merida whispered to Sorcha.

The girl eyed her curiously. But when Merida put a hand to her stomach, indicating that she needed the privy chamber, Sorcha stifled a giggle and nodded for her to be on her way. Merida quickly slipped out of the Great Hall. She caught sight of Lachlan's tall frame just as he turned the corner.

Her heart hammering, she scurried down the corridor, moving as swiftly and quietly as she could.

She halted in surprise when she saw Lachlan enter the privy chamber, having been certain that he'd used it only as an excuse to see Aileen.

Maybe Aileen was already there. Maybe they had

made previous plans to meet between the second and third courses.

Merida slipped between one of the suits of armor and the wall, then waited for Lachlan to emerge. When he did after just a few minutes, she remained in her hiding place, anticipating Aileen's exit from the privy. But no one else left the small chamber.

Merida looked up and down the corridor before stepping from behind the armor and tiptoeing to the privy chamber. Her blood pounded in her ears. Sweat formed on her gloved palms. That anxious feeling in her stomach intensified, the knots twisting and tightening, leaving her breathless.

What would she say if she encountered Aileen or Gregory or the spy? She had been working in MacCameron Castle too long to use ignorance of the castle's layout as an excuse, or to pretend that she did not know that the staff was not to use the same privy that guests used.

She would figure something out. This was too important to allow fear to get in her way.

But when she entered the privy, it was empty. Lachlan Fraser had not left dinner for a clandestine meeting with one of his cohorts.

Merida knew she should be relieved, but instead it only made her more anxious. And confused. What if she had been wrong about Lachlan? Could those conversations she had overheard between Aileen and the others have had nothing to do with King Douglass or the princess?

She had heard their names mentioned, but it *was* possible that it was nothing untoward. Aileen had said that whatever was to be done needed to take place when the other clans were around. What if Lachlan was planning some grand gesture for Elinor that was tied to the betrothal announcement, and he wanted to make sure all in the kingdom were there to witness it? A surprise gift for the princess would also explain why he had been whispering with Aileen in the corridor, if he had asked her to coordinate it.

And here Merida was, accusing them of treason. What was the penalty for bringing a false accusation against someone?

She did not want to find out.

As she returned to the Great Hall, Merida fell in line with the others, taking one of the dishes Sorcha carried from her hands.

"Your stomach still troubling you, lass? You do not have the flux, do you?" the girl whispered.

Merida shook her head. "I think I ate too much of the venison. It had been so long since I had a piece of meat; I got a bit carried away."

"Ah." Sorcha nodded. "Too much of a good thing ain't always good for you."

They carried the dishes to the table, serving what must have been the fourth course. The king, Chieftain Fraser, and Lachlan discussed the upcoming Highland Games while the women sat quietly, picking at their meals.

Well, *most* of the women. Queen Catriona would not allow anyone to silence her. She added to the commentary, remarking on the past year's winners and predicting which member of Clan MacCameron would prove to be victorious this year.

Just as the dinner seemed to be winding down, the chieftain said, "There is one more thing I would like to discuss with you, King Douglass."

The king casually ran his thumb along the rim of his glass. "And what would that be?"

The chieftain looked first to his wife and then to his son. "We think it best that we do away with the reading of the wedding banns."

Elinor dropped her fork. The clatter rang out throughout the Great Hall.

"Sorry," Elinor mumbled.

"Why would we do away with the reading of the wedding banns?" Queen Catriona asked. "It is tradition."

Merida wanted to know the same. It was more than just a tradition; the public proclamation of an impending marriage was required by the church. The couple's intentions were made known three weeks prior to the wedding to allow any objections to the union to be made. It was unheard of to ignore the practice.

"Traditions stand only because they are not challenged. And the children have been promised since birth; there is no mystery that they shall be betrothed. Besides, Douglass is the king. He can challenge the tradition."

"Why would he?" the queen asked. "What reason is there to not read the banns?"

Ignoring the queen's questions, the chieftain looked to King Douglass. "Think about the show of strength it would present if Princess Elinor and Lachlan were to marry *at* the Highland Games. And then, in a few weeks' time, we will hold a splendid gathering celebrating their nuptials."

"You are suggesting the wedding take place at the games?" the king asked.

"Yes. This union between the MacCamerons and the Frasers, on display for all the kingdom to see? It would fortify the alliance between our clans."

Merida watched as the blood seemed to drain from Elinor's face.

"That does sound appealing," the king said.

"Douglass," Queen Catriona said. "Think of the implications. People will assume she is getting married so soon because she *must* get married so soon."

Elinor's pale cheeks instantly reddened at the queen's words.

"No one would dare make such claims to the princess," the chieftain said.

"But they would make them behind her back," the queen retorted. "Speculation would spread throughout the villages and surrounding clans like wildfire."

"Not if I say there is to be no speculation."

"You overestimate your power as king. You cannot change what people think. This cannot—"

"That is enough!" The king slammed his hand on the wooden table.

The queen's face was a mask of stone, but the cold fury burning in her eyes told Merida exactly how she felt about the king's pronouncement. And possibly about the king himself.

King Douglass looked to the chieftain. "I shall think this over tonight. We will revisit it tomorrow, at the start of the games."

CHAPTER THIRTY-EIGHT
Elinor

Elinor sat in silence, feeling smothered by the tension that continued to permeate the room following the exchange between the king and queen. She was counting down the seconds to when the chieftain of Clan Fraser and his family would make their departure. Now that the dessert had been served, it would not be very long. The sooner they left, the sooner she would be able to do so.

She had to get to her chamber. And then she had to go. She had no choice.

An anguished cry caught in Elinor's throat.

The decision was even more difficult than it had been just a fortnight earlier. She had thought there was nothing more important than her freedom, but knowing that her kingdom was under threat made her choice that much harder.

Unbidden, the image of that child from the village popped into her mind. What would become of him and the others on MacCameron land living in dire straits? She was going off in search of others to help when there were many in her own kingdom who were in need.

Why? Why was she doing this?

She glanced at Lachlan and immediately had her answer.

But then she thought about Fergus and how she would be leaving him, also. Elinor could not fathom a time in which a DunBroch was a reason to make her want to give up her much sought-after freedom and remain in her kingdom. Yet, if she were promised to Fergus instead of Lachlan, Elinor was not sure she would be considering this new life in the Lowlands.

No, she knew she would not be, because she and Fergus would work together to save this kingdom. And then they would rule it in a way that put the people of MacCameron Kingdom above all else. Together.

"It is time for us to take our leave," the Fraser chieftain said. He looked to King Douglass. "You shall give thought to what we discussed?"

"I shall," her father answered.

Both men avoided looking at Queen Catriona, but

Elinor did not need to see her mother's face to know she was incensed. She could feel fury emanating from her. The fact that the king and queen had allowed the Frasers to witness their argument still shocked her. Her mother, for one, was always conscious of what outsiders thought about the royal family. But not tonight. Tonight she raged without any consideration of their dinner guests, or what they might share with others.

Elinor was certain the argument would continue once their guests departed, but she could not afford to stay in the Great Hall to hear it. Time was of the essence.

The moment the chieftain and his family left, Elinor excused herself and ran up to her bedchamber. She began pulling kirtles and her earasaid from her wardrobe. She threw three tunics onto the pile, along with a pair of hose and a skirt. She could not pack too much. Not only did she not have time, but she did not want anything weighing her down.

She held in the sob that tried to escape at the thought of never seeing her home again. This was likely the last time she would see Merida, as well. And Fergus.

It felt as if a hand squeezed around her heart.

She would have loved to see him compete against the other clansmen.

This was not the time for tears. She *had* to leave that night, before her father married her off to Lachlan Fraser.

She lifted the tapestry she had been working on for months from the wooden frame that held it and rolled it up. But when she walked to the bed, she could not stuff it in with the rest of her things. The tapestry was not hers to take. It belonged to the castle. It should hang with the others that told her family's story, the rich history of the MacCamerons. Maybe her mother would finish it or assign the task to one of the maids.

It is not a maid's duty. It is mine.

Elinor swallowed past the lump that had stalled in her throat. She'd known this time would come. From the moment she had made the decision to run away, she knew there would be things she needed to leave behind. Bits and pieces of her life that would be difficult to part with, but that had to be left all the same.

Like her family.

She sat on the edge of the bed and buried her face in the tapestry, unable to stop the tears from falling. She had spent hours and hours imagining the amazing adventure that awaited her and the freedom it would bring, but she had never allowed herself to dwell on everything she would have to leave behind. Now that the time was here, it was all she could think about.

And Fergus, of course. These days, thoughts of him were never far from her mind. He was proud, but in a way that had grown charming. And his teasing, while infuriating, had made her smile more in the few days since she had known him than she had in ages.

Could she truly see herself married to Fergus DunBroch?

Yes. She could see it all too well. It looked like years of laughter and delighting in the joys of this beautiful kingdom together. Maybe she could talk to her father, negotiate with him. Maybe she could convince him that they should unite with one of the other clans. Like Clan DunBroch. Then maybe she would not have to leave.

"Stop such foolishness," Elinor whispered.

Of all the clans in MacCameron Kingdom, Clan DunBroch was likely the last one her father would choose to form such a close alliance with. It was not as if it mattered to him that she could not abide the man she had been promised to. What she wanted played no part in the decision. It was tradition.

Why did this stupid, unfair tradition of promising children to others—at birth, no less—even exist? And why did it have to be Lachlan Fraser?

She could sit here and continue to bandy about these questions that would never have a satisfactory answer, or she could leave. Those were her two choices. If she remained, by this time on Sunday she could very well be Lachlan's wife.

"That cannot happen," Elinor said.

She stood and gathered the garments she meant to take with her, wrapping them up in the counterpane from her bed and securing them with two belts. She took one last look around her bedchamber, squelching the mournful cry that nearly escaped. She did not have time to mourn right now. She would do so later, after she had put some distance between herself and the castle.

With one last look, Elinor turned for the door.

And screamed.

CHAPTER THIRTY-NINE
Elinor

"You scared me, lass!" Elinor hissed as she took Merida by the arm and tugged her inside the bedchamber. "I was just coming to get you." She looked up and down the corridor to make sure no one had heard her scream, then closed the door and whirled to face Merida. "I have gathered all that I will take with me to the Lowlands. We shall leave as soon as the groomsmen complete their final check of the horses tonight. We should be able to leave within the hour. Maybe before—"

"You cannot go," Merida said, cutting her off.

Elinor took a step back, unsure if she had heard her correctly. She took notice of the strained expression on the girl's face.

"What do you mean? We *must* go," Elinor said. "That has been the plan from the very beginning. You knew that when you agreed to remain at MacCameron Castle."

Merida shook free from her hold and began to pace back and forth in front of the hearth. "You cannot," she said, emphatically shaking her head. "Not yet."

"I must," Elinor retorted. Guilt washed over her at the thought of leaving MacCameron Castle when there was still a threat hanging over it. "I know I said I would not leave before the threat to the kingdom had been eliminated, but I have no choice." She pointed to the door and the Great Hall beyond it. "You heard them at dinner. My father and the chieftain mean to have me married to Lachlan during the games. They want to do away with reading the banns."

"I know. I heard them," Merida said. "But—"

"But nothing!" Elinor shouted.

She tried to stave off the panic and disappointment rising within her chest. She had thought she could rely on Merida. The girl had been a strong ally in the time since Elinor had rescued her in the woods, but now she was turning on her.

Would there ever be a time when she could count on someone?

There was, she decided. The time was right now. She could count on herself.

She would do this alone. It would have been better to have Merida there to guide her, at least on the first part of her journey, but if the girl would not join her, so be it.

"I will go alone," Elinor said. "I have learned enough to get me to the Lowlands. I will take Alistair and we will be gone within the hour."

Merida rushed over to her and grabbed her by the shoulders.

"Please, Princess."

Elinor wrestled away from her. "Let go. You're hurting me."

Merida looked at her hands, then tucked them within the folds of her kirtle.

"Listen to me," Merida said. "You must trust me."

"Why should I? You said you would help me, and now you are going back on your word. You are just like the others," Elinor said, unable to hide the vitriol in her voice. *Unwilling* to hide it.

A pained look flashed across Merida's face.

"You know better than to think that," the girl said. "I am nothing like the other people in your life. I said I would help you, and I will." She squeezed her eyes tight, then sent Elinor a pleading look. "This journey is as important to me as it is to you. I want to get back home, remember? But if we leave now, something awful may happen. You cannot leave yet."

Her reference to home reminded Elinor of the information she had withheld regarding her actual origin, but before she could bring it up, Merida continued.

"I believe I have figured out the threat to the kingdom. But it is more than just the kingdom at risk. I believe your father is the true target."

"Why would you think that? My father is the most protected man in this kingdom."

"Yet he was almost beheaded by a suit of armor in his own home," Merida pointed out. "And he became violently ill at dinner the other night."

Elinor slowly shook her head. She refused to accept what she was hearing. "You are mistaken," she said. "Those were accidents. The riddle on the parchment—it portends an attack by Mor'du."

"Princess, listen to me. I fear someone in this castle—someone your family knows and trusts—is trying to kill the king."

CHAPTER FORTY
Merida

Merida could tell by the princess's somber expression that she was finally starting to understand the gravity of their situation. The color drained from her face.

This was not the way she had planned to tell Elinor of her suspicions, but after watching her leave the Great Hall in such haste, Merida feared the princess would do something rash, like make good on her promise to run away from MacCameron Kingdom. She knew she had to get to her as quickly as possible. She had to stop her.

"No," Elinor said now, shaking her head.

The horrified look in her eyes pierced Merida's soul. It was as if the princess was pleading with her to be wrong.

She considered the staff at Castle DunBroch, people

whom she had known all her life. Maids like Maudie, who had helped care for her since she was but a wee lass. She thought about how devastated she would have been to learn that one of them had become a traitor, was trying to kill her father. The mere idea of such a thing was too painful to bear.

"I hate that I must share this news with you. I know this is difficult to hear."

"No," Elinor said again. "You must be mistaken. You *have* to be."

"I am not," Merida said. "Think back to the parchment. It said those under the roar's rule will perish. Now, think about Clan MacCameron's crest. What is on it?"

Elinor's eyes widened. "A . . . lion," she said. "A roaring lion."

"The parchment was a signal, Princess. I believe it was a secret message meant for someone who has been tasked with carrying out the assassination of King Douglass."

Merida debated whether to reveal whom on the staff she suspected. She wanted to wait until she had more proof, but she was running out of time. She would need to give Elinor more if she wanted the princess to believe her.

"And I believe I know who is behind it," Merida said.

"Who?"

She took a breath, then said, "Aileen and Lachlan."

"What?" Elinor took a step back.

"I overheard them talking the night Lachlan and the chieftain first came to dinner, when I was still working in the larder." The words rushed out of her, everything she remembered of that night. "Lachlan left the Great Hall to use the privy chamber, but instead of using the privy, he met with Aileen in the small corridor that leads from the wet larder to the kitchens. Neither knew I was there."

Elinor sucked in a quick breath. "What . . . what did they say?"

"I do not know," Merida admitted. "They were whispering."

The princess's brows furrowed with her incredulous frown. "You see two people whispering and assume that they were conspiring to kill the king?"

Merida looked back at the door. The wood was thick, but not thick enough for her peace of mind. She gestured with her head, urging Elinor to follow her deeper into the room, to the space between the wardrobe and the wall.

"It is more than just the two of them whispering," Merida said. "Ask yourself *why*. Why would Aileen and Lachlan be whispering in the corridor together, away from everyone, if they did not have something to hide?"

"Maybe they *do* have something to hide," Elinor said. "Maybe they have been carrying on a secret affair." She released a huff. "I would not care if they were. I would encourage it, even. If Aileen wants Lachlan, she can have him."

Her words gave Merida pause. Hadn't she thought the same thing initially? Could she have gotten this entire situation wrong?

But if this was about an affair between Aileen and Lachlan, it made no sense for the girl to involve her brother.

"That is not it, Princess. Or, rather, that is not the only thing going on between those two, if they are indeed entangled in some type of dalliance."

"It makes more sense than your presumptions. You have no proof that the two are trying to harm the king."

"Yes, I do!" Merida whispered fiercely.

"What evidence do you have, other than some riddle? Lions are not the only things that roar, lass. So do bears. And it is far easier to believe that Mor'du is ready to attack than it is to believe that Aileen would plot to kill my father."

Merida deliberated only a moment before deciding to lay out the feeble bits of evidence she had to back up her claim.

"I need you to consider all that has happened, Princess. Your father fell ill just moments after Aileen and Lachlan's meeting," she pointed out. "She served him a special dessert that night, remember? He was the only one to eat it and the only one to fall ill."

"That still does not mean—"

"She poisoned him," Merida said. "I know she did."

Elinor's head drew back. When she spoke, her voice was shaky.

"Merida, do you realize what you are saying? What you are doing? You are accusing Aileen of wanting to commit murder. And not just any murder, but murder of the King of MacCameron Kingdom. This is nothing to take lightly."

"I am not taking it lightly," Merida said. "I am very, very serious, Princess. Aileen and Lachlan cannot be trusted around King Douglass. And they are not the only ones. There are very likely more involved."

Her heart had begun to slam against the walls of her chest. She could be hanged for making such an accusation, especially if it were proven to be false.

But she felt it in her bones. Aileen was up to something.

Elinor looked to the bed, where her counterpane had been stuffed with something—likely clothing—and wrapped with belts.

"You cannot leave," Merida repeated. "Not yet. Not without warning your father."

"You want *me* to warn the king of *your* suspicions? Are you mad?" Elinor asked.

"He will not listen to me. He does not trust me."

Elinor's eyes trailed from the top of Merida's head to

her slippered feet, as if seeing her in a new light. "Maybe he should not," she said. "Maybe I should not, either."

"Princess—"

"Why did you not tell me you were from the Lowlands? You led me to believe you were of the DunBroch clan that belonged to my father's kingdom. You have been lying to me this entire time."

Merida shook her head. "No."

"It does not matter." Elinor waved her off. "I do not care. And I shall not accuse Aileen of attempting to murder the king simply because she and Lachlan had a clandestine meeting in the corridor." She released a strangled laugh. "Do you think I am immune from punishment? That I would not face consequences for making such a charge?"

Merida wanted to say that the charges would not be as harsh as any she would face. The king would not have his only daughter hanged.

But if she found herself in Elinor's position, would she trust a girl she had known for less than a fortnight? A girl she had found injured in the woods? A girl she knew had been lying to her?

No, she would not. Not without additional proof.

"There is more," Merida said.

Elinor looked to her with raised brows.

Merida was even less sure of the information she was

about to share, but she saw no other way. Her mother's stubborn refusal to see Aileen and her future betrothed for the traitors they were forced her hand. She must make Elinor see reason, and this seemed to be the only way to do so.

"It was not only the meeting with Lachlan in the corridor," Merida cautiously continued. "I heard Aileen, Gregory, and a man *Lachlan*—not your father—sent to spy on you, together. They were outside, near the scullery. They were discussing some sort of plan. When the spy asked Aileen about carrying it out, she said that she would take care of everything."

"What would she take care of?"

Merida hesitated only a moment before she said, "You."

CHAPTER FORTY-ONE
Merida

Merida stepped away from the wardrobe, giving Elinor space to process. It was not the easiest news, that one was possibly at the center of one's childhood friend's nefarious plans. But she had kept the princess in the dark for too long. Elinor needed to know what she was dealing with.

"I do not know if she meant you harm," Merida said. She began to pace again. "At least, Aileen did not say specifically that she would harm you, just that she would take care of it. And, because she was speaking with the man Lachlan had sent to spy on you, I assume that taking care of *it* meant taking care of *you*."

Elinor went over to her bed and sat on the edge of it. Her forehead furrowed, creating a deep vee in its center.

"So this has nothing to do with my father?" she asked. "It is I whom Aileen is after?"

"That is the part that I cannot make sense of," Merida said. "Nothing has befallen you, yet when I overheard Aileen speaking with the others, you were the one they were discussing." She glanced at Elinor. "She said very vile things about you. Because she believes you were sneaking around with a DunBroch."

"Let her," Elinor said. "I do not care what anyone thinks of me anymore."

"But you must care about what people may *do* to you, or do to your family. I do not know if harming the king is Aileen's method of hurting you, but I am certain that she and Lachlan are up to something."

Elinor stared at the floor in silence. After several moments, she looked up at Merida. "What do you suggest I do? Am I to stay and allow this marriage to Lachlan to take place? What if you are wrong?"

Merida was certain she was not wrong. She felt it in her gut. But she also did not know where to go from there.

They found themselves in a precarious situation. If they were to inform the king that he was in danger, it could tip off Aileen and the others. They could decide to abandon their scheme and charge the princess and Merida with making false accusations. It would be Merida's word against Aileen's. She had no doubt whom the king would believe.

Or, worse, Aileen and Lachlan could escalate their plan.

Although, an escalation might not be necessary, because Merida had a feeling the time was near. She was certain they were preparing to carry out whatever they had in store for the princess or the king during the Highland Games. She remembered Aileen telling the spy that it would be better to wait until the other clans arrived, probably so that they could lay blame on one of them. "Well?" Elinor said.

"I am not sure," Merida admitted. "But there is someone in a nearby village who I believe can help."

"You are not going to leave me here," Elinor warned.

"I will be back," she said. "But this person can see things that others cannot."

Elinor eyed her suspiciously. "Are you going to meet a wise woman?"

The leeriness in her voice made Merida rethink her answer. When it came to her parents, her mother courted a belief in witches, wisps, and whimsy far more than her father ever had, but Merida was unsure when that belief started. It was better to keep Freya's identity unknown.

"It is someone who may have answers." Merida squeezed her hands. "Trust me."

"You promise you will come back?"

"I promise," Merida assured her.

Then she took off.

When Merida reached the stables, Ewan tried to question where she was going so late in the evening, but she did not take the time to answer him. She climbed onto Angus's back and charged out of the stable.

She galloped at breakneck speed until she reached Clan Innes's village. She rode past the blacksmith and cobbler shops, heading straight for the small wood-carver storefront.

She quickly tied Angus's reins to a post in front of the store, then entered, calling out for the witch.

"Freya! Freya, I must speak to you."

The front room, which had been bare the last time she was here, was now crowded with hundreds of wood-carvings, just as the witch's cottage had been when she stumbled upon it in the forest. The only thing it was empty of was people.

"Freya?" Merida called, venturing deeper into the shop.

"The shop is closed for the day. Oh, it is you again!"

Merida whirled around. It was the older woman, Freya's mother. She wore the same kind smile as before.

"Hello," Merida said. "Please, where is your daughter? I must speak to her."

"Oh, I'm sorry. Freya is not here, lass. But she must have known you would be calling on her. She told me to tell you that she has gone north to Sutherland to gather supplies. Is she making you a tisane? She tends to go to Sutherland when making a new concoction."

"She is attempting to make one for me, yes," Merida muttered.

Her shoulders slumped, along with her spirits. She did not know enough about the politics of this kingdom. She wanted Freya's guidance to help her figure out if there was a way to keep Clan Fraser out of the games.

But she could not rely on Freya every time she was in a bind. She had to learn to rely on herself.

Still, she needed to talk to someone who knew more about how the Highland Games were conducted, and there was only one other person Merida could think of who could assist her.

She left the wood-carver's shop and, within moments, was back in the forest, heading for Clan DunBroch's camp. She arrived in record time.

The few remaining clansmen were gathered around a fire. One of them was roasting a hare on a spit. Another was filling drinking horns with what looked like ale from a leather drinking skin.

She did not want to break up their party, but . . .

"Fergus!" she called.

He looked up from the bow he was shaping with a whittling tool.

"It is late, lass. What are you doing here?"

"The princess is in trouble," Merida said.

He set the bow on the ground and stood. "What do you mean? In trouble how?"

"I think I have figured out the threat to the kingdom," Merida said.

She laid everything bare, pointing out how the Clan MacCameron crest fit with the riddle they'd found written on the parchment, and then relaying the snippets of conversation she had overheard between Aileen, Gregory, and Lachlan's spy. She also gave him the details surrounding Aileen and Lachlan's meeting in the corridor the night the king fell ill.

Unlike Elinor, Fergus did not question the veracity of Merida's suspicions.

"We must go to the king," he said.

"We cannot," she told him. "We cannot allow Aileen and Lachlan to become aware of our suspicions. Also, there may be others on the staff at MacCameron Castle who are involved. I do not know. What if someone in the king's council is part of Aileen and Lachlan's plan?"

"But we now know that the king is truly in danger.

His guards must know so they can protect him. So they can protect the queen and princess." Fergus punched his open hand, grinding his knuckles against his palm. "Something like this can pitch the entire kingdom into chaos." He looked down at Merida with a frown. "Are you sure about this, lass?"

Merida nodded. She sucked in a deep breath and released it. Then she said, "I believe the next attempt on the king's life will take place at the Highland Games."

He nodded. "You're probably right, if what you overheard is true."

"Is there a way to disqualify Clan Fraser from participating in the games? From attending the games at all?"

Fergus was shaking his head before she could finish her question. "'Tis the clan's right to attend as a member of MacCameron Kingdom." His eyes darkened. "And there is the matter of the princess's betrothal. 'Tis to take place at the games, as is tradition."

Merida was taken aback by the sharp edge to his voice at the mention of the betrothal. It was reassuring. If he felt this way about the princess's upcoming betrothal, Elinor must have meant more to him than he had been letting on.

"There is something else," she said. "The chieftain suggested they do away with the reading of the wedding banns."

Now it was Fergus's turn to look taken aback. "Why so?"

"He would like the princess and Lachlan to be married at the games."

Fergus froze, a blend of alarm and anger shrouding his face. "There is no proper reason for such a hasty ceremony," he said. He looked to Merida. "The question is why."

"There is only one explanation I can think of," she said.

Fergus spoke the answer before she could, horror shining in his eyes.

"If the princess and Lachlan are married, and something befalls the king and queen, then he will assume the position of leader of MacCameron Kingdom. Lachlan will become king."

CHAPTER FORTY-TWO
Merida

Merida tried to tame her heart's chaotic thumping in the time it took to ride from the DunBroch camp to MacCameron Castle, but it was no use. With every yard Angus's powerful legs ate up on the mad dash through the forest, apprehension about what could go wrong steadily built, until it was all-consuming. The plan she and Fergus had hatched continued to play in her mind.

The first part of their strategy was to determine how Princess Elinor felt about Gawin's loyalty. Fergus told her he'd had dealings with the king's second-in-command on several occasions and believed the man could be trusted. If Elinor felt the same way, Merida and Fergus would inform Gawin of their suspicions.

Merida was still unsure about trusting anyone on the king's staff, but Fergus's qualms regarding security were legitimate. Someone close to the king needed to know about the threat. To keep those charged with protecting King Douglass in the dark would have been irresponsible. It could, in fact, cost her grandfather his life.

But first, Merida needed to return to her duties in the kitchens. It had to appear as if nothing were amiss, as if no one suspected that Aileen and her cohorts were up to something nefarious.

She looked to the sky, determining that the others were likely still in the scullery, cleaning up after the evening meal. She would put in her hours at the washbasin, then seek out the princess.

Merida returned Angus to the stable without encountering any staff. She shoved a pile of hay in front of him as a well-earned treat for the hard riding he had done today, and then she took off for the kitchens.

The moment Merida entered the scullery, she was accosted by Aileen and Elspeth.

"There she is," Elspeth said.

Merida backed away as Aileen advanced on her. Before she could comprehend what the girl was up to, Aileen reached out and ripped away the shawl that covered Merida's head. Her red hair tumbled down around her shoulders, framing her face.

Gasps reverberated around the kitchens.

"I told you," Elspeth said. "She's a dirty DunBroch."

Dread sank to the pit of Merida's gut even as fury welled within her. She had been exposed.

"You had better explain yourself, lass," Aileen said. "What is a DunBroch doing working in the kitchens here at MacCameron Castle? Getting chummy with the princess? Have you been spying for your clan all this time?"

"No," Merida said, shaking her head. There was that feeling again, like she was on the verge of losing control. "It is not what you think."

Aileen grabbed her by the collar of her gown and dragged her from the kitchens. "You can tell it to the queen."

She would rather have faced her grandfather than Queen Catriona. She had a feeling that Aileen knew, too, that between the two, the queen would judge Merida more harshly than King Douglass.

Merida's panic skyrocketed. Pain reverberated in her head as a strange sensation began to throb at the base of her jaw.

That was when she felt it: something piercing either side of her tongue.

Fangs. She was growing fangs.

She stumbled behind Aileen as they moved down the corridor toward the Great Hall. Those same gasps that had rung out in the kitchen echoed throughout the castle with every member of the staff they passed. Elinor had been right regarding the MacCameron loyalists' feelings about the DunBrochs. Merida could feel their disdain covering her like a second skin.

The temperature seemed to plummet the moment they entered the Great Hall. Queen Catriona sat upon the raised dais, her regal nose pointed high. It looked as if she had been waiting for them—for *her*.

"What is the meaning of this?" her grandmother asked as they approached. Her eyes zeroed in on Merida's hair.

"I discovered the girl is a DunBroch," Aileen said. "Now we know how the princess got involved with that one called Fergus."

"No," Merida said. "That is not true."

Merida tasted blood from her punctured tongue.

The queen's usually frigid stare burned like fire. "Who sent you here?"

"No one sent me," Merida said. "The princess found me injured in the woods, just as she said. I am not a spy for Clan DunBroch. I promise you."

"Get out," Queen Catriona said in a hard, low voice. "Leave this castle and never return." She looked to Aileen and Elspeth. "If she is not gone within the hour, she is to be put in the dungeon."

Merida's stomach dropped.

She had to get to Elinor, or to Gawin. But in the short time since she had first met her grandmother, Merida had learned enough about her to know she did not make idle threats. She could not chance being thrown in the dank dungeons hidden in the belly of this castle.

"Please," Merida pleaded, even though she knew it would be no use.

"Do you want me to escort you to the gate or to the dungeon?" Aileen asked.

Her snide voice grated down Merida's spine. A red mist flashed before her eyes.

Afraid of what she would do were she to remain near Aileen any longer, Merida left the Great Hall and, minutes later, MacCameron Castle. She did not get the chance to even visit her bedchamber to gather her meager belongings. She guessed she should feel grateful she was allowed to get her horse.

Her first thought was to return to Fergus's camp, but shortly into her journey Merida encountered a clan wearing a tartan she did not recognize. They were riding with haste.

"Get out of here, lass!" a man on a fine steed called out to her.

Merida began riding alongside him, heading back toward MacCameron Castle. "What is the matter?" she asked.

"Marauders. A gang of them. 'Tis not safe for a young lass like you to be in these woods alone. Go home!"

Merida pulled up on Angus's reins.

Where was home? She could not go to Fergus. Even if there was a boarding house in the village where Freya and her mother lived, Merida did not have coin to pay for lodging. There was nowhere for her to go.

She sat up straight at the sound of horses coming from the south.

"Come, Angus," Merida said.

There was but one option she could think of.

Merida did her best to recall the landmarks she had passed the day she had visited the creek with Elinor. The first sliver of relief she had felt in hours washed over her as the dark, moss-covered facade of MacCameron Castle's northernmost curtain wall came into view. She looked intently at the wall, searching for the special stone that looked out of place. Once she found it, Merida knew she had fought only half the battle. The biggest test would be to push those three stones simultaneously so that she and her horse could slip in.

It would seem as if luck was on her side. It took much effort, but she managed to enter the secret passageway.

"This way, Angus," Merida whispered, urging the horse to follow her. She went opposite the way she and Elinor had traveled that fateful day when the king had been waiting for them at the stable.

The area behind this older, unused stable butted up to the curtain wall. Merida moved toward the middle of the structure, and then, with her back against the curtain wall, she lowered herself to the ground and pulled her knees up to her chest. Ironically, now she was grateful for the hair growing wildly on her arms, legs, and torso. It would keep her warm.

Of all the places she had spent the night, this would no doubt be the worst. It was dark and dank and scary, but no one would find her.

At least she hoped not.

CHAPTER FORTY-THREE
Elinor

Elinor tracked the steps of the lad who dragged the large horn to the middle of the field. He blew into one end, releasing a call to all who were to take part in today's competitions.

The carnyx's mournful cry matched Elinor's mood, but she did her best not to show the depths of her melancholy. It was not as if anyone would understand. The guests occupying the grounds of MacCameron Castle thought she should be the happiest lass in all of Scotland. She had suffered through hundreds upon hundreds of well-wishes from citizens who had journeyed from all areas of the kingdom to enjoy this year's Highland Games and cheer on their kingdom's princess as her betrothal was officially announced.

Let them celebrate. Elinor refused to do so, not when she did not even know her own fate.

Her father had yet to share his decision on the Fraser's request regarding her upcoming union with Lachlan, despite her asking—begging—him to do so. It galled her that she could sit there that morning and not know if she was supposed to bed as someone's bride that night. That she had no say in the matter. That nothing about her life was her own.

But she had already known that. Her life had *never* been her own.

Elinor swallowed down the tears that caught at the back of her throat. Tears served no purpose now. She would not allow anyone to see just how badly broken she felt.

Instead, she sat up straight in the chair next to her father's and looked upon the masses from her place on the dais. The colors of the various tartans both clashed and meshed in a chaotic yet beautiful representation of the clans that made up MacCameron Kingdom. As she observed the gleeful faces before her, it was difficult for Elinor to imagine that just a few short years before, many of these same people would not have thought twice about slashing the throat of the men they now shared mugs of ale with.

She considered, just for a moment, what it would be

like to reign as their queen, but then she quickly pushed the thought from her head.

She would allow herself to enjoy the pageantry. It was, after all, the one thing about the Highland Games she took pleasure in. As for the rest of the day's duties, she would endure them as best she could. But she would *not* enjoy them.

Elinor caught sight of Clan DunBroch's scarlet, green, and blue tartan and immediately sought out Fergus, her heart leaping when she noticed his tall frame towering over everyone else in his clan. She chanced a glance at her mother, grateful the queen's attention was directed else-where. She did not want to even contemplate her mother's wrath if she were to see Elinor looking at Fergus.

It would be better that she forget about Fergus DunBroch. Instead, she would think about the *other* DunBroch. The one who had lied to her. All traces of a smile instantly melted from her face.

When she thought back over her life, there were quite a few things that Elinor knew she would always regret, but nothing was more regrettable than her gullibility when it came to Merida. How could she have allowed herself to believe the girl had her best interests at heart? Like every-one else, Merida had left her.

She had waited for her return, certain that Merida

would be true to her word, even though she had turned out to be a liar. But as the hours stretched through the night and into the morning, she had been forced to accept the truth. Merida had reneged on their agreement. She had left Elinor to fend for herself.

Elinor vowed to not spend a second longer being upset over Merida's breach of trust. Instead, she would use it as fuel—as the catalyst she needed to stop being afraid and take that leap she had backed out of taking so many times.

Her father's decision regarding her marriage to Lachlan did not matter, because soon she would not be there.

She had stashed the meager belongings she planned to escape with at the far end of the outer courts. When everyone gathered in the Great Hall for the opening day feast after the first rounds of the competitions were done, she would feign a stomach ailment, then make her getaway.

And she would finally be free.

Elinor looked around, soaking in what was very likely the last she would see of her home. She would take the good memories with her. Though, as she considered them, she realized there were very few from these past five years, ever since her mother had begun to groom her to take over as queen.

If only they could do away with this archaic tradition of forcing her into marriage to a man she did not even like and whom Elinor doubted she could ever grow to love. If only they would allow her to choose her own husband, maybe she would be happy as the queen of this kingdom.

If only her father recognized that, as king, *he* could make these changes.

If only . . .

Entertaining such thoughts was futile, so she would no longer wrestle with them. Instead, Elinor settled in to watch the games. A group of eight young lads from Clan Shaw lined up across from a group from Clan Murray. They retrieved a thick rope from around their feet and, on the count of three, began the tug-of-war. The crowd rallied around their respective clans.

It took only moments for the more seasoned clansmen from Clan Murray to prove victorious. One member of their clan broke out in a jaunty dance, garnering the first laugh from Elinor in days. She laughed even harder when, while attempting the hammer throw, a lad from Clan Cunningham went sailing across the ground instead of the heavy metal ball he had tried to toss.

Her good cheer lasted right up to the call for the final contest of the evening: archery. The crowds huddled in close as representatives from four clans stepped up to participate, each planting a flag with his clan's crest in the ground. Fergus stood proudly next to Clan DunBroch's flag. Elinor

soaked in the sight of him, a warm, tingly sensation bloom-
ing in her chest. Not wanting to stare too long, she directed
her attention to the others.

She could barely disguise her disgust as she watched
Lachlan Fraser strut across the trampled grass. Whereas the
other competitors held simple wooden bows, Lachlan's was
intricately carved with his clan's symbol, a mighty buck's
head. The buck looked to be as arrogant as the man who
carried it.

Clan MacCameron's best archer, Rory, was the first to
shoot at the target. Elinor felt the disappointment of her
entire clan as Rory's arrow landed well outside of the center target. The MacCamerons were better known for tossing
cabers than their skill with the bow and arrow.

Up next was the lad from Clan McNeil. He was young,
with reddish-brown hair and a face peppered with the
McNeils' signature freckles. Elinor applauded his attempt to
appear calm, but anyone who looked closely enough could
see the way his hands shook. Despite that, his arrow still
landed closer to the target than Rory's.

The conductor of the games called the representa-
tive from Clan Fraser to take his mark. Lachlan ignored
the rowdy cheers and enamored sighs from all the lasses
in attendance as he confidently made his way to his flag.
Then, in one smooth motion, he retrieved an arrow from

his quiver, lined it up with the bow, and sent it careening toward the target. He struck as near to the center of the target as Elinor had ever witnessed anyone hit. The crowd erupted into hoots and hollers.

Her father leaned toward Elinor. "Your husband has the crowd behind him. He will make a fine leader one day."

Not her *future* husband, but her *husband*.

The bitter taste of bile collected on Elinor's tongue. If her father was already referring to Lachlan as her husband, there was little mystery as to his decision regarding their impending nuptials.

"And lastly, we have Fergus of Clan DunBroch," the conductor announced. "The DunBrochs claim to be the best archers in the kingdom," he said, earning good- and not-so-good-natured jeers from the crowd. "Let us see what you can do to hold on to that title, Fergus."

Fergus stepped up to his mark. Elinor could not help admiring his quiet yet confident demeanor. Unlike Lachlan, Fergus did not have to boast about his strength and skill. One got a sense of both simply by looking at him.

He reached behind him and pulled an arrow from his quiver, but as he lined it up against the bow, the tip of the arrow fell to the ground. The crowd gasped. Fergus looked at the arrowhead with annoyed confusion, his forehead creased with deep lines.

He pulled another arrow from his quiver, but the same thing happened. It happened again, and again, and again, until he had no arrows left.

The low murmurs that had begun to travel throughout the crowd had escalated in volume until Elinor could scarcely hear what was being said between Fergus and the conductor.

Sabotage.

Her father stood and shouted, "Quiet!"

Just like that, a hush fell over the hundreds of people gathered on the grounds.

"Now, what seems to be the matter?" King Douglass asked as he descended the dais and walked over to where the competitors and conductor stood.

"Fergus of DunBroch is arguing sabotage," the conductor said.

"What else can it be?" Fergus asked.

"Do you have proof of that?" the conductor asked.

Fergus motioned to the discarded arrows around them. "What further proof do you need?"

"How do we know you did not break them on your own?" Lachlan asked. "Because you were too afraid to compete?"

Fergus took a menacing step toward Lachlan.

Elinor's breath caught in her throat as the crowd once again erupted in shocked gasps and frenzied murmurs.

"That is enough!" the king said. He turned to the crowd. "Seeing as there is no DunBroch to compete, Lachlan of Clan Fraser wins by default."

From somewhere in the crowd, a voice Elinor thought she would never hear again rang out. "No, he does not."

CHAPTER FORTY-FOUR
Merida

"Who said that?" the conductor called.

Merida stepped from behind the tent where she had been surreptitiously watching the competition. Something in her gut told her that if an attempt were to be made on the king's life, it would happen today. But, so far, these Highland Games appeared to be just like all the others she had attended over the years.

Until she saw that Fergus's arrows had been tampered with.

Merida had no way of knowing if the sabotage was connected to the threat regarding the king, but something was afoot. She could feel it.

She made her way through the people gathered for

the archery contest. She tore the hooded cloak from her head, letting her rich red locks fly unbound around her head. She hoped her hair would shield the fur that had grown along her jaw the previous night. Without the knife she had pilfered from the kitchens, she'd had no way to shave it off that morning.

"I am Merida of Clan DunBroch," she announced. "And I will be stepping in for my fa—my clansman, Fergus."

The entire crowd seemed to inhale all at once. A flurry of murmurs and whispers began to reverberate around the grounds.

Fergus's eyes grew wide. "Lass, what are you doing?"

"What is the meaning of this?" King Douglass barked. "You were banished from this kingdom."

Merida was grateful for her kirtle's full skirt. Not only did it hide her woolly legs, but it prevented anyone from noticing just how badly they were shaking. Somehow, she managed to pull herself together and stand up straight as she faced her grandfather.

"I am a DunBroch, and as one, I am allowed to remain in this kingdom as is dictated by the peace alliance signed between the clans. I am also allowed to take part in the Highland Games on behalf of my clan."

"Did you hear that?" It was the chieftain of Clan Fraser. He hooked a thumb at her and laughed, then said,

"The lass wants to shoot the bow and arrow. Go back to the dance tent, lass."

Merida stood her ground. "No. I am here to compete."

"Wha . . . what," the chieftain sputtered. "You cannot talk to me this way!"

"I did not plan to speak at all," Merida said. "My archery skills will speak for me."

"Who is this girl?" the chieftain said.

"I am—" Merida saw a swath of royal blue out of the corner of her eye seconds before Queen Catriona arrived. Elinor was right behind her.

The queen caught her by the shoulder and jerked her around to face her. "I warned you of what would happen if you were to return to this castle," she said. "Leave."

Fear knotted in the pit of Merida's belly. She swallowed the lump of panic climbing up her throat before speaking. "I request the right to compete in this contest on behalf of my clan."

"Did you not hear me?" the queen asked. "Leave now!"

The red mist flashed before her eyes again. Merida felt a growl rumbling deep in her belly. Her animal instincts were becoming harder to control.

"Let her compete."

Both Merida and Queen Catriona turned to see whom the words had come from. It was Lachlan. He stood underneath the Fraser flag, his arms folded casually across his chest.

"The lass is correct," he continued, pushing away from the flagpole. "If she is a member of Clan DunBroch, she has a right to take part in the games." His brow quirked in amusement. "It will not change the outcome of the contest, but it will be entertaining."

"Mother," Elinor said, putting her hand on the queen's forearm. "What harm is there? Think about what people will say if you throw this young girl out of the castle."

It was clear by the queen's demeanor that she wanted nothing more than to throw Merida off the castle grounds with her own two hands, but Elinor had appealed to her mother's obsession with appearances. The princess knew her mother well enough to know that she would do whatever was necessary to prevent any untoward gossip.

Queen Catriona slowly released her grip on Merida's arm and took several steps back.

"Well, lass," Lachlan said. "You said you wanted to shoot. Shoot."

Merida took her bow and quiver and stepped up to the mark. She was afraid the gloves would affect her accuracy, and she did not have time to worry about what people would think of her fur and claws. She had to act fast. She pulled off the gloves.

Several people gasped.

"My goodness, lass. You are hairier than ten lads," Lachlan said. "How did that happen?"

"Something I ate," she said. She brought the bow up to her chest and aimed at the target. She closed her eyes, pulling in several deep breaths before she let the arrow go. Time seemed to stop as it sailed through the air and landed on the target.

Directly onto Lachlan's.

The crowd was stunned into silence, but seconds later they erupted into cheers.

"It looks as if we have a tie," the conductor said.

"No," Lachlan said. "No ties will be allowed to stand. We shall have a shoot-off. Best two out of three."

He crossed in front of Merida and took his position, bringing his bow up to his chest once again. He took more time than he had with his first attempt. This time, his arrow struck even closer to the center of the target.

Merida had purposely missed the bull's-eye just to see what Lachlan's next move would be.

She had spent much of the afternoon watching him, along with Aileen and Gregory, waiting for them to act. She wished she had seen the man Lachlan had sent to spy on the princess, but Merida had only heard his voice. He could be any of the men near the king.

But if the plan was to kill the king, wouldn't they have done so by now? The competitions for the day were almost over. The betrothal announcement was to happen soon. Yet there was King Douglass, unharmed.

"It's your turn," Lachlan said, his arrogance on full display.

Merida returned to the mark. Just as she aimed for the target, a ruckus started behind her. Two men in the crowd began to argue, their deep brogues intertwining. More people joined in the fracas. Merida recognized the Fraser tartan, but the other was unfamiliar. Within minutes, several other clans had taken up sides, with both men and women getting in one another's faces.

The king's guards tried to get a handle on the rowdy crowd before things got any more out of control, but the more they attempted to tame the stands, the more disorderly they became.

Then everything happened in a matter of seconds.

Someone cried, "Watch out!"

Merida felt an arrow whizz by her head.

Elinor yelled.

Queen Catriona screamed.

The riotous crowd was immediately silenced.

And Merida turned to find Fergus splayed on the

ground, with King Douglass sprawled underneath him. An arrow stood erect; its point lodged in Fergus's meaty shoulder.

"Dad!" Merida yelled at the same time that Elinor shouted, "Fergus!"

They ran to his side, Elinor arriving first. She sat next to him and cradled his head in her lap. "Get the physician!" she yelled. "Someone, get the physician right now!" Several people scurried off.

"Who shot that arrow?" Gawin, the king's second-in-command, demanded.

"Did anyone see where it came from?" Queen Catriona asked. She knelt at King Douglass's side, along with two of the men Merida often saw with her grandfather. As far as she could tell, the king looked shaken, but unharmed.

Her father, however, bled profusely from the wound in his shoulder. Remembering something he had taught her years before, Merida went into action. She knelt next to him and tugged at Elinor's plaid.

"Give me that," she said. "We need to tie it around his shoulder so we can stop the blood."

"Are you sure?" Elinor said.

"Do as she says," Merida heard one of the men behind her say. "'Tis what we do with warriors in battle."

Merida went to work, looping the plaid underneath Fergus's arm and securing it tightly in hope of stanching the blood.

She looked over her shoulder and said to Gawin, "We must find who let loose that arrow. It was meant for the king."

"The lass is right," the Clan Fraser chieftain said. "If the DunBroch had not stepped in, the arrow would have gone into King Douglass's heart."

"The DunBroch saved the king's life," Queen Catriona said in an astonished voice. She looked from Fergus to Elinor to Merida, her eyes wide.

"Yes, he did," Elinor said. "He was willing to sacrifice his life for his king's." She looked to her mother and father. "He is a *true* hero."

The refrain began to reverberate through the crowd as news of what had just happened made its way among those on the grounds.

The physician arrived, and Merida left him to tend to Fergus's injury while she sought out Gawin. She ran to the king's second-in-command, grabbing him by the arm and pulling him away from the others gathered around the royal family.

"I know King Douglass does not trust me," Merida started. "But what the king does not realize is that it is his own people he cannot trust. This was no accident, Gawin. There is a plot to kill the king."

"What are you talking about, lass?"

"There is no time to explain." She looked around. "Where is Lachlan Fraser?"

"He is right . . ." Gawin said, pointing to the crowd. His words trailed off. "He was just here."

"We must find him. He is behind this scheme," Merida said. "Lachlan, Aileen, and Gregory."

"No." Gawin shook his head. "You're mistaken."

"I am not," Merida said. "I heard them plotting to harm the king. I tried to warn you, but I was thrown out of the castle before I could." She captured his arms in her hands and looked him in the eye. "You must believe me. Lachlan wants to kill the king."

"Why would he want to do that? He is due to marry the princess. If he killed her father—"

"He could rule," Merida said, cutting him off. Lachlan's motives had to be obvious to everyone by now. "If he is married to the princess and something happens to the king, Lachlan is that much closer to ruling the kingdom."

"And you think Aileen and Gregory know about it?" Gawin asked.

She nodded. "They are assisting him. I heard them with my own ears. And I saw Aileen and Lachlan together in the corridor near the larder. I fear they have been planning the king's demise for some time."

Horror and disappointment warred with each other in Gawin's eyes. Merida could tell how greatly this affected him. He had likely known both Aileen and Gregory for their entire lives.

Gawin dispatched several men to go in search of the traitors. When she told him about the unnamed spy, Gawin knew exactly who it was.

"It has to be Lachlan's younger brother, Lennox," he said.

Trusting that Gawin and his comrades would handle those behind the plot, Merida returned to the area where she had left Fergus and Elinor. But they were no longer there. She learned that Fergus had been taken into the castle and was being tended to by the physician.

Merida rushed into the castle to find Elinor sitting by the door of a small chamber just inside the grand entrance. Merida's stomach dropped. Fergus's injuries must have been more serious than she first thought if they could not even take him to a proper bedchamber to tend to his wound.

"How is he doing?" Merida asked.

Elinor looked up at her. "The physician is with him now."

"I figured as much," she said. She began to pace in

front of the door. "Do you know how he is doing? Is he in danger of dying?"

"Dying? The stubborn mule would not allow anyone to help him walk to the castle."

Before Merida knew what she was about, Elinor reached out and grabbed her hands.

"This is why you purchased those gloves in the village, isn't it?" Elinor asked. She flipped Merida's hands back and forth, studying them. "What could you possibly have eaten to cause this? It is as if you are the legend of the black bear come to life."

Merida's breath caught in her throat.

Then Elinor laughed. "Maybe that is what we should tell those who do not believe in our legends. It may scare some into changing their ways. Make them see things from another person's perspective, as the legend proclaims."

Merida's heart swelled at the familiar words. She realized just how much she had changed since she had eaten that cake. And not just on the outside. She was not the same girl who thought only about what she wanted, without considering her duty to protect and support her kingdom. After witnessing the way Elinor had been willing to put aside her plans to uncover the threat to MacCameron Kingdom, Merida understood how important this role was. She no longer saw her responsibilities as a burden; they were an honor.

"I know that *I* now see things differently," Merida said. "And I have you to thank for that, Princess. You have shown me what it means for a leader to take care of her people. Just look at what you did for me—you helped a young lass that you did not even know."

"I believe that was one of the best decisions I have ever made," Elinor said.

Merida could barely speak with the lump of emotion suddenly clogging her throat.

"Enough of this," Merida said. She would turn into a blubbering mess if they continued. "Back to Fergus. Did he really walk to the castle unassisted?"

Elinor nodded, a frustrated scowl on her face. But then her expression softened and a light entered her eyes.

"Fergus of DunBroch is one of the most stubborn men I have ever met, but also one of the bravest. I cannot believe he took an arrow for my father."

"I knew it. You like him," Merida said, unable to mask the delight in her voice.

"I do not," the princess protested. Immediately, she laughed. "Well, maybe I do," she finished.

An infectious smile drew across Elinor's face. Merida did not need any more proof that her mother was well on her way to falling in love with her father. And Merida knew

Fergus felt the same way. For the first time since the start of this harrowing ordeal, she felt true relief.

Just then, the physician exited the room.

"How is he?" Elinor and Merida asked at the same time.

The physician shrugged. "He is made of sturdy stock. It takes more than the tip of an arrow to hurt him."

"Can we see him?" the princess asked. Merida took the urgency in her voice as another sign of her growing affection.

The physician led them into the room. Fergus sat in a chair like he was waiting for a meal instead of being treated for an arrow to the shoulder. Elinor rushed to his side and took both of his hands in hers. She fussed over him in a way Merida had witnessed her doing a thousand times.

"Finally," Merida said in a relieved whisper. Her parents were finally together.

CHAPTER FORTY-FIVE
Elinor

The competitions done for the day, everyone had gathered in the Great Hall for food and festivities. Elinor sat next to Fergus, who had been given a place of honor on the raised dais. She had thought she would have to persuade her father to bestow such a privilege, but the moment Fergus entered the room, the king declared that he and his fellow clansmen were to be his special guests throughout the Highland Games.

The crowd had erupted into cheers. It was a sight Elinor never thought she'd see: a roomful of MacCamerons raising their ale-filled mugs to a DunBroch.

She looked at Fergus now, surreptitiously studying his strong profile. She was astonished at just how swiftly she had fallen for this jovial, irascible soldier. Then again, she was not all that surprised. She was quickly learning that there were myriad things to like about Fergus DunBroch.

He was one of the most kind-hearted people she had ever met. And in contrast to many of the men in her father's army, who seemed hesitant to display even the barest smile for fear it would make them appear weak, Fergus did not shy away from expressing his joy. He laughed with abandon, as he was doing right now as lads from Clan Moray attempted a rather complicated folk dance.

With his eyes still focused on the dance floor, Fergus asked, "Do you like what you see, Princess?" His lips twitched as he brought his mug of ale to them.

Elinor's first instinct was to deny that she had been looking at him, but then she realized she did not want to. She was done hiding her feelings for Fergus from him, and from herself.

"Actually, I do like what I see," she answered. "Very much."

He spun around to face her, his startled expression drawing a laugh from her.

"Do not move so quickly," Elinor said. "You will upset your wound." She inspected the bandages covering his broad shoulder.

"I do not care about my wound, lass," Fergus said. "I

care about what you just said. Now"—he batted his thick red lashes—"tell me all the things you like about me."

Elinor laughed despite herself. "Must you be this way?"

"What way is that?"

"Presumptuous." Then she smiled. "But also extraordinarily kind. It is one of the things I like most about you. You teach stuffy princesses how to fish, and buy enough bread to keep a poor lad's belly full for the night." She touched his arm. "You are a rare one, Fergus DunBroch."

He captured her hand before she could pull it away and brought it to his lips.

Elinor gasped and quickly glanced around the Great Hall. She noticed numerous eyes on them.

"Fergus, what are you doing?" she whispered. "'Tis not proper to put on such a display, especially between two people who are not even betrothed."

"Yet," Fergus said. "We are not betrothed yet, Princess. Don't worry; we will take care of that soon enough."

"Presumptuous," Elinor repeated with amused exasperation. But she could not deny the excitement that flooded her senses. She had imagined often over these last few days what it would be like to rule a kingdom with him at her side, to be a team in leadership, and it looked as if she would get the chance to make that dream a reality. It took all the restraint she possessed not to run to the king and queen this very second and make her desire to marry him known.

"Oh, and another thing you will learn about me?" Fergus said, retrieving his ale and returning his attention to the dance floor. "I do not give a seabhag's feather about what is proper."

And then he let out a full-bellied laugh. Elinor could do nothing but join him.

CHAPTER FORTY-SIX
Merida

Merida stood in the corner near one of the coats of arms, her eyes focused on Elinor and Fergus and the undeniable affection between them. She wanted to soak in as much of her parents' young love as she could.

The time for her to leave was drawing near.

She felt herself becoming more feral with each second that passed. It would not be long before her full transformation into a bear was complete. She could not allow anyone to see it.

Yet she could not seem to make her feet move. She could not take her eyes off her parents.

Merida was surprised by the twinge of melancholy at leaving. She would miss young Elinor and Fergus, and even some of the staff at MacCameron Castle, like Sorcha. But she also could not wait to see the mother and father she knew and loved, along with her brothers, Maudie, and all the others at Castle DunBroch.

And at least now she could go knowing that all would be well in MacCameron Kingdom.

Earlier, when she had gone up onto the dais to inquire about Fergus's injury, Gawin had been speaking to the king. Merida did not catch everything that was said, but she had heard enough to know that Lachlan, Lennox, Gregory, and Aileen had all been captured. The chieftain of Clan Fraser had been as surprised as everyone else by the plot. He was found not to have been involved.

The kingdom was no longer in peril, and based on what she had witnessed tonight, she was confident the rules regarding the princess's betrothal were about to be rewritten.

The crowd began to empty out into the courtyard. Sorcha had explained that the celebration would move outside well before the sun began to set to ensure that the revelers were there to watch as the summer solstice reached its peak.

Which was Merida's signal that it was time to leave. She considered bidding Elinor and Fergus a final farewell, but decided it was better she simply left MacCameron Castle. Let them think she had slipped away to return to her homeland in the south of Scotland.

She took one last look at the dais before making her way out of the Great Hall. In no time, Merida was on Angus's back, racing through the forest.

When she reached the village, she headed directly for the wood-carver's shop.

"There you are," Freya greeted her. She glanced at Merida's hands and reared back. "It looks as if you are just in time, lass. You remain here much longer and you will soon turn into a full bear."

Merida didn't need Freya to tell her that. She could feel it. Her entire body was now covered in fur. Her sharp claws tore through the gloves and the tips of her slippers. She had awoken this morning with what she thought was a toothache, but upon further inspection, she realized two of her upper teeth had doubled in size. They were so long that they had pierced the bottom of her mouth. She now had a full set of fangs.

The only things left of her human form were her face and her mind. How much longer before those transformed, as well? She grew more aggressive at the slightest provocation, like every bear she had ever encountered. She was becoming one of them.

Freya pointed to the window. "The most powerful point of the solstice is drawing near. Come, the spell is complete."

A mixture of excitement, anticipation, and a touch of fear rushed through Merida's veins. Her life had been turned upside down the last time she consumed one of Freya's spells.

They entered the rearmost room of the shop. Sitting in the center of a small wooden table was a tiny cake that looked nearly identical to the one Merida had gotten back in the wood-carver's cottage.

"Go on. Eat," Freya encouraged.

Merida picked up the cake and took a generous bite. She swallowed, then closed her eyes.

Nothing happened.

She took another bite, eager to see her family. But all she saw was Freya and the bear carvings occupying the shelves in the room.

"Should I eat more?" she asked.

"Yes!" Freya said in a panicked voice. She rushed to the window. "Yes, yes. Eat the entire cake. The sun is at its highest. Eat it before it begins to set."

Merida began stuffing it in her mouth so quickly she started to choke.

Freya turned from the window and stared expectantly at Merida.

And stared. And stared.

Merida knew something was not right as she watched the witch's hopeful expression turn to disappointment.

"No," Merida whispered. "Did you forget to put something in the spell?"

Freya shook her head as she headed for the door. She returned a moment later with the book.

"I followed the instructions to the letter. I even made a trip to Sutherland for a specific herb that is only grown there." She looked up at Merida, despair clouding her eyes. "I am sorry, lass. I do not know what else to do."

Disbelief battled with dismay in Merida's head as the reality of what was happening began to settle in. She was still here. Despite her parents falling in love before the summer solstice. Despite that she had fulfilled all the requirements asked of her. She remained in the past, her body changing into a beast.

The urge to fall to her knees and cry out in pain was almost too strong to fight. So she didn't fight it. She fell to the floor and released an earthshaking roar.

Freya jumped back, her eyes widening in fear.

What did this mean for her? For her brothers? For the Clan DunBroch she knew and loved? Would her life as she knew it never be the same?

Merida forced herself to find some sense of calm, to gain some control over the beast fighting to overwhelm her.

"What am I to do now?" Merida asked.

Feeling utterly defeated, she realized there was only one thing she wanted to do. She needed to return to MacCameron Castle. She had to see her parents one last time before she turned into a bear forever.

"I . . . I will continue looking for a spell for you, lass," Freya said as she followed Merida to the front of the store. "I am becoming a better witch every day. I will fix this. I promise."

At the door, Merida apologized for frightening Freya and thanked her for her help, but it was difficult to feel much hope. How long would it take for the witch to gain enough skill to create the right spell? Freya had said herself that the solstice contained the highest measure of magic. Did this mean Merida had to wait until the winter solstice before they could try again? She would not last until then. She would be a bear long before the next solstice.

She bade Freya farewell, then climbed atop Angus and began the ride back to her mother's home. By the time she arrived, the revelers had all settled in for the night; the tents that had been set up around the bailey for each clan were all closed in.

Merida started to look for Clan DunBroch's tent, but despite her declaration at the games earlier that day, she did not feel as if she fit in with these DunBrochs. They were her clan, but only by virtue of their name. She wanted to go home, to be with her family.

She got Angus settled in the stable, then went in search of the family she *did* have here: Fergus and Elinor. Merida found them in the parlor that was just off the side of the Great Hall. They were accompanied by several of the princess's maids, but the maids gave the couple—who were obviously enamored of each other—a wide berth. Merida pulled up her hood.

"There you are," Elinor exclaimed when she spotted Merida near the door. "Where did you go?"

"I . . . I needed to get away for a bit," Merida answered softly, wondering how on earth she could say goodbye to her mother now.

Elinor eyed her knowingly. "You were running off to the Lowlands, weren't you?"

"Yes," Merida lied. "But I came back, because I told you I would not leave without you."

Merida felt a tingling on her face and what felt like something pulling at her cheeks, almost as if she were growing a snout.

She couldn't stay here, not unless she wanted the castle's army to attack her when she transformed into a bear right in front of the princess. But she could not bring herself to leave. Not yet.

"Are you ready to leave?" Merida asked the princess.

Elinor pulled her bottom lip between her teeth. "I am not so sure that I will be going to the Lowlands anymore." She looked over her shoulder at Fergus. "Actually, I am *quite* sure that I will be staying right here in MacCameron Kingdom."

"What brought about this change?" Merida asked.

"I am not remaining because of Fergus," Elinor said with exaggerated haughtiness. "Well, I am not staying *solely* because of him. This is my home," she continued, her voice earnest. "You taught me that there is merit in living up to one's duty, not because it is being forced upon me, but because it is a privilege to be born into this position. I see the value in that now.

"I know that I will have to marry soon enough, but I talked to Mother and Father, and they have agreed that we can wait a bit longer. Not all traditions are meant to be followed."

"I hope you remember that for many years to come," Merida told her. She gathered Elinor in a hug, holding her tightly, letting the tears flow freely now. "Thank you for everything you have done."

"What did I do, save for getting you in trouble with the king?"

"You have done so much more than that," Merida said, her voice cracking. "I was once so selfish. I only considered what I wanted, never thinking about how my actions affected others. But that has now changed, and it is because of you. You have taught me just as much about my duties and responsibilities, and just how important my family is to me," Merida said. "You have changed me for the better, Princess."

Tears glistened in Elinor's eyes. Merida could feel them welling up in her own.

"I will miss you," Elinor said.

"I will miss you, too," Merida said. She looked up at her father, and the tingling along her skin intensified. "You too, Fergus. Thank you both for everything."

Merida returned her attention to the princess and marveled at the journey they had taken together in this short time. She thought back to the morning Elinor discovered her in the forest, to their jaunts through the forest on their horses. Elinor MacCameron was more than just the woman who would have eventually become her mother; she had become a true friend.

Merida choked back a sob.

"I . . . I love you, Elinor."

Her body jolted as something otherworldly rushed through her. It was happening. She was transforming.

"I . . ." She took a step back. "I . . . shall fetch . . ." She stuck out her hand, using the wall to steady herself. "I shall fetch some mead. To toast your upcoming nuptials," Merida finished.

With one last look, she turned and exited the Great Hall. Heading for the kitchen, she rounded the corner and passed out.

Merida opened her eyes and stared up at the ceiling, unable to believe that she had lost consciousness yet again. She had to stop doing that.

She pushed herself up from the castle's cold, hard floor and continued down the corridor toward the kitchen, where she could slip outside through the scullery before she transformed into a beast.

She turned the corner and nearly collided with a short, buxom figure.

"Oh, I am so sorry. I did not see you," Merida said.

"No worries, Princess," came a familiar voice.

Merida went completely still. "Maudie?" she asked, certain her eyes were playing tricks on her.

"Why are you looking at me that way, Princess? It is as if you have seen a ghost."

"I . . . I . . ." she stammered. It felt like her brain had forgotten how to function.

Maudie's forehead furrowed. "Are you feeling well, Princess?"

Merida immediately looked down at her hands.

No hair! No claws!

"Yes," Merida said in a breathless whisper. "Yes!" she said again, shouting this time. She was home! "Oh, Maudie, I am so happy to see you!" She wrapped her arms around the stunned maid. "Where is everyone?"

"We just served the midday meal," Maudie said cautiously. "Now everyone is returning to the grounds for the evening competitions."

"Competitions? Does this mean the Highland Games are still taking place?"

"Of course they are, Princess. Are you sure you are well? Maybe you should retire to your room."

"I am fine," Merida said, joy sweeping over her. "I must see my family."

She took off for the Great Hall and spotted her brothers just inside the entrance. They were tying rope around the legs of an unsuspecting guard.

"Boys!" Merida squealed in delight. Hamish, Hubert,

and Harris took one look at her and scurried away. "No, boys! Come here! I want to see you."

Merida could only shake her head as they scurried off, undoubtedly to cause more mischief. As she elbowed her way through the moving crowd in search of her parents, she heard her father's boisterous voice ahead.

"Father!" Merida shouted. She caught sight of his red hair and went running.

"Ah, Merida, there you are! Not now," he said, when she went to hug him. "The MacGuffin's boy is going to try to toss a caber. I'll bet it lands on his head."

"But, Father . . ." Merida stared at him as he walked right past her. Had he not missed her while she had been gone?

"Where is Mother?" Merida called to him.

"In the sitting room," he said over his shoulder. "Tell her to come down and see the MacGuffin!"

Confused, Merida went upstairs and found her mother folding the tapestry.

"Mother," Merida said. She ran to her, wrapping her arms around her mother's waist and resting her head against her chest. "I've missed you so much."

"We were only apart for a few minutes, Merida."

Merida lifted her head to look up at her. "Has it only been that long?"

"Do you not remember?" the queen asked. "You made such a stink because we would not allow you to take part in the archery contest. Well, I talked to your grandmother, and she made me realize that I was being rather hard on you."

"My grandmother? Queen Catriona?"

"Yes, Merida. Why are you looking at me so?"

"I just . . . My grandmother is here?"

"Of course she is. You know Queen Catriona and King Douglass would not miss the games. They came down from MacCameron Kingdom a fortnight ago."

"So there is still a MacCameron Kingdom?" Merida asked.

Her mother plopped a hand on her hip. "Merida, why are you asking questions to which you already know the answer? How many times has Fergus told the story of how, after he saved the king's life by taking an arrow meant for him, your grandfather convinced the clans under his rule to join DunBroch Kingdom after your father and I were wed?"

"What about MacCameron Kingdom?" Merida asked.

"It is tiny, but it remains under your grandparents' rule," Elinor said. She took a steadying breath. "Once they are no longer with us, it shall come under DunBroch rule like all the others. But that is nothing to concern ourselves with right now. We should enjoy the games.

"And you will be happy to know that your father has just issued an order that anyone, be they lad or lass, can now participate in the games." She pointed to Merida's chair. "Grab your bow and get out there."

Her bow! The one her mother had thrown in the fire. It was there on the seat, unblemished.

"I can shoot?" Merida asked.

"I believe you have spoken about nothing else for the past month," her mother said. "Go and make the DunBroch name proud."

Merida reached for the bow, but then she pulled away and wrapped her mother in another hug.

"Thank you, Mother."

"For what?"

"For being you. You are the best queen this kingdom could ever ask for. I can only hope I am half as effective as you are during my reign."

Her mother leaned back so that she could look at her. "During your reign? So you no longer object to being queen?"

"We will discuss that soon, but I have something I must do first," Merida said. "Do not worry, I will be back shortly. There is someone I must see." She ran to her wardrobe and grabbed her black cloak.

CHAPTER FORTY-SEVEN
Merida

A lightness filled Merida's chest as she traversed the familiar woods on her way to Freya's. She did not need the help of the will-o'-the-wisps this time. She trusted her instincts to guide her exactly where she needed to go.

Relief washed over her as she came upon the grass-covered cottage.

"Freya!" Merida called. She dismounted Angus and took off for the cottage. She pounded on the door. "Freya, it worked!"

The door opened.

"Who goes there?" The witch's eyes widened as they leveled on Merida. "Ah, there you are, dearie. I was wondering when you would show up."

Merida took in her hunched back, wrinkled skin, and wild silver hair and experienced another bout of relief.

"It worked," Merida said.

"So it did. You've had quite the adventure," Freya said. She opened the door wider. "Come in. Let us have some tea."

Merida hesitated before stepping into the cottage. It was just as she remembered: wall-to-wall bear carvings. She looked around for the talking crow, but did not see it.

"Here, here. Sit," Freya said.

"I cannot stay for very long," Merida said. "But I had questions that I believe only you can answer."

Freya turned, a teakettle in her hands. "What sort of questions, dear?"

"Well. First . . ." Merida was almost afraid to ask. "Is everything back to . . . normal?"

The witch lifted her shoulders. "I guess it depends on what you consider normal. King Fergus and Queen Elinor are hosting the clans of DunBroch Kingdom for the Highland Games, just as they have done for the past twenty years."

King Fergus and *Queen* Elinor. It felt so good to hear that. It was as if the past two weeks had been nothing but a bad dream.

And there lay the question.

"Why did this happen?" Merida asked. "If not much has changed, why did I have to go through everything I just endured?"

"Oh, but *much* has changed," Freya said. "The intention of the spell was for you to experience a great transformation."

Merida looked down at herself. "I did transform, but I am no longer a bear. I am back to being me."

"On the outside," Freya said. "You must look in here." She pressed her hand over Merida's heart. "This is where the biggest transformation has taken place. You have changed very much."

As Freya's words sank in, Merida began to fully grasp what this had all been about.

She *had* changed. When she first came to Freya, she wanted nothing more than to escape her fate. But after observing her mother as a young woman and witnessing how Elinor had put aside personal wants for the betterment of MacCameron Kingdom, Merida became more open to doing the same. She was ready to embrace her duties as a member of Clan DunBroch's royal family in her own way.

Merida grabbed Freya's hand and gave it a firm squeeze. "Thank you. For everything."

"Oh, I only did what you asked me to do," Freya said.

"Now go to Castle DunBroch. You do not want to miss the big feast."

Merida wrapped Freya up in a warm hug, then quickly mounted Angus and headed for home.

EPILOGUE
Merida

Tension filled the air as Merida, Queen Elinor, and King Fergus sat at the monstrous dining table in Castle DunBroch's Great Hall. Merida had called her parents here to discuss her future now that the Highland Games were done.

It took a great effort to constrain the smile that threatened to break out across her face. She could tell by their expressions that her parents were expecting one of their epic arguments.

They were in for a pleasant surprise. Maybe.

She folded her hands on the table in front of her and began.

"Thank you both for agreeing to sit and discuss this topic as adults," she opened. "Now, I know we have disagreed on my future, but time stands still for no one, and these decisions must be made." She took a breath. "I am not ready to be married."

"Merida—" Queen Elinor started.

"There is a possibility that I will change my mind if I am to meet the right person. But I want to marry for love, the way the two of you did. I should not have to marry just because tradition dictates it." She paused for a moment, releasing a cleansing breath. "That being said, I *am* ready to step into my role as a member of the royal family."

Her mother's and father's mouths opened simultaneously.

"This land and our clan both have a rich history, and I want to learn as much as I can about both so that I can be the type of leader DunBroch Kingdom deserves. I do not need to be married to do this."

Her mother frowned, seeming to consider this for a moment. "You are right," she said finally.

"I am?" Merida asked.

The queen nodded. "I never considered an alternative to marriage, because, well, that is the way it has always been done. But traditions can and sometimes *should* be broken.

I believe this is one of those times." She tipped her head to the side and smiled. "The lass you were named after would agree with me, I think."

Merida's heart swelled. "She sounds like a fine person, this Merida that was my namesake."

"She was, lass. She really was," her father said. "Now, this decision you have come to—are you sure this will make you happy?"

"Yes," she answered. "It will make me very happy." She looked to her mother. "Having watched you rule, I understand the importance of maintaining peace among the clans while also ensuring all the people in our kingdom are safe and well cared for. I believe, with your guidance, Mother, that I can safeguard the kingdom of DunBroch and make it prosper."

Her mother rose from her seat at the table and came over to Merida's side. She captured Merida's shoulders and gave them a firm but gentle squeeze before leaning over and placing a kiss on her head.

"I am very proud of the young woman you are becoming, Merida."

"I have one more request," Merida said.

"What is that?" Queen Elinor asked.

"I would like it if our family traveled to MacCameron

Kingdom soon. I know that Grandmother Catriona and Grandfather Douglass were just here for the Highland Games, but I would very much like to see MacCameron Castle again. I think we are overdue for a trip to your childhood home."

"I think that is a splendid idea," the queen said. "We were all so busy during the games that we did not have much time for a proper visit. Your grandmother can fill me in on everything that is happening with the family as we work on the MacCameron tapestries, and maybe the boys will finally sit still long enough for your grandfather to learn how to tell them apart." She looked to the king. "What do you say, Fergus? Are you up for a trip to MacCameron Castle?"

Her father shrugged. "Whatever you say, dear. So long as I can challenge your father to another round of chess. I swear he was hiding pieces in his plaid last time."

Her mother barked out a laugh and turned to Merida. "If it is your fate to marry, I hope you find someone who brings as much good humor as this one."

The king grinned. "And I hope you find someone as intelligent as she."

Merida smiled at the two of them. Then she quickly stood, rushing to keep her brothers from tipping over the lit candelabra they were trying to climb. "Maybe no fire for you three." She turned to her parents. "Who's ready for dinner? I promised Maudie I'd help with the venison. Grueling work, that."

Elinor tilted her head. "On the other hand, I think you might have good humor and intelligence to spare, my dear Merida."

Merida met her mother's gaze. And her smile widened.